JUGGERNAUT

STARSHIP JERICHO
BOOK 3

TOBY NEIGHBORS

MYTHIC
adventure
PUBLISHING

Juggernaut (Starship Jericho book 3)

Copyright © 2024 by Toby Neighbors

ISBN: 978-1-952260-90-2 ebook

978-1-952260-91-9 print

Mythic Adventure Publishing, LLC

Idaho, USA

Juggernaut - a huge, powerful, and overwhelming force

NEW OXFORD ENGLISH DICTIONARY

PROLOGUE

NUREK WAS ALONE, which was exactly how the Dudonus slave wanted it. His master was none other than Emperor Vang, which meant that Nurek had more power than any slave in the galaxy. He was surrounded by luxury, traveled throughout the galaxy in the very best starships, commanded the obedience of every other slave he encountered, and yet he was still a slave. Others in his position might have used their position to gain riches or enjoy the luxuries that serving the emperor entitled him to. But Nurek hated slavery and had long ago resolved in his mind to end it.

He stopped at the manual input station and pulled out the analogue control board. He was a tall, skinny alien—a biped with very little muscle in the arms and legs but with a tall, cylinder-shaped head. The Dodonus were not field workers or mechanical slaves, but they were ideal for everyday tasks. Their species only needed a couple of hours of sleep and could maintain light work for hours at a time. They were also incredibly intelligent, making them ideal for protocol work with wealthy, high-ranking officials. All that, added to the fact that they had natural lifespans of three centuries, made them the most valuable slave species in the galaxy.

Nurek had been a slave in the royal family for four generations. In addition, the Dudonus inability to fend off the slavers made them prime targets no matter what planet they settled on.

Nurek had long, delicate fingers that had no trouble with the old-fashioned analog controls. He input the message quickly. Military protocol required that a communications drone with the latest information on the battle be sent back to the Ashi system. There, the information would be conveyed to the Prime Council and sent to whoever else needed to know about such matters. Nurek's long, delicate fingers moved swiftly over the controls as he added his own message to a shadow program hidden deep inside the communication files. Unlike the rest of the information, it would not automatically be revealed. Only those looking for such a program would find it and then only those with knowledge of the rebellion's passcodes could open it.

Like the shadow program, the Dudonus slave rebellion was a secret. Only those involved knew of its existence. The rebels had not yet chosen to reveal themselves, but the time had finally come. Millions of Dudonus slaves on a thousand worlds would, in a coordinated act of rebellion, turn on their masters. Of course, the Dudonus were not the only species that had been enslaved. There were slaves from nearly every race in the Imperium. Soon, the other slaves would hear of the rebellion. Many would rush to join the Dudonus in their sedition. Fighting would break out on hundreds of planets, and with any luck, the Imperium would fall amid the chaos.

But war and destruction were only the first phase of the well-planned revolt. The Dudonus slaves had already designated several free worlds where the oppressed could flee to. Weapons and defensive systems had been stolen and deposited in the free systems but, of course, that wouldn't be enough to stop the Imperium's well-trained military. What was needed was a galaxy-wide disruption of the status quo. For years, the rebellion had been quietly fomenting the naturally independent tendencies of certain star systems and exacerbating the pressures on others. What they needed was an

inciting incident, and it seemed to Nurek that the sudden appear-
ance of the alien ship was just what the rebellion had been waiting
for.

His message composed and hidden in the official communication buoy, Nurek closed down the manual controls and hurried
back to his tiny quarters in the emperor's star cruiser. Slaves
weren't allowed in the control center of intergalactic ships, but
Nurek had easily tapped into the ship's computer system and could
even listen to the comlink chatter if he wanted to. Being a slave
made him invisible to most people. Being the Emperor's slave gave
him access to anything he wanted. It was all too easy to add a
component or two whenever he sent out for something that Vang
wanted. In fact, it was expected. Nurek was the most important
slave in the galaxy and had it better than many free people. But
Nurek didn't want luxury or compensation; he wanted freedom. In
lieu of that, he had built his own computer that could give him
access to many of the things on the ship that were normally
forbidden to slaves. Most important were the classified communications from across the galaxy that were meant for the Emperor and
his Kahn. Nurek had used that information to bolster the plans of
the rebellion. Soon, it would be time for open war. When it came to
that, he had weapons stashed in his quarters as well. They were
also forbidden, but Nurek was about to throw off the yoke of his
oppressors and deliver a blow to the Imperium it would never
forget.

CHAPTER 1

MASTER SERGEANT REMMY STEEL had taken part in dozens of real and simulated planetary invasions. They all felt the same to the savvy NCO. The fact that he was on an alien planet, in a system he had never heard of before, didn't change the way it felt.

"I think I see them," Corporal Ricky Thompson said.

"Me too," Sergeant Dirk Oliver added. "Looks like four ships."

Remmy looked up into the pink sky. Casasil was a beautiful world. The trees they were concealed in had long, flexible trunks and wide, red leaves. The trio of space marines were set up behind some fallen trees with a clear view of the wide plain beyond the tree line.

"You have eyes, Staff Sergeant?" Remmy asked Laila McPherson via the comlink in their helmets.

"Roger that. Four ships inbound," she replied.

"We don't have the firepower to stop them," Remmy said. "Assuming they land here."

"Looks like they will. My helmet says they're slowing and descending."

Remmy's HUD showed the same thing. The computer in his space armor had tactical apps for just such an occasion. Information shown on the helmet's Heads Up Display in light green, semi-transparent letters.

"We need to slow them down, that's all. Give the locals time to get clear. No heroics. We'll work a tactical retreat."

"Where to?" Corporal Tyler "Tex" Fry asked.

The plain was north of Remmy's location. The forest thickened behind him.

"South," he said. "We'll have some cover in the forest. Try to stay in contact as you move back. And keep track of your ammo. We're not getting more any time soon."

Remmy checked his rifle. It was a Nelson LTX automatic that fired thumb-sized slugs or the high-impact explosive rounds. He had mags for both in the loops of his armor. The rifle also had a spring-loaded bayonet for close quarters fighting, which Remmy hoped he didn't have to use.

Above them, two of the alien ships continued descending; the other two fired their engines and peeled away in opposite directions.

"Just two?" Tex said. "Hell, they don't know what they're up against."

"Very funny," Corporal Isabel "Izzy" Berry said.

Remmy didn't know what they were facing either. But he did have an advantage that the other Marines didn't have. His mind was linked to the artifact who called herself GIGI, or the Galactic Information and Guidance Instrument. All he had to do was think about what he wanted to know, and the sentient, alien computer would fill him in.

GIGI, you copy?

I am here, Master Sergeant.

Any idea what's in these invasion vessels?

They are Ashi Imperial troops, the alien device explained. *They are highly disciplined and well armed with laser rifles, according to my data.*

Laser rifles? Any specs on their power output?

Do you desire raw data?

I just need to know if our armor will hold up.

Humans had developed and, in certain instances, still used laser guns, but most Space Marines preferred projectiles like Remmy's LTX. Their space armor was multi-layered to provide protection against hard vacuum and the extreme cold of outer space. But it also contained energy-absorbing fibers and hard ceramic plating that was designed to stop laser fire.

My data suggests it will protect you from individual laser impacts, but not without damaging the suit itself.

And are the Ashi troops armored?

Negative, Master Sergeant. The Ashi are a highly aggressive, militaristic race who view protective gear as a form of cowardice.

An image came into Remmy's mind. It was one of the ways that GIGI communicated with him. He saw a large, almost grotesquely muscled creature. They were bipeds with wide jaws and large tusks that rose up on either side of their lower mandible.

What am I looking at? Remmy asked, forming the question in his mind.

An Ashi warrior, GIGI replied.

How big is it?

The average Ashi warrior is three point nine six two four meters tall and weighs approximately five hundred pounds in standard gravity.

"Heads up, Marines," Remmy called over the comlink. "The aliens on those ships are big ...really, really big. Thirteen feet tall, five hundred pounds."

"Good grief, maybe this was a bad idea after all," Laila responded.

"The good news is that they should have laser weapons and consider armor to be cowardly," Remmy continued. "Let's hit them hard and fast. Odds are they haven't been in a real fight for a long time."

"I'm not quite sure six Marines constitute shock and awe, Master Sergeant," Izzy Berry said.

"Any idea how many are in those ships?" Sergeant Dirk Oliver asked.

"None," Remmy said. "But we'll bloody their nose and see what happens."

"Are we talking bipeds or quadrupeds?" Laila asked.

"The locals have six legs," Ricky pointed out.

"Bipeds, Staff Sergeant," Remmy answered.

"Then they can't be that fast," Laila said. "Something that big and heavy would move slow."

"We hope," Izzy added.

The first ship completed its landing and vented a thick cloud of gas. Remmy could just make out a wide ramp opening.

"Looks like we're about to find out," Tex said.

"Hold your fire until I have the word," Remmy said. "Make sure your tactical apps are synced."

"Copy that, holding our fire," Staff Sergeant McPherson said just as the first of the aliens emerged from their ship.

CHAPTER 2

THE PLANET of Casasil hung over the *Renegade* as she peeked out at the enemy ships from below. The Ashi Imperium didn't mess around, Captain Zeke Darius thought. They had flown in fifteen vessels, fourteen of which were arrayed against him. From those fourteen battleships, dozens of small fighter craft had launched.

In a small way, Darius questioned how he had gotten into such a seemingly uneven fight with an enemy he knew next to nothing about. Taking the Space Defense Force's newest ship out for its shakedown cruise was supposed to be his last opportunity to man the captain's seat. He had reached the stage of his career where the only two choices ahead of him were promotion or retirement. But all that had changed, when the order came in to fly to the outer half of the Sol system to investigate the alien artifact that was waiting in space just beyond Saturn.

That mission had turned into the first trans-galaxy flight for a human-built vessel. The SDF Jericho had left the Sol system in search of a power drive reputed to have enough energy to help protect the system from the Ashi Imperium. That successful mission had led to the search for the *Renegade*, an Arodoni ship of such incredible engineering that it could single handedly save the human race from any opponent. Only Darius had realized that the ship would almost certainly draw the Ashi to him, and so returning home would only endanger humanity.

The fourteen warships seemed to prove that Darius' instinct about being tracked was correct. They had dropped out of hyperspace into the Casa system just in time to stop a slave ship and return the abductees to Casasil. But before their shuttle could return from the planet, the aliens had arrived.

"Here we go, people," Darius said, his battle plan fully formed in his own mind. "Time for our 'A' game. Let's look sharp. Weapons hot! Fire!"

They had already targeted the Ashi ship that their weapons system labeled Tango Fourteen. Weapons specialist Lieutenant Pete Best was in control of the *Renegade's* powerful quad laser cannons.

"Foxtrot One," Pete declared as he pressed the firing button.

The alien controls had been designed for tiny hands and were highly advanced, yet Darius' crew of senior officers had quickly learned to operate the ship. A flash of light, almost like lightning, dazzled their eyes. The *Renegade's* Bridge had a transparent canopy that gave the officers an unobstructed view. The laser light moved too fast to track. It appeared as a flash of light, followed immediately by the complete destruction of Tango fourteen.

"That's a hit!" Pete declared.

Not that it was necessary. The other alien ships, including the neat formations of the fighters, were hidden by the planet. But Tango fourteen had been visible a moment ago. After their laser strike from over eight hundred thousand kilometers away, the alien ship was a glowing cloud of dust.

"Total destruction," Henry Nash, the chief engineer, said.

It was a significant achievement. No human ship could unleash such incredible power. The alien ship was there one moment and reduced to atoms in the next. The *Renegade's* laser cannons, even at half power, were more destructive than a nuclear bomb.

"Evasive maneuver," Darius ordered. "Take us backward."

"Aye, evasive maneuvering initiated," Henry Nash said. "Reverse thrusters engaged."

Darius switched his focus from what he could see through the transparent canopy to the holographic plot. The *Renegade's* hologram projectors were nothing like what humans had designed. It was like seeing everything exactly as it was, vibrant and full of color. The planet shielded their ship from return fire, but somehow, the *Renegade* could still follow everything happening to the aliens.

"Looks like they're accelerating, Captain," Lieutenant Vivian Ramos said.

She was their navigator, a human counterpart to the ship's computer systems, and the only person on board the ship who actually understood how the hyperspace network functioned. Like most senior officers, she had an excellent grasp of the ship's other systems. When they weren't calculating jumps between star systems, she helped with radar and communications.

"Trying to get into range," Pete Best said.

"Take us up," Darius ordered. "We'll snipe at the other end of their line."

"Aye, express elevator to the top of the planet," Lieutenant Nash replied.

It was human nature to orient themselves to a system's horizontal orbital plane. The alien ships were spread in a line diagonal to that plane. Darius didn't know if it was just different because they were aliens or if it was some advanced tactical strategy that he hadn't encountered yet.

"Approaching the planet's horizon," Henry Nash declared.

"How are we looking, Lieutenant Best?"

"Excellent, Captain. Foxtrot one is already back to full charge."

The Arodoni Power Core was by far the most bewildering technology the crew of the *Jericho* had discovered. It was small, the size of a compact washing machine, yet it produced more energy than all the reactors in humanity's Space Defense Fleet put together. Scientists had theorized about dark energy for centuries but had never been able to prove its existence. The Arodoni Power Core somehow collected it and reverted it to usable power. It was the closest thing to free energy that Darius had ever seen and the amount of its output was so incredible that it was hard for his crew to believe.

"Prepare cannon two," Darius ordered. "Let's spread the workload."

"Aye, preparing Foxtrot two," Pete replied.

The seconds between making a tactical decision and being able to carry it out were some of the hardest. Darius understood the stakes in the battle he was in. Not just life and death to his crew but the safety of the planet Casasil and perhaps even the entire human race. The *Renegade* was powerful enough to fend off many invaders. There was still so much about the galaxy and its hundreds of intelligent species, but in his scant experience, Darius knew the Arodoni battleship was a game changer. He couldn't be reckless with it. If the ship was damaged there was no guarantee his crew could fix it. The ship had a fantastic, automated maintenance system that consisted of hundreds of specialized robots, as well as its own manufacturing plant that could collect raw materials and refine them into whatever was needed. But Darius didn't want to rely on anything other than his martial skills to keep the valuable ship intact.

"Almost there," Vivian said.

"Range?" Darius asked.

"Closing on five hundred thousand kilometers," Pete Best said, "but they aren't there yet."

"Excellent. Lieutenant Nash, prepare the main engines. I want seventy-five percent power on my mark."

"Aye, main engines at seventy-five percent, standing by," Nash replied.

"GIGI, what's the range on the smaller ships? The fighters."

"One hundred thousand kilometers, Captain," the computerized voice replied.

"Looks like they're heading straight toward the planet," Vivian pointed out.

"Maybe to use its gravity to slingshot around it and attack us at speed," Pete Best suggested.

"It might be headed for the planet. Do we have word on our Marines?" Darius asked.

"Aye, Captain, I just got word from Ronan One," Ensign Jacee Bertoli said.

"Let's have it."

"They are on the shuttle and returning to the ship, but half the platoon stayed behind to help the locals."

That wasn't what Captain Darius wanted to hear. He scowled but kept his anger in check.

Ensign Bertoli continued her report. "The others, those that are returning, experienced some kind of damage to their armor. They are hoping to refit and return to the planet."

"Negative. Get them on board as soon as possible," Darius said.

"Should we wait to engage the main thrusters?" Lieutenant Nash asked.

Before Darius could answer, Pete Best interrupted. "Tango One in range. Permission to engage, Captain."

"Fire away," Darius ordered.

"Foxtrot two!" Pete shouted as the flash of laser light lit the bridge.

Darius didn't even bother to look up from the plot.

"Send the Marines straight out from the planet," Darius said. "We can't wait on them. Set them on course two-eight-four, and tell them not to dawdle until we know what those Ashi fighters plan to do."

"That's a hit," Pete Best said. "Another ship vaporized."

"Two down, twelve to go," Vivian replied.

"Captain Darius," GIGI's digital voice came over the speakers built into the chairs that had been fabricated on board the *Renegade* and installed once the humans took over the abandoned alien ship. "Permission to launch drones."

"Drones?" Darius asked.

Of course, he knew there were drones on the ship. When the

Marine platoon had first infiltrated the *Renegade* it had been through a hangar that was packed with thousands of vessels. Some were shuttles like the one the Marine platoon was flying back toward space, but there were thousands of small military drones of various sizes. He hadn't had the chance to study the different designs or learn what their purposes were. No one had. They had scarcely been in the ship a week when they left the Vangori Nebula, where it had been hidden.

"There are eight thousand automated fighters for space-to-space engagement and twelve thousand drones for atmospheric operations. I can launch and control both types," GIGI stated flatly.

"You can control the drones by yourself?" Darius asked.

It wasn't a stupid question. Of course, computers could run all sorts of systems simultaneously, but like the alien ship, GIGI was an alien creation. A sentient computer that had waited nearly three hundred years to make contact with the human race.

"Affirmative, Captain. My system is capable of controlling two thousand drones simultaneously. I recommend three hundred ship-to-ship craft to protect the Marine shuttle and another five hundred atmospheric drones to assist Master Sergeant Steel on the planet's surface."

There were not often moments in a battle when a ship captain was stunned in a good way. He had felt that his ship was alone against overwhelming alien forces, when suddenly he realized he commanded an entire army.

"Vivian, Jacee, take control of two surveillance drones and launch immediately. I want eyes on Master Sergeant Steel's forces down on the surface."

"Aye," both women said at the same time.

"GIGI, launch your offensive," Darius continued giving orders. "Can your drones attack their capital ships?"

"If you desire, Captain," the computerized voice said.

"Would they be effective?" He pressed for the answer he needed.

"Affirmative."

"Do it, but focus on the fighters. Nash, as soon as the drones are clear, engage thrusters. Take us straight up, vector two-niner-zero."

"Aye, two-niner-zero, Captain. Standing by."

"Launch commencing," GIGI said.

On the plot, Darius could see swarms of drones launching from the *Renegade*. Now, it gets interesting, he thought.

"Engage the enemy at will," he ordered.

The drones flew into tight formations before streaking away. Some circled the planet, others made straight for it. Darius knew he was going to have to learn an entirely new way to fight, but so far, he was feeling very good about their prospects.

CHAPTER 3

A GOOD MARINE should be ready for anything. That was the thought that went through Remmy's head as he got his first look at the Ashi Troopers. Instead, he felt a hollow sensation in his gut and thought he might be sick.

"Well," Tex said in his typical, slow draw, "they'll be hard to miss."

"They're out of range," Laila said. "I show them just over fifteen hundred meters out."

"Let's see how they operate," Remmy said.

"They just keep coming out of that ship," Ricky Thompson pointed out.

"Like clowns out of a tiny car," Sergeant Dirk Oliver added.

"No movement from the other ship," Laila pointed out. "It's different."

"We wait and watch," Remmy said. "Everyone stay frosty; make sure you're recording everything you see."

"Roger that," Staff Sergeant Laila McPherson replied.

Remmy glanced over at the two Marines with him in the copse of trees. Dirk Oliver seemed solid, while Ricky Thompson seemed almost jumpy. But Remmy knew some people were flooded with nervous energy before a fight. Sitting still was obviously difficult for Corporal Thompson.

"They're forming up around the other ship," Dirk Oliver said.

"The leader must be in there," Laila said. "I wish we had some heavier ordnance."

"If we're making wishes, how about a way out of here," Izzy said.

"I'm counting at least two hundred... what are we calling these things?" Dirk Oliver asked.

"Ogres," Laila replied.

"Giant ogres," Izzy added.

"Looks like the leader is coming out," Ricky Thompson interjected.

The Marines all fell silent for a moment. At first, they were looking for the leader and when he appeared, they were awed by the massive alien. It stepped to the edge of the ship's opening, a long ramp that was high enough that the leader could take in the view of his troops. In the Marine combat simulations, there were all types of aliens, from slugs to dinosaurs. The Ashi leader was more like a villain from a comic book. He was huge, with bulging muscles all across his green-skinned body, which was mostly bare. Even from a kilometer and a half, Remmy could see the veins that covered most of his body, like lightning crackling across the night sky.

The leader wore a kilt around his thick waist and what appeared to be shoulder pads or some type of ceremonial armor with curved horns that arced up toward his wide head. What he didn't have was a gun. The alien leader instead carried a curved sword that looked almost like a curved Egyptian Khopesh. He raised the weapon and shouted to his troops. The translation of his orders popped up on Remmy's HUD: *To War, For Glory!* The ogres all roared in agreement with their leader, then turned and began marching away from the ships.

"They're on the move," Dirk Oliver said.

It was an unnecessary comment. The aliens were marching toward the Marines, their rifles held across their broad chests. Like their leader, most wore very little clothing. Boots and kilts seemed to be the only uniform for the aliens. Some wore tight sashes, either one that angled from hip to shoulder or two that crossed to form an X over the center of their bodies. They had long hair that grew right on the crown of their head and was tied with multiple threads. Their ears were pointed, their eyes small, but their musculature was very reminiscent of humans.

"Easy now," Remmy said. "Make sure your weapons are on full auto, but don't waste your ammo. Short bursts."

"They look a lot like us," Tex said.

"Are you out of your mind, Tex?" Ricky Thompson asked.

"I'm just saying their physicality is like ours. Maybe their vitals are, too."

"He's right," Remmy said. "Aim for the body."

Another shouted order, and the aliens began to jog. Their heavy footfalls made a rhythmic thumping sound that echoed across the plain.

"Looks like they can move pretty good," Izzy said.

"Faster than I expected," Laila admitted.

"Doesn't mean they're agile," Remmy said.

"They're a thousand meters out," Ricky Thompson said.

"I don't have to tell you with numbers this stacked against us; we have to hit them hard in our initial volley. And we need to be moving back as we fight. If we get pinned down, we're dead."

"We'll be more vulnerable if we're on the move," Dirk pointed out.

"That can't be helped," Laila said. "There's too many of them for us to kill them all."

"What about the locals?" Ricky asked.

"They won't be much help," Remmy said. "They're not fighters."

But he glanced over his shoulder anyway. He could see the elephantine Casians trundling down the plain. There would be no help from them.

"Any chance the LT makes it back?" Izzy asked.

"I'm kinda wishing I had one of those MECH suits right about now," Dirk Oliver said.

"Don't count it," Laila said. "They haven't had time to get to the ship and return."

"Not to mention the ship will be under heavy fire, too," Remmy said. "We have to remember we're on our own."

"More ships," Ricky Thompson said.

Before Remmy could respond, GIGI's voice broke into his thoughts. *Master Sergeant, I have five hundred drones inbound to your location.*

"This could be a slaughter," Tex said.

"We knew this was a last-stand situation before we volunteered," Izzy said. "I can live with that."

"From what we've seen, things are not good on this planet," Laila said. "The locals don't stand a chance against the ogres."

"Hold on, platoon," Remmy said. "GIGI, repeat that."

I have five hundred drones inbound to your location, Master Sergeant. I suggest that you take cover immediately. ETA is twenty-seven seconds.

"Marines," Remmy said. "Get down. Take cover. Those ships are from the *Renegade*."

"What?" Laila asked.

"Reinforcements, baby! Hell yeah," Dirk Oliver said.

"Let's go!" Ricky Thompson added.

"Get down," Remmy ordered. "Take cover now."

The aliens saw the drones, too. Remmy was watching, his head just slightly above the fallen trees he was sheltering behind. They turned, looking up. Orders were shouted. The alien troops began to fan out. It was like watching a military parade. They turned, moving backward, their rifles coming up to their shoulders in a firing position.

Remmy's tactical app showed the drones at over four kilometers from the ground. The aliens couldn't shoot them out of the sky with their laser rifles. But as the drones began to drop small yield warheads, the aliens started shooting. The bombs fell fast, and many were hit with laser fire as they dropped. Those that were shot exploded in the air. Some of those explosions set off more of the bombs. Only a few got through, but they landed among the troopers with deadly force. Howls and screams were heard as the bombs dropped. Thunder rolled from the explosions overhead.

"Why don't they take cover?" Laila asked, her voice barely more than a whisper over the comlink.

"There isn't any," Dirk Oliver pointed out.

"That's some kind of courage," Tex said. "It's like they aren't afraid to die."

The troopers weren't the only things targeted. More bombs dropped onto the ships which had been left unattended. They were blown to pieces of smoking rubble. The bombs that hit the ground left blackened craters.

Drone squadron is turning for another pass, GIGI warned Remmy. *Sixty seconds.*

"Copy that," Remmy said. "Drones are coming back around. If you have a shot, take it."

Most of the aliens were still out of range, but they continued fanning out so that the bombs didn't take down larger numbers of them. A few were at the edge of Remmy's effective range. He steadied his LTX rifle on the log he was kneeling behind. The rifle was loaded with heavy slugs. He flipped the firing switch from auto to semi-auto and synced his rifle to his helmet's long-range targeting app. Crosshairs appeared on his HUD. He steadied them on the closest alien, took a breath, held it, and eased the trigger back.

His rifle rocked against his shoulder as the round shot out. A full second later, the bullet arced down and smashed into the unsuspecting alien's back. The huge brute stumbled for a second, then straightened and continued backing up.

"They aren't going down easy," Remmy said as he switched to a three-round burst mode and pulled the trigger again.

Across the plain, Laila McPherson was having the same luck. Her weapon of choice was Bericuda Supreme 5.96. It was a rugged, fully automatic rifle that fired stub-nosed shock rounds that split apart on impact, the jagged edges sliced through flesh easily. Her first shot took one of the alien troopers in the back of his neck. The alien reached up, felt the wound, glanced at his bloody hand, and turned. Her second shot punched into the left side of his chest. The alien swayed but didn't fall. Instead, he raised his laser rifle in his right hand and fired a strafing shot at the trees where Laila's fire team was hidden.

Her third shot hit the alien high in his chest, just below his throat at the top of his sternum. The bare-chested alien dropped his rifle and went down to his knees as navy blue blood flooded the front his body.

Remmy's bursts had more impact. The three bullets landed like a supersonic combo punch, twisting the massive alien fighter and knocking it off its feet. But it wasn't an immediate kill. The alien ended up on its hands and knees and surprised Remmy by crawling toward the rifle it had dropped.

Remmy ducked back down under the cover of the fallen logs as the aliens started to shoot toward the trees. His hands moved quickly, ejecting his magazine of soft alloy slugs for a fresh clip of explosive rounds. He darted back up and fired quickly. It was the type of weapon handling that could only be effective after hundreds of hours of practice. His shots hit one of the aliens on the right side of its chest and shoulder. The bullets punched into the fleshy muscles and then exploded, ripping the alien's arm from his body. To Remmy's horror, the alien ignored the wound, bent over, plucked the rifle from its amputated arm, and began firing.

"They're unstoppable," Ricky Thompson complained.

"Aim lower," Tex said. "I think maybe their vitals are in the lower abdomen."

Remmy hadn't been spotted. The aliens were simply shooting

blind into the forest. Laser bolts ripped bark from the narrow tree trunks and sizzled overhead. He had time to test Tex's theory. He fired another quick trio of explosive rounds. They hit the alien across the wide leather belt at the top of its kilt. The entire middle of its body blew outward from the explosive bullets, and for the first time, the alien toppled backward and didn't move.

"That did it," Remmy said.

"Hell yeah! I got one," Dirk Oliver exclaimed.

But the aliens weren't stupid. In fact, Remmy didn't think he had ever seen a more disciplined force. They were turning, moving in an erratic fashion that was ideal for evading fire. Most were still out of range, but they had turned their attention from the drones above to the Marines on the ground. And they were moving quickly. Not quite sprinting like a human might but running faster than before. They were huge targets, and Remmy knew that diving to the ground wouldn't save the big aliens. None were trying, not even taking cover behind their fallen comrades, as Remmy had seen other Marines do countless times.

"Incoming!" Remmy shouted. "Take cover."

The sky was marred with smoke from the first wave of bombs, making the drones harder to see. And they were too high up for Remmy to hear them. The aliens didn't seem to have heard them either. Most were still firing at the tree line as they zig-zagged across the open field.

The bombs fell like rain. All Remmy could do was to get as low as possible behind the fallen log. He was thankful for his armor as the ground shook from the heavy explosions. In all his time as a Marine he had never experienced the amount of firepower dropped onto the battlefield. It was a massacre. Well over half of the aliens were killed in the second wave of bombing. When the explosions stopped, Remmy slowly raised his head. The battlefield had become a smoky nightmare. It was dark, and there were bodies burning across the charred field.

"Woah," Tex said.

"I got no bogies in range," Izzy added.

"Stay put," Remmy said. "It's not over."

"Feels like it should be," Dirk Oliver said. "How can anyone keep fighting after that?"

"They've got nowhere left to go," Remmy reminded them. "And there's no one more dangerous than an enemy with nothing left to lose."

CHAPTER 4

THE *RENEGADE* SHOT up past the planet faster than anyone on board thought possible. One minute, they were cruising at normal speed, but once the main engines kicked in, the ship rocketed through space.

"Bogies are scrambling!" Vivian Ramos said.

"They're moving to cut us off from escaping," Henry Nash replied.

"Range?" Captain Darius asked.

"Six hundred thousand kilometers and rising," Vivian said. "We're out of their effective firing range."

That didn't stop several of the alien ships from taking shots at them. Most were clear misses. Those that were on target weren't strong enough to penetrate *Renegades's* sonic shields.

"Should we turn and shoot back?" Pete Best asked.

"Negative, we're not in danger yet," Darius said. "GIGI, can you tell us what your drones are doing?"

"Circling the planet to engage enemy fighters, Captain."

"Very good. This is all, very, very good."

"Sir, I have contact with the Ronan One," Ensign Jacee Bertoli said.

"Put them through."

"Shogun, this is Ronan One actual, we are inbound for your location. Can you give a rendezvous point, please?"

"Lieutenant Colt, you've jumped from the frying pan into the fire," Darius replied. "There are fighters in high orbit. Head straight out and wait for rescue."

"But sir, there's a fight on the ground. We need to reequip and get back down there," Colt said.

"Can't do it," the captain said, watching the alien ships on the plot. They were spreading out and gaining speed as they rushed back toward the hyperspace portal. "We are facing multiple capital ships, Lieutenant. This isn't a simulation."

"Sir, I know that, but my new MECH armor could make the difference between life and death on the surface."

"You'll have to wait to test your new toy, Ronan One. But rest easy; we launched drones to help Master Sergeant Steel. Proceed to the rally point you've been sent, Lieutenant, and let us do our work. Shogun, out."

"Passing seven hundred and fifty thousand kilometers, sir," Vivian said.

"Alright, let's slow down and turn," Darius ordered. "Weapons?"

"Fully charged and ready, captain," Pete Best said.

"Good. Can we target more than one ship at a time?"

"Staggered firing is possible, Captain," Pete Best said.

"I want to hit them all," Darius ordered. "Begin tracking the capital ships for a staggered laser burst at ten percent power."

"At ten percent, we won't destroy them," Pete Best said.

"That's okay," Darius said. "The point now is to show them what we can do."

"Fighter weapons are in range," GIGI said as laser flashes twinkled around the planet below them. "Evasive maneuvering initiated."

In some ways, the battle felt like a game. The fighters and drones were listed as a number total on Darius's display. The three hundred drones sent to stop the fighters were declining, and it took a few moments for the drones to close to their own effective firing distance. By the time the drones started shooting back, a third of their number was gone.

Darius pressed the comlink transmit button. "Commander Lee, are you tracking the battle?"

"Aye, Captain," Lori Lee said.

"Systems report."

"All systems are green, sir."

"Power output?"

"We haven't even begun to tax the energy core, Captain. We're in good shape down here."

"Have Ensign Stanislaus run manufacturing sims on the drones we launched. We're going through them fast."

"Roger that, Captain. We'll get right on it."

"Sir, I have surveillance from the planet," Vivian said.

"Show me," Darius said.

The *Renegade* didn't have big display screens, but the holographic projectors could mimic them perfectly. And it wasn't just the plot that was high resolution. When the video feed from the surveillance drone popped up, it was like a huge window had been opened directly onto the Bridge of the ship. Through that window, the officers could see the surface of the planet from ten thousand meters above it. The image zoomed down. A wide plain came into focus, with forests on either side. Much of the ground itself was masked by smoke. And there were flashes of laser fire. Darius saw a neat formation of drones making a wide turn over one of the forested areas.

"Drones have dropped their warheads," GIGI explained. "Preparations for strafing runs are being made."

"There's a ship headed straight toward the fighting," Vivian said.

"Take evasive action," Darius ordered.

But before the drones could react heavy laser fire issued from the alien ship. Half of the drones were reduced to ions in a blink of an eye.

"Should we send reinforcement?" Pete Best asked.

"We're too far out now," Darius lamented. "They'll never get there in time."

"Captain, I have a communication from Tango Eight, sir," Jacee Bertoli announced.

Darius took a deep breath, then stood up. "Let's have it, Ensign."

Another video projection showed a massive creature with green skin. He had a thick, black beard over the bottom of his wide jaw and short, curved tusks. When he spoke, his voice was deep. The language was rough and guttural. Fortunately, GIGI translated for the alien.

"Greetings from the Ashi Imperium," the green-skinned alien said. "My name is Ulrach Sheika. I am the Emperor's Kahn. I will accept your surrender and the transfer of your ship."

Darius had to fight back a smile. He wasn't sure if the alien could see him, but he assumed that he could.

"I am Captain Zeke Darius. Return to orbit, and we will allow your crews to live."

"The Ashi Imperium does not lose in battle, Captain," the alien said.

"You are outgunned."

"You are outnumbered."

"Your forces on the ground will soon be slaughtered," the Kahn said. "And there is nowhere in the galaxy where you will be safe from the Imperium."

"We'll take our chances," Darius said, glancing at the numbers that indicated the drones and fighters in combat near the planet. "Your attack force is on the verge of complete annihilation."

"This is but a sample of what the Imperium can bring to bear. Even now, there is an armada on its way to reinforce us. You cannot beat us to the hyperspace lanes. If you try to escape the system, we will destroy you."

"I think you overestimate your abilities," Darius said.

"Doubt us at your peril, Captain Darius. But there is another option. The Emperor has long admired the Arodoni civilization. Surrender, and we see to it that your people are treated with dignity and respect. Whatever you desire is ours to give."

"We've seen what the Imperium is about. Slavery, conflict, oppression, these are not traits that we value in an ally."

"The only other alternative is death."

"So be it," Darius said. "If war is what you crave, we shall give you all you can handle."

"Spoken like a true warrior. Prepare for death, Arodoni. Yours is coming soon."

The image vanished, and Darius turned to Pete Best. "Are we ready?"

"Aye, Captain," the weapons specialist said.

"Fire away!"

CHAPTER 5

"SIR, the aliens have not been identified," the shipmaster said in a tremulous voice.

"They are not Arodoni?" Sheika Kahn asked.

"Not according to our records. We ran the images through the entire database. There were no hits. This is an unknown species."

"How did they know our language?"

"I cannot say, Lord. They must be using the ship's computer database to translate. We have no record of their spoken language either. They are completely unknown, perhaps not even from our galaxy."

"But the ship?"

"The ship is Arodoni. It was last seen nearly eight centuries ago. Classified as a Star Killer. It disappeared."

"But now it's back," Sheika Kahn said as he scratched at his thickly bearded chin.

A sudden flash was immediately followed by a slight dimming of the lights on the *Vexation*. The Khan's eyes narrowed as an officer called out.

"Multiple shots fired. Our shields held, Shipmaster."

"What happened?" Kahn asked.

"They fired on all our ships, sir, but our shields held."

"How is that possible?"

"They must have weakened their lasers."

"A warning. Get us the hell out of here, Shipmaster. Before we're all destroyed."

"But sir, what about the emperor?"

"We will return for Emperor Vang. He is safely on Casasil. Recall our fighters and prepare to jump out of this system."

"Aye, Lord Kahn. We will make the preparations, but our fighters were destroyed, sir. The last ship was disabled a few moments ago."

"I thought you said our shields held," Sheika thundered away. "Now you tell me our fighters were destroyed?"

"They were attacked by small, unmanned attack craft," the Shipmaster explained. "There were hundreds of them. Our fighters fought valiantly and died gloriously in battle, sir."

Ulrich Sheika was an Ashi and he understood the cultural ideal of dying well, but of course, he was much more interested in living. Let Emperor Vang die a glorious death battling the new species. Sheika Kahn would live.

"Order the other ships to move in a shielding pattern between us and the Star Killer," Kahn ordered. "Send word to the Emperor that we will return with more ships."

"Ordering a shielding pattern," the Shipmaster called out. "Communications are sent, Lord Kahn."

"Set a course for Min'Hoi Station," Kahn said. "Have the fleet gather there for an attack on this Arodoni ship."

The Shipmaster hurried away. Kahn brought up the information about the new species which had been gathered during the communication. It was not lost on Sheika that the Captain did not correct him when the Kahn assumed he was Arodoni. They were clever, this strange new species, and bold. Of course, anyone could be bold with an Arodoni warship. Its destructive power was unfathomable. Khan wasn't fascinated by war the way many of his Ashi kinsmen were, yet he knew that a weapon strong enough to overcome a battleship's deflector shields would have to be substantial. Sheika knew that only a mega-cannon could do that with a single shot, but those were massive weapons that required so much energy that they could only fire once without needing to refuel. The standard warship of the Ashi Imperium was a frigate-class battleship with multiple cannons and a squadron of fast attack fighters. Their cannons relied on multiple shots to disable a ship's deflector screens, and while a ship could, in theory, be totally destroyed, nothing in their arsenal was capable of reducing a ship to atoms. Even fission bombs left debris when used to scuttle an Imperial ship. Yet the Arodoni vessel had destroyed two of Sheika's vessels with a single shot.

The new aliens certainly had no qualms about using the Arodoni weapons, and that told him something about them. The hologram from the alien ship had shown a trim, pale looking species. They were not unlike the Ashi, although obviously smaller. He knew full well that the images he had seen of them might be fabricated, but that seemed unlikely. If Sheika were going to pretend to be something other than an Ashi, he would have created something large and intimidating. The new aliens were too small, too weak to be a threat ... and yet somehow, it was Sheika's forces that were in full retreat.

He leaned forward and pressed a button to record a message for Emperor Vang.

"Lord," Kahn said, bowing as he spoke. "The Arodoni ship is too powerful for our forces. We have lost two frigates and two squadrons of fighters. I have, therefore, ordered a full retreat from the system. We will return as soon as possible. Hold on, my liege. I am fully aware that no threat can harm you and no enemy can defeat you. I am sure we will return to find you victorious, my Liege. Until then, I will do my best to carry on as you would have me do."

He bowed again and then stopped the recording.

"Send this message to Emperor Vang on the planet," the Kahn ordered.

"As you wish, sir, but I must inform you that Emperor Vang's ship was destroyed."

"What?" Sheika replied, feigning outrage while secretly rejoicing that his plan had worked.

"We have no word from the emperor, but the *Devastation* reports that his ship was destroyed by drones from the Arodoni vessel, just like our fighters."

"They are cowards who do not fight their own battles," Sheika raged. "What is the enemy vessel doing now?"

"It remains just outside the effective range of our cannons," the Shipmaster replied. "But it is not moving to cut off our retreat."

"Excellent. What is the *Devastation* doing?"

"They report troops still on the ground, but there are casualties, my Kahn. The emperor's forces were caught in the open."

"The Emperor will survive. He cannot be defeated."

It was propaganda and the Shipmaster clearly didn't believe it, but neither could he contradict the Kahn. He looked uncomfortable.

"Send the message," Sheika Kahn ordered. "Then take us out of the system."

"And what if the alien ship fires on us again?"

"They will not," Sheika declared. "They have used their power reserves, I'm sure. And they have what they want. Let them believe they have victory. It will be so much sweeter when we snatch it away from them."

The Shipmaster bowed. "Aye, my Lord."

Sheika Kahn should have been worried, but he wasn't. The Imperium was on the verge of a revolutionary change that would usher in a new dynasty. He felt confident that his time had come at last. He meant to ensure that no one could challenge his ascension to the throne.

CHAPTER 6

"FALL BACK," Remmy ordered calmly. "Slow and silent."

Above them, a battle was taking place. The drones had just begun strafing runs, but the smoke was impairing their effectiveness. And then came another of the alien ships. It hit the drones with heavy laser fire. Remmy didn't need GIGI to tell him it was a one-sided affair. The drones that were shot down fell into the forest behind his position, most of them burning, and it didn't take long for the forest to catch fire. Between the falling drones and the aliens shooting lasers into the woods, it was inevitable, and Remmy had planned for it. The smoke moving among the trees would offer the Marines cover.

"Roger that," Laila replied. "Bravo team is on the move."

Remmy waited for Ricky Thompson and Dirk Oliver to slink deeper into the woods before peering up over the top of the fallen log he was lying behind. Down low, he could see a little better through the smoke. There were a lot of bodies strewn across the battlefield. Most were in pieces from the second wave of bombs the drones had dropped. The once beautiful meadow had become a blackened killing ground, with craters and debris everywhere.

It was impossible to count the exact number of aliens. Their leaders had ordered them back into a small throng. Remmy wasn't sure if they were protecting someone or simply falling back to let their ship mop up the drones, but it was a good time for the Marines to move. He rolled to his knees and got up slowly. He kept his weapon held, ready to fire. His sense of impending doom was gone. The drones had changed the tide of the battle and given Remmy hope that they might survive the fight. At the very least, GIGI could pilot a shuttle down to rescue them if all else failed.

"Are we retreating or just maneuvering for a better position?" Dirk Oliver asked.

"Let's wait and see what the enemy does," Remmy said.

"Every minute we keep them engaged here, more of the locals have time to escape," Laila pointed out.

"Looks like we've lost air support, though," Ricky Thompson said. "And we're still outnumbered."

Remmy understood the stress of battle. It was impossible to ignore the feeling that you were going to be left all alone to face the enemy by yourself. He had felt it during every engagement he had fought in. The human mind could be tricky that way. Remmy's natural instincts were, like every person who ever lived, to avoid danger. Some were drawn to dangerous activities or professions, but they still had to overcome the instinct for self-preservation. And Remmy didn't want to stay on the battlefield for one second longer than he had to. But his duty required that he stay, to face his enemy ... if possible, to defeat him.

"There's no telling what ogres might do," Izzy said.

"I'll bet they're thinking the same thing about us," Tex told her.

"Look sharp," Laila cut in. "They're on the move."

"Looks like scouts," Remmy said. "I count ten. Five moving my way, five moving toward your location, Staff Sergeant."

"Copy that," Laila said. "Orders?"

"Let's find a place to welcome them to the jungle," Remmy said. "Pick a good spot with cover. Wait until they're close, then make 'em pay."

"Oh, yeah, now you're talking," Tex said. "I'll show these big green ogres how a country boy does it."

"I can't get much tactical response on my app with all the trees and smoke," Dirk Oliver complained.

"Don't rely on the computers here," Remmy said. "Pick up your visual scanning. These guys are too big to hide."

"They aren't moving cautiously either," Ricky Thompson said. "They have no fear."

"There's a difference between having it and showing it," Laila said.

"Let's give 'em a reason to be afraid," Remmy said.

He was slinking between the trees and soon came to a pair of them growing close together. The two trunks gave him plenty of cover. Through the shroud of smoke came the first of the alien scouts. Ricky was right; it seemed fearless. The big, heavy-bodied alien wasn't being cautious. It marched boldly into the forest, looking around, but not slowing. Remmy could hear the heavy footfalls. It was headed close to him, not straight to his position, but he would pass by within a few meters.

"Keep in mind they may light things up once we start shooting," Remmy reminded the Marines. "Heads down, eyes open."

"Roger that, Master Sergeant," Laila responded.

Remmy went down on one knee and brought his rifle to his shoulder. His heart hammered hard in his chest. Fear told him to cower down and hope the alien passed him by. But fear didn't rule Remmy Steel. He leaned out, sighted the approaching alien, and fired.

If the alien spotted him, it made no move to target him or protect itself. Remmy's three-round burst was loud in the forest. The explosive rounds punched into the alien's waist and nearly cut him in half. The alien dropped to the ground with a thud, and everything was quiet again. A few seconds later, Remmy heard a rifle report from across the meadow. Then, shots closer to his own position. The Marines were taking down the aliens one by one.

Remmy heard a savage roar; then, laser fire ripped through the forest. One of the aliens was charging forward. Remmy didn't know if it was bravery or if the stress of hunting an enemy it couldn't see had gotten to the alien. Either way, he was shooting too high. Even shooting from the hip, the aliens were aiming high. They were more than twice the height of the average human and they hadn't learned to adjust their aim yet. Remmy let the alien charge toward him, then fired from between the two trees. The alien was at an angle to him. Remmy's shots blew off the alien's leg. It fell, and the laser rifle dropped out of reach, but the alien wasn't dead. It lay shuddering on the ground as blood pumped from its severed leg. It didn't scream, but it couldn't keep from moaning and breathing heavily. Remmy didn't know how they communicated and stayed out of sight. The last thing he wanted was to reveal himself to the dying alien and have it communicated to the rest of its companions.

"We took down three," Laila said. "The other two are retreating."

"I got one," Dirk said.

"Me too," Ricky Thompson added.

That was four. Remmy didn't have eyes on the fifth alien. It could be retreating, or it might still be hunting them.

"Stay alert; they'll send more the next time."

"We may have a bigger problem, Sergeant," Laila responded. "The fire is getting close."

"It's spreading fast on our side," Tex said.

"Bravo team, get out of there. Fall back. Once you're clear of the fire, we can set a rally point."

"Roger that," Laila said. "Bravo team is out."

"Let's start moving back, too," Remmy said. "Just keep in mind, there's one more of those things out here."

Sergeant Dirk Oliver and Corporal Ricky Thompson acknowledged the order. Remmy waited a few more seconds. He could hear the crackle of fire nearby, but it wasn't a roar yet. And he knew his armor would protect him from the heat and smoke as long as he didn't get caught in the actual flames.

GIGI, what's the status of your drones? Remmy asked, forming the question in his mind instead of his mouth.

We are down to ten percent, Master Sergent. I have them hovering in the trees to avoid detection.

What are they armed with?

A single-barrel machine gun for precision strikes. They are armed with what you would call flechettes.

I'm guessing they're not much use against the Ashi.

There was no time to rearm the drones, GIGI explained.

But you've depleted the bombs?

Correct.

Then hold them back, Remmy ordered. *We can use them for surveillance.*

Captain Darius ordered two surveillance drones launched before the Renegade left orbit. One is circling your position at ten thousand meters, but I cannot share the video feed with your brain.

That's okay; just give me the gist.

I am unfamiliar with that vernacular.

A report, GIGI. Tell me what you see.

Smoke mostly. The initial bombing run was successful in destroying the emperor's shuttle, as well as the troop carrier that was sent to accompany him.

The emperor? As in the leader of the entire Imperium is on the ground out here?

The data would warrant a seventy-two percent chance that the emperor is there.

That changes things, standby, Remmy said.

"Bravo team, I just got intel that the emperor is on the battlefield," he reported.

"The emperor, as in the king of the bad guys?" Laila asked.

"Affirmative. I've sent the rest of Alpha squad south through the forest. I'm going to linger here a bit, move around, and see if I can get a shot at this guy."

"We should join you if you're planning an attack on the emperor," Laila argued.

"Negative. I'll take a shot if I have one. Otherwise, I'll fall back, too. We're going to have to stay alive for a while down here. Don't take any unnecessary chances, Staff Sergeant."

"That's good advice. You should remember it."

"I will. Don't worry, I won't reveal myself unless I have an excellent chance to take down their leader."

"Good luck, Master Sergeant. Keep us in the loop."

"Will do. Remmy out."

He moved slowly, looking in every direction before venturing out from behind the trees. Smoke was filling the canopy above him. He knew it would get thicker and lower as the fire intensified. It was flushing the Marines out of position, but it also offered a barrier to the aliens. They could pursue the locals down the open portion of the plain between the forests, but that bottleneck would make them vulnerable to an ambush, and from what Remmy had seen, the aliens weren't too keen on chasing them down.

On the battlefield, many of the craters were still smoking, which made it difficult to see very far. Remmy angled his way closer to the tree line. He could just make out the jumble of alien fighters. Even from a distance, they were intimidating. Their size and obvious strength made him feel like a child fighting adults. Fortunately, his rifle was effective in disabling and killing the Ashi warriors.

Part of him couldn't help but admire the aliens. They looked like beings from a fantasy game, but they were real. They would have been better off in a firefight to wear protective armor, but by baring their hulking physiques, they sent a powerful message to their enemies.

What else can you tell me about the Ashi we're fighting? Remmy wondered.

They are a martial race who hold a strict, warrior ethos, GIGI replied, the words forming straight into Remmy's brain. *Having conquered most of the galaxy, I surmise that they are anxious to prove themselves against a potent enemy.*

How's the Renegade *holding up?*

Excellent. Captain Darius is a daring and skilled tactician.

Good to know.

You should also be aware that the Ashi battleships are fleeing the system.

Wait, are you sure about that?

They have vowed to return, but they are making their way toward the hyperspace portal at speed after losing two of their ships in battle with the Renegade and two squadrons of fighters against our drones.

But you said the emperor is here.

There is a high probability that he is.

How are you coming to that conclusion?

The emperors of the Ashi Imperium have traditionally piloted a certain kind of ship. It is made from four interlocking segments. Such a ship is in orbit now. The three hybrid craft separated from the ship's mainframe and descended to the planet. They consist of the emperor's command ship and two protective vessels. One of the protective craft destroyed most of the support drones I was operating above your position, Sergeant. And the command craft that traditionally comprises the emperor's personal quarters was destroyed in the bombing.

But you haven't seen the Emperor?

It is impossible to make a conclusive identification through the smoke from the battlefield and without current data on who the emperor is.

How will I recognize him? Remmy asked.

He will wear more regal attire and will command the other warriors.

Remmy was about to ask another question, but as he stepped around a crooked tree, he found himself face-to-face with an alien scout. The warrior must have seen or heard him approaching. Remmy would have cursed his lack of attention if there had been time, but before he could do anything, the alien shot him.

CHAPTER 7

THERE WAS a flash as the laser hit Remmy. The focused light was powerful enough to burn through metal, but his armor was a high heat-dispersing polymer backed by insulation. He felt the impact of the laser, but it was nothing like the kinetic exchange of a projectile. To Remmy, it felt more like he was thumped; it didn't even knock him backward. His suit registered the hit, though, and internal sensors set off sirens inside his helmet.

Remmy didn't need electronic warnings to alert him to the danger. His instincts kicked in without a second's hesitation. He simultaneously dropped to his knees and, at the same time, raised his rifle. There was no time to aim and really no need either. The alien was huge and less than ten meters away. Remmy fired a burst in the alien's direction. Two of his rounds missed, but the third ripped into the warrior's muscular shoulder. The explosive round worked almost like a piston. The pointed tip drove into the flesh, while the charge at the rear of the bullet had a split second to rush forward and set off the small explosive. Remmy saw a flash of light as a second laser blast flashed over his head, and then the eruption of flesh as his own bullet exploded. It missed bone but shredded the alien's flesh. Muscle, skin, and blood flew out in a spray as the big alien was pushed backward.

There was a look in the alien's eyes that hadn't been there a moment before. Not fear, but surprise mixed with anger. To Remmy's shock, even though the big alien had lost its grip on the laser rifle when it was hit by the exploding round from Remmy's LTX, it quickly regained its composure. The gigantic warrior didn't fall down the way a human would have. Instead, once it regained its balance, it charged forward. Remmy was so surprised that, for a moment, he did nothing. There was something valiant about the alien charging down its foe. Remmy found it hard to pull the trigger, but he did it. The second three-round burst all found their mark, stitching across the alien's wide chest. The explosive energy blew the creature backward. Remmy saw his feet fly up as if he had slipped on a patch of ice. He also felt the ground vibrate with the impact as the big body hit the dirt.

His knees ached as Remmy stood back up. The space armor he was wearing had pads for the knees, but dropping straight onto them had taken a toll. His joints had years of wear and tear from running and fighting. But pain was just another sign that you weren't dead. Remmy ignored the pain as he got to his feet and moved carefully toward the alien.

It wasn't dead. The pectoral muscles had been shredded, but unlike humans, the aliens had a solid plate of bone across their chests. Remmy could see it through the gore of blackened flesh. It didn't even seem to be fractured. But the alien was in a lot of pain. Without the pectoral muscles, it couldn't get up. Just moving its arms was agonizing for the alien, but it watched him approach with rage in its eyes.

"Sucks, I know," Remmy said softly. "We use stunners in military training. They make you go numb, but you're still conscious. But I'd say you're in a bit of a worse situation."

The alien growled, then barked at Remmy. He ignored the warnings on his HUD and glanced at the translation that popped up: *Kill me with honor.*

"No time for that, buddy," Remmy replied, not that the alien could understand him. But it did understand the barrel of the rifle Remmy pointed at his head. He hissed just before Remmy squeezed the trigger. Three rounds punched through the bones in the alien's ugly face, and his head exploded.

Normally, Remmy would want to move away from where he had just killed an enemy combatant. There was no doubt that the aliens had heard the gunfight. There was still too much smoke to see what they were doing clearly. Despite the danger, Remmy had an opportunity and seized it. After stopping the warnings on his HUD, which alerted him that his suit's heat-deflecting plate across his chest was compromised, he activated a trauma scanner and pointed it along the alien's body.

The information came up on his HUD, showing a ghostly outline of the big alien. The scan penetrated through muscles and reflected off bones. The trauma app tried to identify the organs, which were alien but familiar in some respects. The gut, for example, had a similar digestive system with long coils of intestinal tubes that would break down whatever the aliens ate. It had bones, ligaments and muscles that were very similar to humans. The circulatory system was powered by two heart-style muscular pumps. One clearly circulated blood through the body and the other cycled oxygenated blood from a single, large lung sack that was near the alien's back. The trauma app also showed him that the blood contained hemocyanin rather than iron-rich hemoglobin. An informational description popped up. Hemocyanin utilized copper, which gave the blood a blue color. On Earth, certain cephalopods use hemocyanin rather than hemoglobin in places with low oxygen and cold temperatures.

Most of the vital organs were inside a protective shell of bone plates that connected together to form a kind of tube inside the aliens' bodies. The weak point was their waist, where a flexible band of cartilage held the upper section to the lower section while allowing for freedom of movement. There was no chance to scan the head for the brain, but the alien had a nerve core inside the bone shroud that ran up toward where its head had been. There was a lot of dense muscle all over the body but not a lot of nerve endings, which probably explained the alien's high pain threshold.

Remmy saved the information, which was vital to their fight with the aliens. It was important to know as much about one's enemies as possible, especially how to kill them. Tex's suggestion to aim low on the body was a good one. He sent the information to his team. The smoke, heat and distance were starting to interfere with their comlink, but the digital stream of information would cut through even when audio transmission wouldn't.

His scan of the alien complete, Remmy moved on. He was more careful, too. There was a time and place for breaking down intel; the battlefield wasn't one of them. Remmy needed to know as much as possible about his enemy and how to hurt them. But not at the expense of his focus while moving closer to them.

The forest angled northward. He followed the tree line, hoping to find a gap in the smoke. Eventually, one opened up. He settled by a tree stump. An old tree had been cut at some point in the past. The loggers had left a wide stump that was waist-high to Remmy. Kneeling behind it gave him cover, leaving only his head exposed. Through the smoke, he could see the enemy troops. They were formed into small groups, which in turn encircled a smaller group of what Remmy could only guess were the senior officers.

Using his tactical app, an infrared laser measured the distance from his stump to the group of aliens. They were seven hundred meters away, beyond the range of his rifle. In fact, he would have to expose himself on the open plain to get close enough to take a shot. His space armor had no camouflage technology. And Remmy had no idea how good the aliens' eyesight was or what equipment they might have to detect him.

But Remmy had other options.

GIGI, can you locate my exact position?

Affirmative, Master Sergeant.

Outstanding! Alright, get a couple of the drones ready due east of my location.

En route, Sergeant, please stand by.

Remmy waited, praying that he wouldn't be too late. The leaders were giving the small groups of fighters their instructions. Every once in a while, Remmy saw a flash of red. Someone in the group was wearing red, and he hoped it was their emperor.

I have five drones three kilometers due east of your location, the Artifact responded.

All right, that's good. Now, seven hundred meters from where I'm sitting, the aliens are bunched up. They are west, by northwest, just eighteen degrees from my location. I want you to fly your drones in a staggered formation and fire at full auto.

Commencing strafing attack.

Remmy held his breath. The drones were nearly silent as they flew. They raced over the forest, flying low to the canopy, then streaking out over the open plain and firing. The drone ammunition was razor sharp, finger length blades. Remmy wanted to shout with excitement as the incoming fire rained down on the aliens. A few went down, their bodies shredded by dozens of flechettes. Many more of the aliens were hit but seemed unfazed by the small arms fire. Remmy saw aliens with blue stains across their nearly naked bodies raising their rifles and shooting down the drones.

And then the emperor appeared. He was big, his chest and shoulders wider than his narrow hips. From his shoulders, there were big metal plates with curved horns angling up toward his head. And a red cape hung from the shoulder pieces. It had to be the emperor and Remmy was staring right at him.

It worked! Remmy thought.

The drones were damaged, Master Sergeant. Flight capabilities were destroyed by enemy laser fire.

That's okay. I want to do it again but from both sides this time.

I have twenty-two drones still in operation. Your suggestion would cost us half our remaining aerial support vehicles.

I'm aware. The loss is worth it.

I will move the units into position.

Keep them low, Remmy warned. *We don't want to give the enemy any clue of what we're up to.*

CHAPTER 8

NOTHING HAD GONE RIGHT from the moment Emperor Vang had landed on Casasil. His battalion of foot soldiers was massacred, and there was not even a single enemy laying cold and dead on the ground. The enemy was a coward but a tactically smart one. They had drawn his force into the open, then devastated his forces with drones from the air.

"Sir, the scouts report that the enemy is fleeing," proclaimed Chief Harker, the last remaining leader whose sole duty was to carry out the emperor's orders in battle. "Should we pursue them?"

"We will hunt them down and crush them," Vang growled angrily. "Their cowardly drones have been destroyed."

"Mostly," Harker pointed out.

"Enough to level the odds," Vang said.

He was still struggling with the strangeness of his first real battle. He had fought many times in his young life. Usually dualing, often to the death, and he was always the victor in those contests, but war was different. It felt nothing like the glory and honor he expected. Instead, he had marched from his spaceship with confidence and pride, only to have it all shattered as the bombs fell.

His ship and the troop carrier were both destroyed. They lay shattered and burning. Across the wide field smoke rose from craters in the ground. The carnage that had once been his regiment bothered him. He told himself it was fury, but it felt like fear, which only made him even more angry.

"Divide our force," Vang ordered. "We will pursue both groups of enemy figh—"

"Incoming!" Someone shouted.

Harker dove into Vang, knocking the emperor to the ground and covering him with his body. The royal leader's first impulse was to push his chief off of him. But before he could act, the sound of projectiles thumping into flesh and pinging on the ground around him caused him to hesitate.

Harker grunted with pain but didn't scream. From where he lay, Vang saw a squad of drones racing by overhead. His well-trained troops opened fire. Their laser rifles filled the sky with energy. The drones were hit, disabled, and destroyed.

Vang pushed his chief off of him. Harker groaned a little. His back was bleeding from a row of small projectiles.

"Can you stand?" Vang asked him.

"Of course, your Excellency."

Vang lent Harker a hand.

"You need medical attention," Vang said, unable to keep the disappointment out of his voice.

It didn't matter that it wasn't Harker's fault he had been shot. Nor was it relevant that he had actually taken his wounds in the course of saving his Emperor. Vang needed his chief. Therefore, it stood to reason that Harker's injuries were an annoyance to the emperor.

"Forgive me, my Lord," Harker replied. "I can fight. The wounds are minor."

The chief's back was covered in blood, but he could move. He could hold a rifle and fight.

"We must make for the trees," Vang said. "Their little needles won't be nearly so efficient through the foliage."

"Agreed, my Lord. I shall give the orders now."

"And someone message Sheika Kahn," Vang demanded. "Tell him we need air support at this location."

"Sir, word just arrived from the armada," an underling said. Vang never bothered to learn anyone's name beyond his chieftains. "Shieka Kahn has ordered a retreat from the system."

"What?" Vang said, fighting back another wave of terror. "He's left us here?"

"Two ships and two squadrons of fighters were completely destroyed, sir. The cannons on our ships don't have the range to stand and fight with the Arodoni ship."

Vang lashed out. It wasn't uncommon, but it was unexpected. He drew his battle sword, a short, double-edged, sickle-shaped weapon. The underling delivering the message died instantly as his head was severed from his shoulders. The big head flew a short distance, then dropped ignominiously into the mud. But Vang wasn't finished. He roared in defiance, his terror mixed with rage at what he felt was the ultimate betrayal.

"They will return, my Lord," Harker said through clenched teeth.

Vang didn't know if his subordinate was angry that the under-ling had been killed or if he was in pain. The skin on the Chief's back was swelling and Vang wondered for the briefest of moments if the darts from the drones could be poisoned. Time would tell, he decided.

"I will have Sheika Kahn's head," Vang snarled. "He's grown fat and cowardly. Contact our support ships. We will head toward the capital. Once we have a proper base of operations, we will track down the Arodoni and destroy them."

"Excellent, my Lord," Harker said.

But before the orders to withdraw could be given, more drones appeared. They flew low and fast, first from one direction and then another.

"Protect the Emperor!" Harker shouted.

A group of fighters surrounded Vang. He didn't want to be protected but he despised an enemy that fired weapons at him from a distance that he could not attain. Regret was filling his mind like a roar that encompassed everything else. As he knelt on the ground, huddling under the living shields that were his warriors, he couldn't help but question why he was there. Why had he longed for war? Never before had he ever felt so close to death and he didn't want it. He wanted to live. To his horror, he found that his hands were trembling. Death had come for him and Vang wasn't ready.

CHAPTER 9

REMMY WAS ON HIS BELLY, crawling toward the enemy. Out in the open, he should have been seen. But he was moving slowly and there were plenty of craters left by the bombs to hide in. Plus, the field was littered with bodies. All of the dead were bigger than Remmy, even those who had been blown apart. He had little trouble crawling through the carnage of the battlefield without attracting attention, especially since the Ashi warriors were looking up, just as Remmy had predicted they would.

Settling into a slight depression behind the body of a fallen alien warrior, Remmy had just enough space to aim his Nelson LTX rifle through a small gap under the body. He raised his head slowly. Information was flooding into his helmet and displayed clearly across his HUD. There were still close to a hundred alien warriors. Remmy had no chance of fighting them all but that wasn't his goal. Maybe if the drones had heavier munitions than just flechettes ... but they did not. And the gigantic aliens seemed unfazed by the aerial attacks. Many had been hit and were bleeding. He could see that. Their blue blood oozed across their green skin but they didn't show any signs of being injured.

Near the center of the group stood their leader. He was

surrounded by hulking warriors but his red cape was a dead give-away. Remmy had to wait for a clear shot. He knew one was all he would get.

Aerial drones are down to just twelve units, GIGI informed him.

Alright, that's okay, Remmy replied. *Do you have a fix on the range of their laser rifles?*

Scans of their weapons show adequate power for up to one hundred meters.

Stay out of their range but show them the last of the drones on the western side of the enemy.

Moving units into position.

It didn't take long, and it had the desired effect. As the enemy turned to face the drones, which they expected to come racing toward them, guns blazing, just like the other drone assaults had done. And as the huge alien warriors turned, an opening between them appeared. It was narrow. Not the straight on shot Remmy would have liked. The alien Emperor was standing so that Remmy could only see his profile. But it was enough. He took aim at the big head and fired.

It was a long shot. The report was loud. The explosive round was on target, but the gravity of the world pulled it down. The bullet impacted on the Emperor's shoulder armor, right at the base of the curved horn, which shattered. Tiny bits of bone tore into the emperor's face, and the explosion was small but enough to sear parts of his flesh. The emperor fell, roaring in pain and fury, just as the report from Remmy's rifle reached them. He had already ducked back into the crater, using the ground and the body of the fallen alien to shield himself.

Laser fire filled the air above him. He could hear the aliens barking and shouting. The emperor was wounded but not dead. Remmy had missed, or at least he had failed to make a kill shot. There was no way to know how badly the emperor was hurt. And Remmy had no intention of sticking around to find out.

Attack runs, Remmy ordered, barking the commands in his mind—*two by two. Go!*

Commencing attack runs now, GIGI replied in the ever-calm, robotic diction.

Remmy squirmed around, waiting for a lull in the shooting. It came as the drones drilled into the aliens from the western side of the open prairie. Remmy was only fifty yards from the tree line. But it still seemed like an impossible distance. As soon as the laser fire dwindled, he jumped forward and sprinted for the trees.

Flashes of light showed the laser beams. Remmy was right at the edge of their effective range, but still, it was terrifying to think that, at any moment, his life could be over. The first hit felt like a shove in the back. Alarms went off in his helmet. There was no pain; his armor had held back the deadly energy burst, but it was wreaking havoc on his space armor's computer sensors.

Another shot hit his leg and nearly tripped him up. He dove into a crater, rolled to his knees, and opened fire back at the aliens. His rifle was on fully automatic and ripped out two dozen explosive rounds in just three seconds. Then another laser hit him, this time in the shoulder. It knocked him backward, and he could feel the heat on his shoulder.

Warning! Warning! Warning! His helmet blared. **Armor compromised. Suit integrity twenty percent.**

Remmy scrambled from the crater and ran for his life. There was no need to look over his shoulder to know he was being chased. Another laser hit him just as he reached the trees. The impact was near the suit's main power core, and his helmet's HUD vanished as Remmy staggered into the trees.

"Maybe not the best idea I ever had," he said. "But I know I'm faster than you."

He popped the seals on his helmet. His suit had already scanned the atmosphere on Casasil several times and showed it to be safe. He ripped off the helmet, threw it aside, and kept running.

Laser fire ripped into the trees around him. He heard the bark and wood sizzling. Remmy slid to a stop behind a wide tree and dumped his magazine, which only had a few rounds left inside. He rammed home a fresh one, tried not to think about the fact that he only had six full magazines left, and fired back at the rushing mob.

They were close enough that Remmy could feel the ground shaking as they ran. But he saw that they were lumbering, their faces covered in sweat, their mouths open as they panted hard to catch their breath. Two went down under quick bursts from his LTX. Then he sprinted away again.

The air was tinged with smoke. Normally, his helmet would filter it out, but not without power. Remmy hit the emergency release that held the air tanks and heavy power batteries in a reinforced section of his suit. They dropped away, thudding on the ground behind him, and he felt much lighter as he sprinted ahead.

As a Marine, he had run almost every single day of his adult life. From boot camp to training between missions, running was a cardiovascular mainstay in his workout regimen. The only times he hadn't run were on missions when he was pinned down, sometimes for days at a time, or on watch. He had once spent twelve days lying on a hilltop, waiting for a chance to take a shot at the leader of a rebel faction that never materialized. But running was second nature to Remmy. He didn't love doing it like some people, but he didn't hate it either. To him, it was a way of preparing for whatever he might encounter in combat.

Remmy ran through the forest, his boots flying over fallen logs and around trees. There was no doubt in his mind that he was faster than his enemy. But he wasn't invincible either. He took another laser blast. It ripped across his hip and tore a fat chunk from his suit. Pain registered on his hip, but he didn't have time to stop and check on the wound. He hadn't fallen either, which was a big win, considering he might really hurt himself if he fell. A sprained ankle or twisted knee, even a hard bruise on his thigh, could slow him down considerably, and speed was the only advantage over the hulking green aliens that Remmy had.

As the laser fire slacked behind him, Remmy immediately began to angle to his right. He kept running, turning his sprint into a slower pace that he could keep up for a while, as he circled wide. Eventually, he came to a group of tall, skinny trees and decided it was safe enough to catch his breath. His chest was aching, his eyes burning, and his mouth felt swollen inside. He had to move his lower jaw back and forth several times to work up enough spit in his mouth to swallow. He needed water but had none. His suit had water in it, but without the power to pump it out, he couldn't get to it. And it wasn't the freshest water either. Most of it was collected sweat and urine. He wouldn't trust the busted suit to filter it properly into potable water.

There was no sign of the enemy. He had outrun them. But that wasn't really his purpose or at least not the ultimate goal he was aiming for. His job was disruption. And Remmy was well versed in guerrilla tactics. He would hit the aliens again, hopefully where they didn't expect it, then disappear once more. It was a tried-and-true strategy that had been used with great effect through the centuries of human warfare right up to the present. That was why he had circled around as he ran, angling through the trees to curve back around the group of aliens.

But his speed had bought him a little time. He pulled off his utility belt with its holster, knife sheath, and survival pouch. The contents inside were valuable. It wasn't until he looked at his pistol that he realized that it, too, had been damaged by the last laser bolt that hit his hip. The handle was half gone, and the battery compartment was smoking. He tossed the useless weapon aside. He couldn't imagine it having much effect against the thirteen-foot-tall aliens anyway.

Remmy shuddered a little as he remembered how big the Ashi Warriors were. Remmy had no qualms about accepting his fears. They were natural and he knew that everyone had them. Anyone who denied their fear was just lying to themselves. So, Remmy let the tremor pass through him. His fear died for lack of attention. Sure, the aliens were frightening, but Remmy focused on the job he had to do. It was a task he knew how to do well and one that he enjoyed. Maybe it was crazy to enjoy combat, but he did. He loved pitting himself against an enemy. He loved considering various strategies and utilizing different tactics. Of course, combat was also terrible. Seeing his friends die was the most awful thing he could imagine, much worse than his own death would be. Combat was pure adrenaline, and afterward, his soul paid a heavy price for his love of it. But Remmy couldn't change that. He was who he was, and he was at peace with that fact.

He pulled off the stretchable, tactical vest he wore over his armor that held his rifle's magazines and a few other tools of his trade. Then came the suit itself. Normally, space armor was fluffy, even after a long training session. It was made from multiple layers, which helped insulate the wearer. But in many places, the layers had been fused together in Remmy's suit from the laser energy the suit had absorbed. That was its function and he was alive because of it. Remmy tightened the laces on his boots and pulled out the hard case first aid kit from his tactical vest. The burn on his hip wasn't bad, but he sprayed it with antiseptic, which included an analgesic to numb the pain. He followed that with a simple protective patch that adhered to his skin around the burn and would keep the wound from chaffing. The only clothes he had were the compression pants and shirt he wore under his armor, but the dark color wouldn't stand out in the forest and the world was warm enough that he didn't need anything else.

He strapped on the utility belt and ignored the stab of pain from his burned hip. He had endured much worse, and the pain was only momentary. Next, he put on the tactical vest. It was mostly webbing made of stretchable cords so that it fit him with armor and without. Once he had everything in place, he checked his survival supplies. Inside was a hermetically sealed water filtration straw. If he could find some water, any water at all, he would be in business. The thick tube could filter out toxins, organic matter, and debris down to a microscopic level. He closed the pouch and checked his rifle. It needed a good cleaning. The Nelson LTX was a rugged weapon built for intense combat environments, but he had already put it through a lot, especially crawling across the open battlefield. As soon as he got a chance, the weapon would need to be taken apart and each piece cleaned and oiled.

A fire burned to his right. The smoke was creeping toward him, which was a hazard both to his health and to his stealth. It was impossible to be silent when smoke was making you cough. He picked up the last item from his discarded space armor. It was a standard breathing filter, not much more than a plastic shield with slits in the side and thick filters that could keep out things like smoke and debris. He slipped it over his head and fit the mask around his mouth and nose. He was ready to take the fight to the enemy again. Only this time, without his protective armor, he would have to be much more careful. Hit and run. That was the name of the game. And that was exactly what he intended to do.

CHAPTER 10

"THEY'RE MAKING the jump to hyperspace, Captain," Vivian Ramos announced.

"I'd call that a win," Henry Nash added.

Captain Zeke Darius wasn't as sure, but he kept his thoughts to himself. The battle had been too easy; his single ship, plus the drones, were more than a match for the armada of alien vessels. But they had wisely retreated once the *Renegade's* powerful weapons and surprising maneuverability had been put on display. They were no longer an unknown enemy asset. The Imperials would be more prepared for the next fight and Darius was already worrying about it.

"Should we set course to pick up the Marines in the drop ship?" Pete Best asked.

"Negative," Darius ordered. "Stay on station. I want proof that all ten of those alien ships are out of the system."

"What are the odds that they can still keep tabs on us while they're away?" Henry asked.

"Excellent, would be my guess," Darius said. "This is a settled star system in their control. Even if they don't have direct access to the satellites and orbital scanners, there are probably plenty of people on Casasil who are loyal to the Imperium."

"So, what option does that leave us?" Vivian Ramos asked.

"I'd say that we need to be gone soon," Darius replied. "Why don't you plot us a course to unoccupied space."

"Aye, Captain, plotting now," Vivian said.

"We're leaving?" Nash asked.

"Not before we gather our people," Darius replied. "Do we have eyes on them?"

"Negative, Captain," Jacee Bertoli replied. "The fighters have moved into the forest. We can't get visuals through the canopy."

"Comms?" he pressed.

"Negative, sir; our surveillance birds are much too high."

"Lieutenant Nash, turn us around. Let's go pick up the drop ship."

"Aye, Captain, reversing course now."

"The last of those enemy ships just transitioned out of the system," Pete Best announced a moment later. "No bogies on the board."

Darius pressed the transmit button on his communications controls. "Commander Lee, run a full ship diagnostic check. Did we suffer any damage in the battle?"

"Not directly, Captain," Lori Lee said from the systems control room two levels down from the Bridge. "We lost a lot of drones, mostly the midsized units. Ensign Stanislaus is overseeing the production of replacements as we speak."

"How's that going?" Darius asked.

"It's simple, Captain," Stanislaus replied over the comlink. "The computer already had the plans for all the drones and shuttles. And the automated processing plant is mass producing the parts. There are robotic assets doing the final assembly, and I believe they'll move them to the hanger, too. All we had to do was press a button."

"Manufacture our own troops," Henry Nash said. "We're a traveling army complete with reinforcements."

"Are we manufacturing warheads, too?" Pete Best asked.

"That does appear to be possible, although it requires a different configuration of the processing plant," Stanislaus said. "Essentially just a different order from the computer, and a little bit of set up time, then we can produce a wide range of munitions. For now, it appears the ship already has stores of ammunition laid up for the drones. No need to produce more to arm the new units once they're constructed."

"What's the timeline?" Darius asked.

"If we crank out all eight hundred that were sent into combat," Stanislaus replied, "we're looking at two days."

"Unbelievable," Henry Nash said. "That's more efficient production than anything I've ever heard of before."

"It's all automated," Darius said. "No human error to account for."

"And no need for the robots to sleep or take a break to rest," Vivian said.

"How are our stores of materials?" Darius asked.

"We're still at high levels," Commander Lee replied. "And the computer has lists of locations to harvest rare minerals."

"In a ship like this, there is never a need to go home," Henry Nash said. "Unlimited power, unlimited resources; it's hard to believe the Arodoni ever walked away from her."

That fact still bothered Darius but he was also relieved at how well the ship had performed in combat. Maybe, he thought to himself, it was possible to go home. With the *Renegade* in the Sol system, they were more than a match for almost any threat. At least any threat they had come across so far.

"Let's not forget who we are," Darius said. "Whatever the *Renegade* was built for, it is now a ship of war. And we are officers with a duty to our people that supersedes whatever wonders the ship can accomplish. I want full reports on the engagement with a specific emphasis on the enemy ships and their capabilities. We cannot afford to get caught by surprise."

It took an hour to reach the shuttle and get it safely back on board. Dr. Lanski gave the Marines a full scan and declared them fit for combat.

"We weren't injured in the fighting," Lieutenant Colt insisted. "Just stunned. The slavers used some type of disruptor beams that shut down our armored suits."

"We'll need to study that tech," Darius replied.

The two men were standing in the hanger bay. The five Marines with Lieutenant Colt were gearing up to go back down to the planet. They were swapping the heavy space armor for lighter combat gear used in habitable environments.

"I brought back one of the weapons, and we took scans of the slavers themselves," Colt said. "My people are itching to get back down to the planet, sir."

"I understand that, but we don't have contact with the Marines down there. And there are two enemy ships still in that area. We can't risk you going down until we know for sure where the others are. Gear up and stand by; we'll launch your shuttle just as soon as we have confirmation that our people are still alive."

"Roger that," Colt said.

Darius left the Marines and made his way back through the ship. He didn't like being so far away from the bridge. The hanger with the drones and drop ships was a full four kilometers from the command section. Walking that distance, even at a fast pace, took thirty minutes. That was too much time in Darius' mind. He was used to being minutes away from any section of a ship. Human vessels were small, cramped, and utilitarian. The alien ship was the complete opposite. It was massive. Every compartment was lavishly spacious, from the maintenance areas to the lavatories. He could imagine a crew of a thousand on the ship. There were plenty of berths for that many people, from the standard crew quarters for the officers below the bridge to the apartment-style compartments that overlooked the lavish park in the center of the ship. There were working facilities for all kinds of artisans and craftspeople, along with laboratories for scientists and researchers. There was plenty of food, air, power and storage, not to mention the manufacturing plant on the lower section of the bow that could produce anything that might be needed.

But Darius didn't have a thousand people on board. And he wasn't on an exploration mission. The *Renegade* currently had a crew of just under one hundred Naval personnel and a single Special Operations Marine platoon. The priority had to be getting those Marines that stayed on Casasil to help the locals fight the Ashi army. It would have been a suicide mission if not for the drones from the *Renegade,* which were just another part of the fantastic ship they knew almost nothing about. Darius was certain he could spend the rest of his life studying the alien ship and not discover all her secrets and capabilities, but that wasn't his mission. In fact, his mission was just as much a mystery as the ship. He still wasn't sure what he was doing.

They had left the Sol system in the *Jericho* specifically to find the Arodoni Power Core, which he had been led to believe was essential to defending the Sol system. The acquisition of the alien technology then led to a decision to seek out the *Renegade*. In some ways, Darius felt as though he had been manipulated by GIGI. The alien artifact clearly had an agenda and it just so happened that his own beliefs about what was best for his crew to do fell in line with what GIGI wanted. Which was why he was on the massive alien vessel in an alien star system, opposing what could only be described as a very formidable enemy. If not for the *Renegade,* the situation would have been hopeless. But Darius was far from hopeless; he was invigorated. It was as if his life suddenly had meaning and purpose again. They could go home, but he would be removed from command at the earliest opportunity. The *Renegade* wouldn't be filled with craftsmen and explorers but technicians who would take her all apart in hopes of understanding how she was made. The thought of that seemed profane, especially after the Arodoni ship had saved their lives on more than one occasion.

The long walk gave him the time to consider what they should do next. They had picked a fight they weren't prepared for. Going home was a dangerous prospect. They still had no idea just how much firepower the Ashi Imperium could bring to bear. It could be catastrophic if they led the enemy back to the Sol system and then failed to protect humanity. On the other hand, the Casa system wasn't their home. They needed to find a place of refuge and decide what the best way to move forward was. Darius was a firm believer in the concepts of mobility and fighting on good ground. Not that there was ground in outer space but if they were going to fight, he wanted to choose the place of battle, one that suited his needs and maximized the *Renegade's* advantages. The problem was that humanity actually knew very little about space outside the Sol system. They had mapped the stars and studied the various celestial phenomena, but he had no idea where to go where they might be safe.

And was it even important for a ship of war to be safe? He was still thinking like the SDF Captain. One of humanity's ships could be powerful but all alone with no hope of reinforcements or resupply, that ship would be in a desperate fix. The alien ship Darius and his crew occupied was completely different. They could slip off into deep space and never be seen again. The *Renegade* didn't need anything, not fuel, not air, not supplies, or even, for that matter, a crew. It was a perfect design, at least as far as he could tell. Despite being occupied by his crew for over a week, the ship was still spotless. He knew it was well over four hundred years old and yet it looked pristine inside and out. With the dark energy power converter, the ship had so much electrical power that it could project sonic screens and fire the enormous laser cannons in quick succession. He had to start thinking like the captain of the *Renegade,* not of a regular human ship.

When he reached the Bridge, his officers were waiting there for him, including Commander Lori Lee, who had taken the con while Darius was away.

"The dropship just launched," she told him.

"Do we have word from the Marines?"

"Not yet. The drop ship will stay in orbit until there's word."

Darius suppressed a frown. Having the ship in orbit would

make getting to the Marines on the ground faster, but he didn't like having assets outside his ship. If they were attacked again, having the drop ship in orbit would make them vulnerable. But he tried not to think that way. They had beaten the enemy, who would need time to gather their forces before they returned to try again. By then, the *Renegade* and all her crew would be gone.

CHAPTER 11

LAILA MCPHERSON FELT a cold knot of dread in her gut when Master Sergeant Remmy Steel's comlink went offline. There were any number of reasons why they might lose contact, including distance, which was relevant since she was leading her small team of three Marines south, away from the battlefield. There was also the possibility that the fires and smoke were interfering with their radio signals. Not to mention, they were on an alien planet that could have any number of effects on human technology, from varying magnetic fields to solar radiation.

But Laila still felt the cold knot and feared that something had happened to him. He certainly wouldn't be the only friend she had lost in combat. But he would be the first love she had lost. It still boggled her mind that she could even entertain the word 'love' about Master Sergeant Steel, but he was more than just an interest, more than just a crush. He embodied everything she wanted in a partner and she couldn't deny that her feelings for him were stronger than she had ever felt for anyone. Almost from the moment she had let herself believe they could be a couple, her emotions had soared to new heights. But she had to put all of that out of her head. She was the Staff Sergeant in charge, with Marines still in theater. Until they were safe back on board the *Renegade*, she couldn't let her feelings bother her.

"Staff Sergeant, we have movement ahead," Tex said.

"Hold your position," Laila ordered him.

"Copy that," Corporal Tyler Fry responded.

"Izzy, let's approach slowly."

"Yes, Sergeant," Corporal Isolde Berry said.

They were spread out in a line, weapons ready. The enemy was behind them, massing in the wide meadow between the two forested sections of land. Laila was in one section, Remmy was leading a three-man team in the other.

"Alpha team, do you read me?" Laila asked, using her helmet comlink.

"Five by five, Staff Sergeant," Sergeant Dirk Oliver said.

"We have movement in the forest due south of our position. What's your status? We've lost contact with the Master Sergeant."

"Us too," Dirk replied. "He was staying to keep tabs on the enemy. We're moving south and west in hopes of meeting up with you."

"Alright, approach with caution. Standby for more instructions."

"Copy that, Sergeant. Alpha team, standing by."

His words were like a dagger in her heart. Alpha Team, without Remmy, seemed terribly wrong somehow.

"I've got eyes," Tex announced. "Looks like the tall, lanky aliens we set free from the slave ship."

"Let's approach with caution. They may be armed or recaptured by militant forces."

The trio of Marines moved from tree to tree in quick bursts. Despite their bulky armor, they were nearly silent as they pressed forward. Laila caught sight of the aliens quickly. They stood out among the dark tree trunks and nearly black soil. She knew almost nothing about them except that they seemed intelligent.

"Alright, hold positions," Laila said. "I'll make contact."

She raised the barrel of her rifle. Laila preferred a Sterner M88 Classic with a modified barrel that suppressed both the gun's report and recoil when firing. It had a piston stock, which made it even easier to fire and it shot simple .223 rounds which had been a mainstay in the military for centuries, hence the use of Classic in the name. She held the rifle with one hand, leaning it against her shoulder as she stepped out from the trees into a small clearing in the forest.

The aliens looked up at her. There was terror in their large eyes. They were bipeds with grey skin and long, skinny limbs. Their heads were conical in shape. One stepped toward her and opened both hands in what seemed to Laila like a placating gesture. It spoke in a soft voice and in a language she didn't know. But her helmet's translation app, updated by GIGI, displayed the words on her HUD.

"Welcome, we mean you no harm?"

"Are you alone?"

"We are. Most of us were not taken from this world by the slavers. We have nowhere to take refuge."

"I'm Staff Sergeant Laila McPherson."

"One of the brave warriors who helped us to escape," the alien said. "I am called Lodus. We are the Dudonus people."

"It's nice to meet you," Laila said. "But it's not safe here. The forest is on fire, and the Ashi forces are moving south."

"Unfortunately, we have no place to go," Lodus said.

"Better come with us then," Laila said.

Tex and Izzy joined her with the aliens, who seemed not just friendly but relieved to have the Marines with them. An hour later, they connected with Sergeant Dirk Oliver and Corporal Ricky Thompson.

"It's good to see you, Staff Sergeant. Looks like you've made friends," Dirk said.

"These beings have nowhere to go," Laila replied. "Any word from Master Sergeant Steel?"

"No, Sarge. Nothing. But there were some attacks by the

drones. Not many, but some. I'm hoping he's still with us somehow."

"That man has a way of staying alive despite all odds. What are the enemy doing?"

"We think they're in the forest. It's hard to say for sure. There's a lot of smoke and we weren't looking to engage, but we did see some movement after we took out some of their scouts."

"If they're moving this way, it would be best to find a place to fight from," Laila said. "We can't run forever."

It was sound advice, and she hoped it wasn't driven completely by her desire to avenge Remmy. She didn't know for certain that he was dead, but she felt like it was a very likely possibility. He wouldn't have shut down his comlink without a very good reason.

The group turned due south, and the terrain began to change. The forest of tall, skinny trees began to open up around rocky hills. When they reached a place where a wide, open valley appeared between two boulder-strewn hills, Laila knew she had found what she was looking for.

"This is perfect," she said.

"Hell of an ambush site," Tex agreed.

"Good cover, too," Sergeant Dirk Oliver added. "We should see what's on the far side of the valley."

To their relief, they found a river flowing through a gap in the hills. It bypassed the valley at an almost perpendicular angle.

"We'll stage here," she announced. "Izzy, Tex, head back up the valley and stand watch. Once you see the enemy, fall back to this position. I want you on the southern hillside."

"Yes, Staff Sergeant," Izzy said before she and Tex jogged back up the valley.

"Thompson, you're with me. Sergeant Oliver, I want you to take the Dudonus downriver at least a mile. You can return once you are certain they're safe."

"Roger that," Dirk said.

"May I have your permission to stay?" Ludus asked. "I would

very much like the chance to see who is leading the Ashi troops against us."

"Very well, but you stay close to me ... and when I say move, you move."

"I will do as you command," the alien replied.

"Thompson, we're taking up station on the northern side of the valley. Find a spot with good cover. If we get cut off, circle wide, find the river, and keep moving south until you catch up with the others."

"Got it," Ricky said.

Laila climbed the hill with Ludus at her side. The hills were steep and rocky, with only tufts of grass growing in a few places. The hillside was littered with boulders; some were the size of basketballs, others were as big as cars. She settled in behind a wide stone that stuck up out of the ground. It was only waist-high and made a perfect rest for her rifle when she stood up.

"There are only five of you," Ludus said. "Is that enough to strike at the band of Ashi warriors?"

"If they come through this valley," Laila said, "we'll hit them with gunfire from both sides. We have the high ground and cover. They'll be out in the open. With any luck, we'll cut them all down before they can mount a counter-offensive, but we'll have to see."

"You must be a great hero to your people," Ludus said.

Laila chuckled. "Not really. I'm just a grunt in the Space Defense Force," she explained. "Many of our people serve in the military."

"My kind are not fighters. We do not have the strength for such endeavors."

"Compared to the Ashi warriors I saw, I'd say we don't either. They're pretty damned big."

"Their's is a war culture. Selective breeding has ensured they are as big and strong as it is possible to safely get."

"We tried that for a while," Laila said. "But it can't be maintained for long."

"May I ask you a question, Laila McPherson?"

"Sure, and Laila is fine."

"Laila, it is an exotic name. I like it very much."

"Thank you," she said, checking the breech on her M88 Classic to make sure it was free from debris.

"Why did you rescue us? From the slavers, I mean? You risked your life for species that are not your own?"

"Slavery is especially repugnant to my people," Laila said, her battle helmet translating her words into the Dudonus language via the communications app. "I doubt that any human could just turn a blind eye to it. We knew we could help, so we did. Plus, we needed to learn more about them."

"The slavers?"

"Yes, and the other species in the galaxy."

"It seems we may be able to help one another. My people are among one of the oldest races in the galaxy. We were once welcomed on nearly every inhabited world along the hyperspace lanes."

"But not anymore?"

"The Ashi declared us to be a slave race after many of my kind were involved in fomenting rebellion against the Imperium."

"A slave race?"

"We can be enslaved without consequences wherever we're found. Once the rebellion was crushed, my people fled from Dudon Prime, our home world. Those who stayed were soon captured and enslaved. Since then, we have lived as refugees wherever we go. There are more Dudonus in slavery than living free."

"That's terrible."

"We would tend to agree, but we are not strong enough to resist our captors."

"It doesn't take much strength to pull a trigger," Laila said.

"Weapons like yours are outlawed on all Imperium planets. Only the Ashi, as the Empire's guardians, can carry weapons."

"Sounds like every tyrannical government I ever heard of," she replied, which only made the alien blink. It clearly didn't understand. "I'm sorry," she finally added. "My people have debated the right to own firearms for generations. It's one of the central pillars of our right to be free."

"My kind had no such weapons when the Ashi rose to power. We have always been a peaceful race."

"Then I envy you," Laila said. "My people have always been plagued with war."

She had to raise one hand to silence Ludus as her comlink sounded inside her helmet.

"Contact," Izzy said. "We have movement due north of our location, Staff Sergeant."

"Is it the enemy?" Laila asked.

"Affirmative. Looks like a large force moving this way. They're huge."

"Make the trees look like toys, don't they?" Tex added.

"How many?" Laila asked.

"Hard to say," Izzy replied. "Dozens. They've got a lot of wounded with them. Master Sergeant Steel has chewed them up."

"And spit them back out," Tex said with a chuckle. "We're falling back, Staff Sergeant."

"Outstanding. Move back and find good cover. We'll hit them in the valley. Wait for my command."

"Roger that," Tex said.

"On the move now, Staff Sergeant," Izzy added.

"Looks like the enemy is almost here," Laila told Ludus. "We'll need to remain silent from this point forward."

The alien nodded. He didn't seem frightened at all. Even unarmed and virtually helpless, he wasn't daunted. Laila was reminded of Remmy. That memory was bittersweet. She had hoped he might wander into their valley ahead of the aliens, but he was nowhere to be found. She pushed the memory away and focused on the task ahead. If the enemy was going to walk into her trap, she had no qualms about making them pay for it. And the cost would be their lives, every last one.

CHAPTER 12

"WE HAVE ISOLATED THE ATTACKS, my Lord," Harker said.

"How many of the cowards do we face?" Emperor Vang demanded.

"A small number, your Excellency. Three at the most. Maybe as few as one. They are small and fast."

"They are cowards who will not stand and fight."

"True, they hit us from behind with their projectile weapons, then flee back into the forest. What strategy do you propose?"

"There is no effective strategy against such a small force. Sooner or later, they will make a mistake. Have everyone prepared to return fire at the Arodoni cowards, but we will continue moving."

"Sire, we could spread out."

"We will not waste our time," Vang said, spitting out a mouthful of blood. "This Arodoni is a stinging bug, nothing more. We must reach a suitable place to make our stand against the enemy until more of our ships return to the system."

"As you wish, your Excellency," Harker replied.

What Vang wished for was something to make his face stop

burning. The pain was great. The flesh on the left side of his head was shredded and burned. Blood ran down his face and into his mouth. The burned flesh throbbed with terrible pain. But Vang was an Ashi warrior, and he would never complain about a battle wound. So, he suffered in silence, plodding on through the forest, surrounded by guards who were themselves nursing wounds. The only positive thing to happen so far was the thinning of the forest. Vang was no student of geography and certainly not of a fringe world like Casasil, but he had studied the map on his ship's computer before landing. They were one hundred kilometers north of Surtan, a major city. That was Vang's goal. He would lead his decimated army to Surtan, route whatever paltry defenses it might have, and make that his base of operations. From there, he could send troops out to hunt down the Arodoni fighters. There certainly didn't seem to be many of them.

They came to a clearing that led into a valley between two rocky hills. Emperor Vang stopped long enough to get a count of his surviving troops.

"Ninety-two, counting yourself, Lord," Harker said. "More than enough to take Surtan."

"I've no doubt," Vang said.

The truth was, he didn't care how many troops were dead or alive; he just wanted to stop and rest. But he didn't want anyone to know how tired he felt. Maybe it was the blood loss, or perhaps just the shock from the alien attacks, but his body felt heavy, and of course, the pain was difficult to endure.

"We could make a stand here," Harker suggested. "Perhaps draw the Arodoni out into the open."

"They are not so foolish," Vang said. "In the open, we are more vulnerable. Let's press on."

"As you wish," Harker said.

Vang saw the glimmer of doubt in the chieftain's eye. Once they reached Surtan, Vang would dispose of Harker. It didn't do to have a chief who had lost faith in his emperor. Normally, Vang would have challenged him outright, but he was too weak to duel.

Harker's time would come. He might question his emperor but he would not disobey.

They pressed on through the valley. It was a mistake. Vang was a student of war, but perhaps not a good one. He loved stories of valor and heroic sacrifice, but ideas like defensive strategy bored him, which was probably why he led his force into terrain that was ideal for ambush. One moment, they were marching along, making good time. Emperor Vang was fantasizing about getting some type of medical aid that would numb the pain in his face. Then, suddenly, booming reports sounded around them.

"Attack!" Someone yelled.

"It's an ambush," another warrior bellowed.

"Protect the Emperor!" Harker ordered.

Vang was already in the center of his battalion and surrounded by some of the biggest warriors who remained alive. Weapons fire rained down from various points on both hills. Dozens died within the first few seconds. The enemy weapons spewed deadly projectiles at an incredible rate.

"Return fire!" Vang screamed, but he was hardly heard over the reports of gunfire and the screams of the wounded.

"We must retreat!" Harker shouted. "Get him out of here!"

Suddenly, troopers on either side of him took hold of Vang's arms and dragged him back through the panicked forces. Not that he was resisting, but his mind was fuzzy. Clear thought alluded him. He wanted to escape and yet he couldn't quite understand what his guards were doing.

"Make way! Make way!" Harker screamed.

It didn't help. The warriors were crowding together as each side tried to move back from the hail of gunfire. But clumping together only made them easier targets. Harker pushed and shoved his way through the throng in a heroic effort to save the emperor's life. He might have succeeded, but just as he broke through the mass of panicked warriors, gunfire ripped into his body. The bullets hit low, between his thick hips. They tore through his kilt and punched into his abdomen. He fell to his knees and died without saying a word.

"Retreat!" Someone screamed.

It wasn't Vang, but he realized it was the correct order. Half his remaining force was dead or wounded in the valley, including his last chieftain. The mass of warriors was shooting back, but their lasers never seemed to find the enemy, who were hidden behind rocks and boulders. It was a slaughter, even worse than the drone bombing had been. Fear gripped Vang's heart in a way that he knew he would never recover from. The most valiant warrior in the Imperium was injected with fear that he couldn't escape from ... or deny. Warriors around him were running from the valley, and he joined them, still flanked by guards.

Some threw down their own rifles as they ran. The most valiant warriors in the galaxy were caught in panic. They raced back up the valley and straight into steady gunfire laid down by Master Sergeant Remmy Steel. He stood just inside the tree line and fired from between two trees that grew close together. All around Vang, his troopers died, starting with the guard on his right side. The warrior grunted with the impact of bullets, then fell. Some turned and tried to flee up the mountains, but suddenly, there was gunfire everywhere from both ends of the valley.

One projectile hit Vang's arm just below the elbow. It tore through muscle and tendon before shattering the bones inside. The pain was terrible and Vang couldn't lift his arm or hold onto anything in that hand. All around him, there was a maelstrom of death. Then suddenly, it stopped as Vang dropped to his knees on the bloody ground.

CHAPTER 13

REMMY HAD FOLLOWED the troop of Ashi Warriors. He reached the edge of the valley just as the shooting started and knew instantly what was happening. He took a good position and waited. It didn't take long before the survivors came rushing back up the valley.

There are times in battle when a warrior simply does what he or she has to do with no real thought about it. Remmy wasn't really aiming in the traditional sense. He was so in tune with his Nelson LTX that he was simply selecting targets. His muscle memory did the work of aiming his weapon. The aliens died. It didn't take long before more Marines joined him in the slaughter. They came from down the valley, moving along the hills to either side, making short work of the stragglers and those trying to climb over the hills to safety.

The battle only lasted a minute. Remmy had depleted all his magazines of explosive rounds and was down to just one mag with soft slugs. Before him, the emperor, in his red cape and shattered ceremonial armor, dropped to his knees. His compatriots were all dead or dying. It was the perfect tactical ambush.

Remmy stepped out from behind the trees and stood where the

other Marines could see him. Normally, they would be connected via comlink, but Remmy's had been destroyed by enemy laser fire. He had to wait until the other Marines recognized him and ensured that it was safe to join him on the valley floor.

Only one came and he recognized her instantly. He was honestly surprised at the way relief flooded through him when he saw her.

"You're alive," Staff Sergeant Laila McPherson said, her voice sounding strange coming from the helmet's tiny speaker.

"All my life," he said. "Hell of an ambush, Staff Sergeant. Your tactical brilliance is on full display."

"Well, at least you haven't forgotten how to talk to a girl," she said with a chuckle. "What happened to you, Master Sergeant?"

"I was shot up," he said honestly. "The laser fire fried my suit's electronics. I've been harrying this bunch, but not very effectively."

An angry growl caused the pair of Marines to shift their focus back to Emperor Vang.

"How's your ammo?" Remmy asked.

"I'm out," she admitted. "Sergeant Oliver has some extra ammo, but not much."

"And the others?"

"Down to the dregs. If there are more of the aliens, we're in serious trouble."

Remmy nodded. "Me, too. Last mag, but that's it. From this point out, survival is the best we can hope to achieve."

"At least we captured their commander," Laila said.

"Not just the commander," Remmy replied. "According to GIGI, this is the 'Emperor'."

They both turned toward Vang, who was getting back to his feet.

"How are we supposed to secure him?" Laila asked.

"We don't. I think the fight's gone out of him anyway. Let's see if we can make contact with the Renegade. Lieutenant Colt should be back by now."

"Unless they were destroyed by the Imperium forces."

"That's not a happy thought," Remmy said. "I'm still in touch with GIGI, so it can't be all bad. Why don't you translate for me with this big fella."

"Why not?" Laila replied. "What do you want to ask him?"

"Tell him he's our prisoner and then ask if he needs anything."

They stood back several meters just to ensure they weren't in Vang's reach. He was unarmed and wounded but still gargantuan by human standards. If he managed to get even his one good hand on them, he could do real damage.

"What is your name?" Laila asked, her helmet translating the question into the guttural language of the Ashi.

The emperor didn't respond. She asked again, but he still would not reply.

By that time, three other Marines and Ludus had descended into the valley. Tex and Ricky Thompson were busy collecting weapons and finishing off the wounded. It was gruesome work but the charitable thing to do in that situation.

Izzy led Ludus to where Remmy was questioning the emperor with Laila. The Dudonus bowed as he approached Remmy, then turned and spoke to the emperor.

"Your days of tyranny are over," Ludus said.

The emperor growled menacingly, but the Marines all raised their weapons toward him, and the alien in the cape backed down.

"He's not very friendly, huh?" Izzy said.

"No, he's not," Remmy said. "Who's your friend?"

Laila made the introduction. "Master Sergeant Remmy Steel," she said, her helmet translating the words so that Ludus could understand her, "this is Ludus of the Dudonus people."

"It's a pleasure to meet you," Remmy said. "Let's move this party someplace with a little more cover and I'll touch base with the *Renegade*."

"There's plenty of tree cover downriver," Laila said. "Sergeant Oliver is there with more of Ludus' people."

"Let's go," Remmy said. "Tell the emperor he can come with us or die where he stands; it's up to him."

Laila translated and soon they were moving down the valley. Vang moved slowly, cradling his arm. The Marines were spread out around him, two in front, leading them through the valley and three behind. They kept their weapons ready even though most of them had little or no ammo left. They all had the big laser rifles that had been dropped by the Ashi warriors. They were too large to wield effectively but it was better than nothing if they had to fight again.

Ludus confirmed that Vang was the Ashi Emperor. Remmy thought it was hard to believe that they had actually captured the leader of the Imperium, but Ludus explained that a ruling council actually governed the galaxy. The emperor's main task was defense, even though there hadn't been a viable threat to the Imperium in several hundred years.

Remmy spent most of the time communicating with GIGI, who gave him a direct connection with Captain Darius.

"You're alive," Darius said. "That is excellent news."

"We're all alive and well, sir," Remmy said. "The drones made the difference. And Staff Sergeant McPherson laid the perfect ambush on the enemy fighters who remained. They walked right into it, sir. It was a textbook battle. To my knowledge, we killed all the Ashi warriors on Casasil."

"Spectacular achievement, Master Sergeant. GIGI has noted your location and Lieutenant Colt is heading down to retrieve you, but there are two enemy ships still in the air. We're tracking them and neither are near to you, but we'll have to be careful."

"Roger that, sir. What should we do with our prisoner?"

"Lieutenant Colt will take charge of the prisoner. If it really is their emperor, we can't just leave him down there."

"Agreed, sir. My thoughts exactly. There is also a group of former slaves that need refuge. What should I tell them?"

"How many?"

"A couple dozen, I think," Remmy replied.

"Let me think on that. For now, we want your platoon and the prisoner safely back on board the *Renegade*. Perhaps, if it's safe enough, one of their representatives could join us. The system is safe for now, but that won't last."

"I'll let them know, sir. See you soon."

"I look forward to that, Master Sergeant. Shogun out."

"Looks like we're going home," Remmy told the Marines. "Or at least back to the Renegade."

"Good enough for me," Ricky Thompson said.

"Yeah, this place is great, but a hot shower and good meal would be awesome," Tex added.

They didn't have to wait long. They reached a small clearing next to the river where Sergeant Oliver was waiting with the rest of the Dudonus refugees. Fifteen minutes later, Lieutenant Colt arrived in the drop ship with the rest of the Marine platoon. Lieutenant Colt, in his MECH suit, sprayed Vang in the face with an aerosol sedative. The massive alien dropped to the ground and had to be carried on board the drop ship, where he was secured with kevlar ratchet straps to the deck.

Ludus was only too happy to leave with the Marines, and they promised to do whatever they could for the refugees, even leaving them with the Ashi laser rifles to protect themselves with.

"Looks like we've got company," Lieutenant Colt said. "One of the Ashi ships is on an intercept course."

"How much time do we have?" Remmy asked.

"Two minutes at most," the Lieutenant said.

"Don't worry, we stocked up," Hugo McManus said, taking a shoulder-fired rocket from the armory inside the back of the dropship.

"Everyone check your harnesses," Lieutenant Colt ordered. "I'm going to open the rear hatch."

"Sir?" Laila asked. "Who's flying this ship?"

"It's automated, Staff Sergeant," Lieutenant Colt said. "Hang on."

The rear hatch opened to a rush of air. Everyone was in space armor except for Remmy and Ludus. Remmy pulled out air canisters. The mask didn't fit the alien's features exactly, but he didn't seem to have any trouble getting enough air to breathe.

With the rear hatch open, Sergeant McManus, Sergeant Jay Thorne, and Corporal Leigh Ann Poh aimed their missile launchers out the back and fired in quick succession. Then Lieutenant Colt climbed on top of the ship in his MECH armor. The Ashi ship used countermeasures to try and stop the missiles, but one got through. The ship's armor held until Colt fired two more rockets. They blew up on the alien ship's front section and it immediately began to descend. The second ship was making its way toward them but was too far away to be a threat before they reached orbit.

Ludus, who had been tense, seemed to relax when the rear hatch closed with everyone back inside. The entire flight to the *Renegade* lasted less than an hour. The crew of the ship used the gravity beam to pull them back into an empty hanger. There, a medical crew waited with what appeared to Remmy to be a cargo skiff. The emperor was still sedated or pretended to be. The transfer was smooth, and Doctor Lanski whisked the alien away once the huge emperor was lashed securely to the skiff.

"Did I hear right?" Gunny Rand asked. "Is that their leader?"

"The supreme poohbah," Remmy replied, "at least according to GIGI."

Gunny Rand pulled Remmy to the side. "How much do you trust that thing? I mean, it's a computer right, AI or something?"

"An alien version of that, I suppose," Remmy said. "Trust is a broad term, too. It's more like the way you know your favorite weapon. You know what it's capable of and how to use it in a fight. That's how I feel about GIGI. She's reliable."

"This is all like a dream," Gunny Rand confessed. "Ever since that monster got me on Lawash, I feel like I'm in a dream and not necessarily a good one."

Remmy understood how his friend felt. Stress affected people in different ways. The Gunnery Sergeant's belief about his own capabilities had been shattered on Lawash. And that horrific experience had been followed by things that were completely new to all of them, from the ship they occupied, to the battles against aliens they were fighting.

"Let's talk about it once we get settled again," Remmy said. "You're not alone, Chad. I've got your back."

"Thanks, brother. I'll take you up on that."

Lieutenant Colt, fresh from his MECH suit, joined them. "Making plans?"

"Tentatively," Remmy replied.

"Well, it might have to wait. Captain Darius wants us to meet him in the park with your new friend."

"I think Ludus is more comfortable with Staff Sergeant McPherson," Remmy admitted.

"Then bring her," the Lieutenant said. "Med scan, then straight up to the park."

"On my way," Remmy replied.

He walked over to where Laila and the alien Ludus were getting scanned by a medical tech with a handheld device.

"I'm next," he announced.

"Wait your turn," Laila teased.

She was fresh out of her space armor, her face red and sweaty, but Remmy thought she looked beautiful.

"Can't," Remmy said. "The captain wants to meet our guest."

Ludus made a cooing sound. Laila waited a second, then spoke into a translator she held in one hand.

"The captain of our ship wants to meet you," she said.

The device translated, and Ludus bowed. Remmy let the med tech scan him with his wand. Nothing appeared on the readout that bothered the technician, who cleared them to proceed to the park. They joined Lieutenant Colt at the anti-gravity lift. The four of them drifted up through the lower levels of the ship and came out near a pavilion surrounded by flowering shrubs.

Ludus' eyes grew wide with wonder as he took in the incredible sights of the park. The trio gave him a moment to take it all in, then led him to the pavilion where Captain Darius was waiting with

Commander Lori Lee and their civilian counterpart, Connor O'Dell.

"Welcome," Darius said, waving a hand toward one of the padded benches. "Would you be so kind as to join us?"

His words were translated by a small machine. Ludus bowed and moved to the padded bench. He sat delicately, his long, thin legs folding neatly beneath him.

"You are kind," Ludus said.

"We believe in treating our guests with hospitality," Captain Darius said.

"You have rescued me from the slavers. I cannot ask for more kindness than that."

"It was the least we could do," Captain Darius said. "But we're a little lost here. Can you tell us what you know about the Imperium?"

"It is a long history," Ludus said.

"We're mainly concerned with what's going on now?" Commander Lee said. "How will the Imperium respond to our taking their emperor hostage?"

"The Ashi are extremely ambitious. What happened to the ships that accompanied the emperor?"

"They retreated after we destroyed two of them," Darius said.

Ludus nodded. "I suspect that the emperor was left at your mercy on purpose. Another will rise up in his place."

"They used us to do their dirty work," Remmy said.

"Yes, that is correct. But the Imperium will strike back. The Ashi are prideful and covetous. They will want your ship."

"What would happen if we left the system?" Darius said.

"That I do not know," Ludus said. "I have spent my life trying to avoid the Imperium as much as possible."

"The Dudonus are considered a slave race," Laila said. "They're fair game anywhere in the Imperium."

"Slavery is repugnant," Connor said.

"I need to ask you another question," Captain Darius said. "We got a message from the emperor's ship. Someone by the name of

Nurek claims to have information we need. Does any of that ring a bell?"

"Nurek is a traditional Dudonus name," Ludus said. "I do not know him, but few can speak our language without an accent. I might be able to determine if he is one of us. I know the emperor had a personal Dudonus slave."

"Is that unusual?" Lieutenant Colt asked. "I only ask because Staff Sergeant McPherson said your kind is regularly taken as slaves."

"That is so. But we are few in number and can be very expensive at market. Often, only the wealthiest of families can afford a Dudonus slave. For the Emperor, his slave would be a sign of his wealth and power."

"What's the message say?" Remmy asked.

Commander Lee pressed a button on the translator device. It played the message, first in Dudonus and then in English.

To the Arodoni ship, my name is Nurek. I have served the Imperial family for two generations, but no longer. I seek asylum on your vessel and can bring with me news of a budding rebellion. Please respond to this message when you have decided if I am welcome among you.

Ludus seemed excited by what he heard. "That is a true Dudonus," he exclaimed. "And the rumors must be true."

"What rumors?" Darius asked.

"For a long time, it has been said that agents of descent stand ready on every world of the Imperium," Ludus said. "They wait only for a precipitating event to launch their revolt."

"So, this Nurek might be telling the truth?" Darius asked.

"That is my very great hope," the alien replied.

Darius nodded. "Thank you, Ludus. You have been a big help to us. We need to plan what we will do next. Would you mind if Mr. O'Dell spoke with you and showed you around the park?"

"It would be an honor," Ludus said.

Connor got to his feet. "Right this way," he said.

"Should I go, too?" Laila asked.

"No, stay," Darius said. "Your perspective might be helpful."

They waited as Connor took the translator and led Ludus out into the park proper. The ship's officers watched the alien go, marveling at how different Ludus was from humanity.

"Things are getting complicated pretty damn fast," Darius said. "My first impulse was to make a run for an uninhabited system where we could regroup."

"We aren't going back home?" Lieutenant Colt asked.

"I don't think we can risk it," Darius said.

"Not until we're sure they can't track us," Commander Lee said. "And it's bothersome that an armada showed up here not long after we did."

"You think they tracked us?" Remmy said.

"Unless they normally travel with that many ships," Darius said. "There were thirteen, counting the emperor's vessel. And two of those ships contained several dozen small, one-man fighter craft."

"So, what's there to think about?" Lieutenant Colt said. "We go to where we can be safe."

"But can we just leave this system?" Laila asked. "They're helpless?"

"Is that our fault?" Colt insisted.

"We brought conflict to this planet," Darius said. "I'm not inclined to just run away and leave the people here to fend for themselves."

"They're not fighters," Remmy said. "The Casasil people are six-legged pachyderms. They can't hold weapons. They're pretty much helpless."

"And Ludus told me that weapons are prohibited in the Imperium," Laila added. "We left the refugees with weapons taken from the Ashi warriors, and they could hardly lift the bulky rifles."

"So, if the Imperium army returns, they'll be overrun?" Commander Lori Lee asked.

"Overrun and maybe declared a slave race," Laila replied.

"Alright, that's what I needed to know," Captain Darius said.

"Lieutenant, see to your platoon. Do we have enough space armor for everyone in case it's needed?"

"Yes, sir," Colt said. "And my people are eager for action."

Remmy didn't think that was true. It certainly wasn't true for everyone. But there was no time to argue and he wouldn't counter what his Lieutenant said at any rate.

"Good. I'm going to give GIGI the order to launch drones and take down the last of the Ashi ships."

"Should only be one, sir," Colt said. "We downed one on the way up."

"Outstanding," Darius said. "In the meantime, we'll bring this Nurek on board. I want you both with us when we debrief him."

"Yes, sir," Lieutenant Colt and Master Sergeant Remmy said at the same time.

"Staff Sergeant McPherson," Darius said, standing up.

"Sir?" Laila said, jumping to attention.

"It's come to my attention that we have captured the emperor because of your outstanding leadership and tactical brilliance."

"I was just doing my job, sir," Laila said.

"Excelling in a difficult theater of war," Commander Lee said, "against an enemy we know very little about."

"It was a group effort," Laila said.

"Your contribution has not gone unnoticed," Captain Darius said. "I'm recommending you for a commendation when we get back home."

"Yes, sir. Thank you, sir."

"You made us all proud," he said. "Keep up the good work."

"Yes, sir!"

Captain Darius led Commander Lee from the pavilion. Remmy stood up and shook Laila's hand.

"Well deserved, Staff Sergeant," he told her.

"Thank you, Master Sergeant."

"Let's get cleaned up and grab some chow," Lieutenant Colt said. "Then I want everyone geared up. We need to be ready to roll when the call comes our way."

"Copy that, sir," Remmy said.

He left and Remmy lingered behind with Laila.

"That was you, wasn't it?" She asked.

"What?"

"Tactical brilliance?"

"I may have mentioned what a fine job you did, Laila, but I would have done that for anyone in that situation."

"It was a basic ambush."

"There were over ninety aliens in the valley," Remmy said. "You knew where and how to stage the ambush."

"Some of them would have escaped, if not for you."

"I've been meaning to ask how you knew I would seal off that valley?"

"I didn't. I thought you were dead."

"Me? Nah, I don't want to die."

"But you almost did," she said, speaking softly. "That was a major risk you took."

"I had drone cover," Remmy said.

"You were all alone, facing over a hundred enemy fighters."

"The opportunity came up to take down their leader," he said. "You would have done the same in my boots."

"Not by myself."

"It's easier by myself. I don't have to worry about the people I care for getting hurt."

"Just remember, if you get hurt or killed, we'll have to live with that pain."

"Never thought of it that way," Remmy said.

"Well, you better start. Because I don't plan on losing you, Master Sergeant. We got a good thing going."

"That's for sure," Remmy replied with a smile.

They left the pavilion side by side, uncertain what the future held but happy to be together, no matter what was coming their way.

CHAPTER 14

AN HOUR LATER, Remmy was showered, shaved and fed. He still needed to collect his gear and get a new suit of space armor, but Captain Darius had summoned him. The *Renegade* didn't have a medical facility, so the humans had taken most of the gear from the *Jericho's* sick bay and set it all up in a large room just off the command section. It had human-sized beds, scanners, therapy pods, surgical bots, and lots of supplies, including a blood bank. Everyone on board had contributed or was scheduled to.

Right in the middle of the big room was the cargo skiff. The emperor was awake and furious but unable to move. His arms and legs were secured with multiple kevlar straps, and there were more across his chest and abdomen. His head was left free, but that was the only part of his body that wasn't tied down to the skiff. At first, he had roared in anger as he strained against his bonds but it didn't take long to realize how futile his efforts were.

Doctor Lanski had scanned his shattered arm, stopped the bleeding, and secured it with a temporary cast. He had also dug the shards of bone from the alien's face, stitching up the wounds and applying a burn salve where needed.

"I got the bullet fragments out of his arm, but the explosive round destroyed the bone," Lanski was explaining to the captain when Remmy arrived. "I could probably do something about it with surgery, but I'm still studying his anatomy. It's very different from our own."

"Different, how?" Darius asked.

"His blood is different for one thing," Lanski explained. "He has two hearts and a completely different nervous system."

"Is he stable?"

"He is, but he'll never use his left arm again unless we operate."

"And you don't want to operate because..."

"Because I don't know how to keep his body and brain oxygenated while under general anesthesia. Not to mention, we have no blood supplies for him. He could bleed out and there would be nothing we could do about it."

"I see," Darius said. "Good work, doctor. Master Sergeant, will you walk with me?"

"Yes, sir!" Remmy said.

They turned down the corridor toward the gravity ring. At first, the captain was silent. Remmy had no idea why he had been called to meet with Darius, but he was content to wait until the captain told him.

"I sent Commander Lee to pick up Nurek," Darius said. "Lieutenant Colt took Alpha Team with her."

"She's in good hands then."

"They made a quick inspection of the emperor's ship. It's just the framework now. The crew flew down in the two escort vessels, and the third part of that ship was the emperor's quarters, which were destroyed by the drones."

"I see," Remmy replied.

"Nurek had already killed the two crew members still on the frame. It didn't take Alpha Team long to search the ship."

"Nothing but the engineering section left, I suppose," Remmy said.

"That's right," Darius said. "A couple of big hyperspace engines. They'll be back here soon. I've sent word to the planet that we would like to discuss the security of Casasil with their officials. I'd like you to lead that discussion."

"Me, sir?" Remmy asked.

"Yes. Look, I know this isn't within your normal scope of duties, but I need someone who really understands what we're up against here."

"Why not Commander Lee?"

"She could do it, but I need her up here with me. The Imperials are coming back; there's no doubt about that. We must be ready for them, which is why I'm going to move the *Renegade* back in the system. Once they arrive, the fighting should be away from the planet, not toward it."

"Makes sense," Remmy said.

"But there's always the possibility that when the Imperials come, they will send more ground troops to the planet, which is why I'm asking you to do this for us, Master Sergeant. You can handle the diplomacy but also help prepare the people down there for whatever might come."

"You're talking about a ground war?" Remmy asked. "I don't think I could have the locals ready for that if I had an entire year to prepare."

"The fight is coming no matter what we do," Darius said. "We can't stop it from happening. Hell, we may not be able to stop them at all. But on board the ship, you can't do much. Down on the ground..."

"I see your point. Are you sending me alone?"

"No, the entire platoon. I hate to risk you all on this crazy enterprise, but that's what gives us the best chance of surviving. I want you to take GIGI, too. She'll launch in her own dropship and return to orbit and lead the drones once the fighting starts. That should even things up some."

"A last stand, sir?"

"Something like that," Darius agreed. "If we leave, we'll live to fight another day, but I can't imagine what could happen to the people down there. And we have their emperor. Maybe that will be enough to make the Imperial forces surrender."

"Not likely, sir."

Darius nodded grimly. "It's worth a shot. In the meantime, you do all you can for the people on the ground."

"Yes, Captain. I can do that."

"Good man. I knew I could count on you."

"Sir, if I may ask. What about Lieutenant Colt?"

"He'll lead the platoon. You'll lead the efforts with the locals, including leading them into battle if necessary."

"I see."

"Can you handle it?"

"I can give it my best effort, sir."

"That's all I ask. Load up as much gear as you can. Weapons, ammunition, whatever we've got on board. Take as many dropships as you need; they're all going to launch with you anyway. I'm sending a couple of medical techs, too. If we can hold this ground and repel the Imperium's attack, there's a good chance we'll save this system. If Nurek is right about fomenting rebellion across the galaxy, what we do here and now could mean the difference in humanity's future."

"You're talking about revolution."

"I am. It's a cause worth fighting for, wouldn't you agree?"

"Yes, sir. I saw the prisoners on that slave ship, remember?"

"I do remember," Captain Darius said. "And I remember your advice to me. I think it was spot on. Which is why I think you're the right man to communicate what we can do and what we can't do to the people down there."

He extended his hand, and Remmy shook it.

"Just in case we don't see each other again, it's been a pleasure, sir," Remmy said.

"The pleasure has been all mine, Master Sergeant. Let's make sure this isn't the last time."

"Copy that."

The captain propelled himself up into the gravity ring with a small jump. Remmy stepped out into the ring and then pushed himself down. His mind was racing with the possibilities of what lay before him. But even his imagination couldn't prepare him for what was to come.

CHAPTER 15

"RADAR? ANY SIGNS OF THE ASHI?" Captain Darius asked as he strode back onto the Bridge."

"Negative, Captain," Vivian Ramos said. "There's no movement in the system but us."

"Excellent. We've got a little more time then. Status?"

"Green across the board," Henry Nash said.

"Power to weapons is one hundred percent," Pete Best said.

"Any word from the planet?"

"Our message was received, and any help we wish to share with the Casians is welcome," Ensign Jacee Bertoli said.

"You're plans are coming together," Henry said. "Who knows? If the alien is right and there is a rebellion, maybe there won't be a retaliatory attack on this system at all."

"I wish we could count on that," Darius said.

"It seems to me our work here is nearly done," Pete Best said. "Once the Imperium falls, there's no reason we can't go home."

Darius didn't reply. He knew his weapons specialist was simply being optimistic, but they all knew that empires didn't fall in a day. And going back to the Sol system was still a huge risk they couldn't take, even if the Casa system was out of danger.

"Captain, I have word from Commander Lee. She has Nurek and is returning to the *Renegade*. ETA half an hour, sir."

"Very well. I'll make plans to meet them in the park. In the meantime, Lieutenant Ramos has the con. I want to know the instant any other ship arrives in this system."

"Aye, Captain, we'll let you know," Vivian replied.

"As for the rest of you, take turns getting some rest. We'll need everyone at the top of their game when the Ashi return."

Darius left the Bridge and stopped at his office. There was nothing that he needed but he was nervous. They had picked a fight with an enemy they couldn't even begin to estimate. The Ashi could return with a thousand ships. What would he do then? The thought was terrifying. But a ship's captain had to be supremely confident. He could never let his doubts, much less his fears, show to his crew.

Part of him loved the action and adventure of being in the Arodoni ship and being the first humans to leave the Sol system. His life had been on the cusp of a great change if he hadn't been ordered to retrieve the mysterious artifact that turned out to be a Galactic Information and Guidance Instrument. He had been staring at a promotion to an administrative role in the SDF or retirement. Yet somehow, he had been swept away in a grand adventure across the stars. It was the kind of thing he had dreamed of as a young officer. His professional life had turned out to be more of a manager on star ships. He could count the number of times he had been in a real fight on one hand. And in those instances, he had been a small part of a Fleet squadron.

He had to admit he loved the *Renegade's* power and speed. He had essentially stumbled upon a ship with nearly limitless resources. Between the lasers, the shielding, and the drones, the Arodoni ship was a force to be reckoned with. And the fact that he could command her with just a skeleton crew was unbelievable.

He left his office and made his way down to the systems control room. Ensign Alex Stanislaus was there. The young officer was a computer phenom and Darius needed some answers. In his mind, a new vision for the *Renegade* was forming. One that was much more than simply running back to the Sol system as soon as possible.

"Captain," Stanislaus said, getting quickly to his feet as Darius walked into the Systems Control room.

"As you were, Ensign. How are things looking?"

"Awesome, sir, if I can use that term. Everything is in optimal condition."

"Excellent, that's what I like to hear."

"Aye, sir."

"I have a security question for you," Darius continued. "Is it possible to lock down the forward section of the ship?"

"Lock it down, sir?"

"There are refugees on the planet," Darius explained. "I'm toying with the idea that maybe we take them on board. If we were to do that, I would want the entire fore section of the ship, say from the gravity ring forward, to be secure so that only the crew has access."

"Oh, I see what you're saying. I don't know, but I can find out."

"Would you do that for me, Alex? No decisions have been made. We're still out on a limb here in this system, but I like to know my options."

"Of course, Captain. I'll get right on it."

"Excellent," Darius told him.

The walk from the Command section of the ship to the park was becoming familiar to him. He took the gravity ring down to Epsilon deck, which led straight down the middle of the ship to the park. The Pavilion where he met with Ludus was only a hundred meters from the entrance to the agricultural center of the ship. And like most of the crew, the park was Captain Darius' favorite part of the *Renegade*. It was like stepping out of a spacecraft and into a world that was vibrant and grand. The sheer amount of open space was breathtaking. And the oxygen content in the park was rich too, as were the smells. During the early days of exploring the alien ship, Darius and every other member of the crew had removed his boots and walked barefoot on the grass. It was a luxury beyond the imagination of human engineers. Even on the big space stations, there had never been such a perfect agricultural environment.

Darius reached the Pavilion just as Commander Lee led Nurek into the park from the gravity lift. He looked almost identical to Ludus, only with different clothing. The alien wore a robe of pale ivory. Unlike Ludus, he made no outward show of surprise at the grandeur of the ship's park. Commander Lee led him to the pavilion, where Darius was on his feet waiting to greet him.

"Nurek, welcome to the *Renegade*."

"Thank you, Captain. I regret that I do not speak your native language."

Commander Lee was carrying a handheld translation device that had been produced by GIGI using the ship's manufacturing facilities and programmed with her extensive list of known languages.

"Maybe in time, we will be able to learn from one another. Please, sit down and tell us about your plight."

Nurek sat down, followed by Commander Lee and Captain Darius. Like Ludus, the Dudonus alien was graceful. He folded his legs under the wide bench seat and kept his hands in his narrow lap.

"My name is Nurek, and I have been a slave in the Imperial household for over one hundred cycles. In that time, I have served four Emperors. Vang Na'Raj is the latest after he killed his father nearly a full cycle ago."

"Emperor Vang killed his father?" Darius asked.

Nurek nodded. "Along with his mother and younger siblings. It is not uncommon among the Ashi elite. Vang is strong. He challenged his father, and once he had taken the throne, he had the rest of his family murdered."

"Sounds like a wonderful person," Commander Lori Lee said.

"I only explain this to help you understand the enemy that you have made," Nurek said. "The Ashi are militant. They thrive in times of war. Your victory here in the Casasil system could be the spark that ignites them. But there are other factors at work in the galaxy, too."

"You mentioned a rebellion," Darius said.

"Yes," Nurek said. "For several decades, preparations have been underway. The Empire has grown fat with bureaucrats who only care about themselves. Many worlds have been neglected or abused. Many races have been shamed. But for all the planning and preparation, the Ashi have one thing that keeps us from acting. They alone have access to ships of war."

"That's what Ludus told us," Commander Lee spoke up.

"Classic tyrannical move," Darius said. "Restrict the ownership of weapons so that the populace can't rise up against the corrupt."

"Exactly," Nurek said. "My people are not warriors. Most races in the galaxy are not suited for fighting. Our rebellion will disrupt supply chains and make waging war difficult for the Imperials, but we still need a strong ally that can fight for our freedom. Otherwise, we will be crushed eventually."

"We're just one ship," Darius said. "I'm not sure we can do what you need."

"You already have," Nurek said. "Your fight with Sheika Kahn's flotilla was a spectacular victory, although I suspect the Kahn was all too happy to retreat."

"Why is that?" Commander Lee asked.

"He is Ashi. They are all ambitious. Ulrach Sheika has served as Kahn for many cycles, and although he hides it well, he has no love for Emperor Vang. I believe he manipulated the young emperor to challenge his father and destroy his family so that the Kahn would be in place to seize control. Vang harbors visions of military greatness. Your presence in the galaxy began a chain of events that would allow Sheika Kahn to have Emperor Vang destroyed."

"He's not dead," Darius said. "We captured the emperor. He's in our medical facility."

That was a surprise to Nurek, and for once, he could not keep his shock from showing on his face.

"He is here?"

"Yes. We have him under light sedation and tight restraints," Darius said. "We come from a system that knows nothing of the Imperium. We didn't come looking for a fight."

"But you are warriors," Nurek said. "It is said the Arodoni are the only race the Ashi fear."

Darius looked at Commander Lee. He wasn't sure how much to share with Nurek. He certainly wasn't about to tell the alien about humanity or the Sol system. Perhaps it was better to let him believe they were Arodoni. But if he spent much time on the ship, he would soon discover the truth. And Darius didn't want to start a new friendship by telling a lie.

"We are not the Arodoni," Darius said.

"But this is an Arodoni ship. It is in the Imperial records."

"True," Darius said. "But we are stewards of this ship, not the creators of it."

"Are you people, not warriors?"

"We can fight," Darius said. "Right now, our Marines are preparing to return to Casasil and help them prepare for the retaliatory strike from the Ashi."

"And what will the ship do?"

"Stay, fight, whatever we can do to help these people," Darius explained.

Suddenly, Nurek stood up. Darius turned and looked to see what the alien had caught sight of. It was Ludus and Connor O'Dell walking toward the pavilion.

"You have Dudonus slaves?" Nurek asked, his voice tight.

"No," Darius said. "Ludus was on a slave ship that we stopped and returned to Casasil. He is one of several of your kind that are refugees on the planet below."

"We don't practice slavery," Commander Lee said. "It was outlawed on our home planet long ago."

"Ludus is a guest here, like yourself," Darius added.

"Brother!" Ludus called. "Look at this. They have Tanga fruit!"

Nurek turned to Captain Darius. "He is free to leave?"

"As are you, any time you desire."

Ludus jogged to the pavilion, his thin body springing on his surprisingly flexible legs. He held out a dark fruit the size of a large orange.

"Can you believe it," Ludus said. "Tanga fruit. I didn't think they could grow anywhere but Dudon."

"Nor did I," Nurek said, taking the fruit.

He raised it to his mouth. "I had one once as a child." He took a bite. His narrow mouth curved into a smile.

"It is a miracle. This ship is unbelievable," Ludus said. "I have learned so much."

"And you are well?"

"I was rescued, defended and brought here to meet with Captain Darius to plead for our people on Casasil," Ludus said.

Nurek turned back to Captain Darius. "I cannot thank you enough. My people have been exploited for centuries. Your kindness will not be forgotten."

"I am glad you feel that way," Darius said. "For now, we must prepare for the Ashi to return. You are welcome to stay here with Ludus or go down to the planet. Neither option is necessarily safe, I'm afraid. But we won't leave the people on Casasil to deal with our problems. When the Ashi return, we're going to face them."

"You are brave. I will stay and help however I can," Nurek said. "I have known Sheika Kahn for many years. I may have insights that will help in your preparations."

"Any help you can give would be greatly appreciated," Darius said.

"It is most likely that Kahn fell back to the Rologani Exchange," Nurek said. "My guess is that he will take his flagship back to the core systems to declare himself the new Emperor. His flotilla will be joined by other Ashi warships. As many as thirty or forty would not be surprising."

"Forty or fifty ships would be difficult to manage," Commander Lee said.

"Once we're in position we can strike at them the moment they emerge from hyperspace," Darius said. "I've already taken steps to ensure that the Marines are ready for a ground invasion. They'll have GIGI operating the drones to back them up."

"GIGI? Nurek said.

Ludus looked at Nurek, "Can it be possible?"

"What?" Darius asked.

"You have a Galactic Information and Guidance Instrument?" Nurek asked.

It was Darius' turn to be surprised. He wasn't even sure that the acronym would translate, yet somehow it did.

"We do," he said, not quite sure if admitting it had been a good idea or not.

Ludus threw back his head and yelped.

"I think that's how they show delight," Connor suggested. "He did the same thing when he found the Tangi tree."

"It is indeed a sign of great delight," Nurek said. "Long ago, before our kind was considered a slave race, our ancestors helped lay the groundwork for a rebellion. They enlisted the help of the Correll, who built the Guidance Instruments and sent them to prospective systems that had not yet been discovered by the Imperium."

"Your people were behind sending GIGI to our system?" Darius asked.

"It was a Dudonus idea, carried out by others, in the hopes that someday one of those races might rise up and help us defeat the Ashi. It has become a sort of fable among our people, although it is never spoken of openly. We all secretly harbor hope that one of you might turn the tide and help us overthrow the Imperial regime."

"It's a small galaxy, after all," Lori Lee said.

"I suppose so. Commander Lee and I have work to do. Nurek, Ludus, I leave you in the capable hands of Mr. O'Dell. Be sure that you keep your comlink on at all times, Connor. We may need to get information from our guests."

"Yes, Captain," Connor said.

"Do you have any idea how long it will take the Ashi forces to return?" Darius asked Nurek.

"It could be hours, or it could be days," he said. "Sheika Kahn will have his plans ready. It won't take him long to act."

"And there's no chance they'll just forget about what happened here?" Lori Lee asked.

Nurek shook his head. "The Kahn's first act as new emperor will be to defeat you and parade the Arodoni ship through the core systems."

"Then we know what we have to do," Darius said. "We had best be about it."

CHAPTER 16

THE MARINES LOADED EVERYTHING. Every ship in the fleet had a Marine detachment and they, in turn, brought all sorts of gear and munitions. The *Renegade's* maintenance droids helped move everything and by the time Lieutenant Colt returned from escorting Commander Lee, they were ready to launch for the planet.

"Hot damn! I'm ready to have my feet on the ground again," Rip said.

"Yeah, maybe this time you don't get shot before the real fighting takes place," Tex teased.

"Enough chit-chat," Lieutenant Colt barked. "We load up by teams. I'm with Alpha. Master Sergeant Steel, you're with Charlie Team."

"Copy that, sir," Remmy said.

"Let's look alive, people," Colt continued. "There's a whole planet down there depending on us."

"Good luck," Remmy told Laila and Gunny Rand.

"See you in the dirt," the Gunnery Sergeant replied.

They were all in full armor and carrying weapons. Having fought the Ashi, everyone knew what they wanted. Remmy still carried his LTX and a dozen extra magazines of explosive rounds in the loops of his tactical vest. He replaced his ruined laser pistol for a Yagger HC, or as most people called it, a Hand Cannon. It was a five-round revolver that fired shotgun-style shells filled with Buzzers. They were small, disc-shaped blades designed to eviscerate flesh. The pistol had a very short range, only fifteen meters before the Buzzers lost velocity, but he guessed the weapon would be effective against the Ashi.

He also had a dozen thermobaric grenades. It was protocol for Marines moving from space into the atmosphere to wear space armor on the off chance that their vessel was compromised during descent. But with no enemy ships in the system yet, Master Sergeant Steel had opted to go with standard battle armor. It was sturdy enough to stop laser fire but not as bulky. He didn't need the extra insulation or the oxygen tanks that were standard on space armor. Better mobility was a higher priority to Remmy than extra protection.

He boarded the drop ship with Charlie Team. They had only a few boxes of supplies on board and GIGI who was strapped to the deck.

"We got trouble, Master Sergeant?" Dirk Oliver asked.

"Anticipating the possibility," Remmy replied, strapping into a jump seat.

Rip fastened himself into the seat on the opposite side of the ship. The launch was no small feat. GIGI organized over a thousand space drones that were put into orbit. Then, the sentient machine took control of eight hundred atmospheric craft, including the drop ships with the Marines and cargo. The entire operation took over an hour before every ship was launched, but soon, the *Renegade* was making her way into the outer system, while eighteen hundred drones and drop ships stayed by the planet.

"What's our destination?" Rip asked.

"A city called Kipbur in the northern hemisphere," Remmy explained. "That will be our base of operations, although the platoon may branch out to other points."

"Kipbur their capital?" Dirk asked.

"Yeah, biggest city, too," Remmy told him. "I'll be meeting with their ruling council there. Our job is to protect them, but the best way to do that is to teach them how to defend themselves."

"Copy that," Dirk said.

"Hell yeah," Rip added. "Teach 'em how to fight their own battles."

The trip down through the atmosphere was slow. GIGI was careful to pilot down the drones, so they didn't get overheated by friction in the upper atmosphere. When they finally reached the planet's surface, the Casians had already set up a large area for them. It was winter in the northern hemisphere. A light pink snow fell in beautiful flakes and covered everything. The Casians used geothermal energy to power their city and were ready to recharge the power cells in the Arodoni drones when the Marines arrived.

"Unload the cargo," Remmy ordered Dirk and Rip. "I've got to find the LT."

He stepped out into a magical, alien winter. The pink snow looked like flakes of cotton candy. The city nearby was a series of large buildings with sloping roofs that were covered in snow. Icicles hung from the corners. The streets were paved with large, gray flag-stones. And Remmy could smell the scent of fragrant wood being burned.

Lieutenant Colt had been the first to land. He stood out in his MECH armor. With the suit's powerful servos and hydraulics, he was able to put up a large tent within minutes and carry the heavy pallets of communications equipment into it. When Remmy reached him, he was setting up a huge receiver dish with an antenna protruding from the center.

"Sir, I'll be going to meet with the locals now," Remmy said.

"Your people offloading their ship?" Colt asked.

"Yes, sir. They'll be done in a few minutes. Then GIGI will take the ship back up to orbit."

"Very well. Report your progress with the locals as soon as you can."

"Roger that, sir," Remmy said.

He turned to the city and found a group of officials waiting. They were mostly Casians, the six-legged, large-bodied aliens with a tensile trunk like an elephant. Remmy was wearing an open-faced helmet with a comlink built into one ear and a translator in the other. He approached the group and held out his empty hands.

"My name is Remmy. I'm a Master Sergeant in the Space Marine Corps. I'm here to help you prepare for a possible invasion."

"You led the team in overthrowing the slavers who took our people," one of the Casians said. "We are in your debt."

"No, you don't owe us anything," Remmy replied. "Odds are very high that your planet will be invaded by an Ashi army."

"Your warriors defeated them before," another of the leaders pointed out.

"That was different. It was a very limited force and we had the advantage of surprise. We could be facing a much larger threat."

"Will you stay and help us?" The oldest looking alien asked.

"Yes," Remmy said. "We will stay and help."

"Then that is all we can ask for from you. Come, we will show you what you need to know."

Remmy followed the group into the town. There were plenty of Casians around. They were clearly a timid race, even though they were all bigger than Remmy and could have easily trampled him down if not for his weapons. Yet they all seemed scared and he couldn't blame them. The humans were aliens and they were fighting a war with a powerful foe who had dominated the galaxy for thousands of years. It wasn't surprising that they didn't have a lot of hope in the newcomers.

Eventually, they came to a large building made of stone and timber. Inside, there was very little furniture. A large round fire pit dominated the space. Several dozen of the elephantine aliens lingered in the warm space. A table was set up with maps on paper that were unrolled and held open with small, smooth stones. The Casians were herbivores and had troughs full of various kinds of foliage, from hay analogues to clover look-alikes. There were also stone basins large enough that Remmy could have laid down in them and been completely submerged in water. He also saw several large jugs with what appeared to be wine in them. The wine was poured into ornate bowls for the Casians to drink from.

But there were more than Casians in the building. At the map table, a pair of Dudonus stood by, along with a tall alien with a face like a grasshopper and long, powerful legs that folded up under the alien's smooth body.

"This is Rodan," one of the Casians said, waving his trunk at the grasshopper-faced alien. "Their kind have a city in the southern mountains."

When Rodan spoke, it was a series of chirps and clicks. The galactic translator put the sounds into words for Remmy: "Casasil has become our home."

"And you've met some of the Dudonus who once had several colonies on our world," the elderly Casian said. "We do not practice slavery, but the Imperial slavers discovered their existence. Only a few still remain here."

"I met some of you from the slave ship," Remmy said.

"Your rescue of the unfortunates on that terrible vessel is a great victory for all our kinds," said the Dudonus.

"I hope so," Remmy said. "Because it was also a blow to the Empire. And there is little doubt that the Ashi will return."

"In greater numbers," the elderly Casian said. "I am Ernhard, Chief of the Casians here in Kipbur. These are my fellow Chiefs from other locations. What can we do to be ready for what is to come?"

"We have weapons," Remmy said. "Some can be automated, but others you will need to use."

"We are not warriors," said another of Casian Chieftains.

"No, but you will have to become defenders unless you want the Ashi to destroy your world."

"They can simply bombard us from orbit," Rodan said.

"We have measures in place for that," Remmy said. "I hope everything I'm going to tell you here is confidential."

"There are those who would share such news with the Empire," Ernhard said, "but not in this room."

"Good," Remmy said. "Then know that our ship is in the system. It has the capability to fight whatever the Imperium sends. To draw the destruction away from your world, it is moving deeper into your system, beyond the hyperspace portal."

"The Imperium will send dozens of battleships," one of the Dudonus said.

"Trust me when I say the *Renegade* can handle it. But it is a possibility that some of the Ashi ships will be troop carriers that will make straight for the planet."

"Then we are doomed," said one of the Casians.

"No, we have attack drones in orbit. Over a thousand space-craft whose job is to defend your world."

"Then why are you here?" Rodan asked.

"Redundancy," Remmy said. "The battle will begin in space, and hopefully, it will end there, too. But because we cannot antici-pate how many vessels the Ashi will send or what types of craft may come through the portal, we will do all we can to defend your people."

"Why?" The Dudonus asked. "What reason can you have for risking so much for a race you do not even know?"

"That's a good question," Remmy said. "We don't know you, yet. I hope to change that. I hope to prove that we are friends, not foes. But the fight that is coming here is because of us. We attacked the Imperial ships. They will return to fight us and perhaps to punish you. We find that outcome unacceptable. We will not leave you to fend for yourselves after we started the war."

"There are rumors of rebellion," one of the Dudonus aliens said. "I am called Helzo, and there are whispers among the people of revolt."

"I hope they are more than rumors," Remmy said. "Although we didn't start them."

"Your kind is not behind the rebellion?" Ernhard asked.

"No," Remmy admitted. "My people want peace, but not at the cost of subjection to an Empire that does not share our values. We acted against the slavers because we do not believe any intelligent species deserves to be treated as property to be bought and sold. And while we didn't come looking for war, we will not run from it either. If the Ashi Empire tolerates and encourages slavery, we know that we, as a race, want nothing to do with it."

"Lofty words," Rodan said. "But many have said as much, only to be exterminated."

"Or enslaved for their trouble," Helzo added.

"We may die," Remmy said, "but we'll go down fighting."

"Then let us learn what we can to be able to defend the people of Casasil," Ernhard said.

CHAPTER 17

LAILA AND IZZY BERRY were carrying a belt-fed remote weapon in a hard case up a ramp toward the roof of a building on the edge of town. It was cold, and she halfway wished she had worn space armor.

"At least we would be warmer," Izzy was arguing.

"A little snow never hurt," Laila said, although secretly she agreed with her subordinate.

"It's wet and cold; that's a terrible combination," Izzy said.

"You sound like someone with experience."

"I have plenty. I grew up in Canada. If you think space is cold, try making it through a winter in Saskatoon."

"I'll take your word for it," Laila said.

They stopped at the top of the ramp and set up the tripod that would hold the weapon. It was a heavy, rotating barrel machine gun that fired .50 caliber rounds at a rate of thirty per second. It was controlled via computer or, if synced up, a Marine's battle helmet. The weapon would cover two sides of the city for nearly a thousand meters. The one thing Kipbur had going for it was the wide open spaces all around it. An army on foot would have to cross a deadly no man's land to reach the city. And they were setting up the autocannons on all four corners of the neatly arranged community.

The entire day was spent preparing fortifications and setting up their communications lines. Signals were sent up into orbit where GIGI could relay them through the system to the *Renegade*. Fortunately, they had no word about the enemy appearing in the system. The longer it took the Ashi to come back, the better off the people on the ground would be.

That evening, the platoon gathered in their mess tent. The locals only ate foliage, which meant the Marines were left with combat rations. Laila didn't really enjoy any of the Meals Ready to Eat, or MREs, as they were more commonly known. She ripped the top off a package of Mac and Cheese with bits of broccoli and small protein wafers. It wasn't hot, but not really cold, either. Somehow, the containers kept the contents from getting too cold. It was all mushy, the cheese sauce too heavy and not quite right. Still, it filled her stomach, which was all she could really ask for. She washed it down with a bottle of water flavored with electrolytes and amino acids. It gave the water an orange flavor, again, not her favorite, but not what she hated most. Peach was the worst, in her opinion, and fortunately, Izzy and Leigh Ann Poh preferred it.

"Alright, platoon," Colt said, finally coming into the mess tent after spending most of the day in his MECH suit stomping all around camp. "Perimeter motion detectors are up and operational. Let's do single duty watch, two hours. Gunny Rand will set the schedule. Make sure if any word comes in from the *Renegade* that you alert me immediately."

"Will do, LT," Gunny Rand said. "Alright, people, you heard the man. I need four volunteers for watch duty tonight."

No one wanted the four am to six am slot, so Laila took it. It was the worst watch duty since it meant rising early to stand watch before the day truly began, plus no hope of getting more sleep before having to go to work. Still, as Staff Sergeant on a Spec Op platoon with three NCOs, it was up to her to set the example for the platoon. She went off to sleep as soon as she finished her dinner.

Next to the chow tent was a barracks tent. It had a small, liquid fuel heater, but the tent couldn't hold in the heat. Laila took off her boots and her armor but then added a hoodie from her gear and crawled into the sleeping rack that was laid across her field cot. She set her watch to wake her up five minutes before she was due in the communications tent and then pulled the hood up on her sweatshirt, zipped up her sleeping bag and fell asleep.

Six hours later, her watch buzzed on her wrist. She shut it off and got dressed in the dark. When she got to the command center, she was delighted to find a working coffee maker with a fresh pot.

"High octane," Rip Van Winkle told her as she made straight for the coffee maker. "You're gonna need it."

"Slow night?"

"Watching the snow fall is mesmerizing," he told her. "It'll lull you right to sleep if you ain't careful."

"Roger that," she said, pouring the hot liquid into a disposable cup and then moving to the camp chair near the monitors. She slipped a set of headphones over one ear, then studied the motion sensor camera feeds. They were on night vision, which lit everything in green but made it possible to see, even if all there was to see was snow falling.

She had almost finished her first cup of coffee when the flap moved, and Remmy appeared. He had been gone most of the day working with the locals.

"What are you doing up?"

"Thought you might like some company," he told her. "And I need some of that coffee."

She joined him at the pot and refilled her cup. Laila added some sugar to hers, and they both returned to the monitors.

"Anything moving out there?"

"Negative," she told him. "No word from the *Renegade* either. What are the locals like?"

"Peaceful, content, and communal."

"Communal?"

"They live together in groups. Each one of the structures is like a big open space with several families living together. There's very little electronics, although they do use electric vehicles."

"Will they be much use once the fighting starts?"

"They say a man fighting to defend his home and loved ones is worth three professional soldiers," Remmy declared.

"But they aren't men," she said pointedly.

"Fair enough. Only time will tell. They aren't physically capable of fighting in the traditional sense."

"So, we're on our own?"

"For the most part," he admitted. "We've made plans but mostly to move their vulnerable out of the cities. Tomorrow, we'll set rally points and start looking for more defensible locations."

"Who would have imagined that Remmy Steel, winner of the Medal of Honor, would become a diplomat?" She teased.

"Yeah, well, I'd rather be a drill instructor, but they didn't give me that option. So, I'm stuck trying to convince the locals to do what's best for themselves. Unfortunately, they don't seem to get it."

They sipped coffee and talked about the duties that waited for them once the sun came up. It had just begun to lighten the cloudy sky when word came in from the *Renegade*.

"Ronan One, this is Shogun actual. Be advised we are picking up energy readings from the portal. Enemy ships could be entering the system."

Laila leaned forward and compressed the transmit button on the communication unit.

"Roger that, Shogun. We are standing by."

Laila looked at Remmy. It had been a pleasant hour, but the threat was back and there was no more time for casual conversation.

"I'll go alert the LT," Laila said.

"Go," Remmy said. "I'll monitor things till you get back with him."

She left quickly, dashing through the fresh snow and into the barracks tent. Lieutenant Colt's cot was nearest to the door and also closest to the heater. She shook his arm.

"What?" He asked.

"Energy signature at the portal. Could be enemy vessels inbound."

"Yeah, okay, wake everyone else. Let's get suited up and ready," he said. "Who's monitoring the communications unit?"

"Master Sergeant Steel."

A look of surprise crossed the lieutenant's face.

Thinking fast, Laila said, "He stopped in for coffee."

"Ah, yeah, I could use some too. Thank you, Staff Sergeant."

Laila nodded, then moved to the next cot and started waking up the platoon.

CHAPTER 18

DARIUS CALCULATED that he had managed to squeeze in four hours of sleep in the last thirty-six hours. His coffee wasn't helping much, but the adrenaline that surged into his veins when Vivian Ramos alerted him to the energy build-up at the hyperspace portal was burning off his fatigue.

"Get Lieutenant Best and Lieutenant Nash up here. Sound the alert. I want the crew at their duty stations," Darius ordered.

"Aye, Captain, sounding the alert now."

"Did you message the Marines?"

"Yes, sir, a few minutes ago. We should be getting a reply any moment."

The *Renegade* had spent the last twelve hours moving into position. They were on the far side of the portal from Casasil, hiding in the lee of a small moon that orbited the system's largest gas giant. But, according to their calculations, they were still within effective range of the *Renegade's* big laser cannons.

It took less than sixty seconds for Nash and Pete Best to reach the Bridge. They dropped into their seats just as the message from Casasil came in.

"Alright, this could be it, people," Darius said. "Let's get the cannons fully charged and ready to fire."

"Aye, Captain," Pete Best said. "Activating cannons. We are at full power capacity, sir. Ready to fire in thirty seconds."

"Lieutenant Nash, keep your engines warm," Darius said.

"We're purring like a kitten, Captain. Ready for evasive maneuvers."

"First vessel is coming through," Vivian said.

Darius noticed the tension in her voice. She was nervous. They all were. There was no way of knowing what the Ashi forces would bring to bear.

"Get ready to alert the ground forces," Darius said.

A ship suddenly appeared. It was just a speck of light in the distance, but on the plot, the high-resolution hologram showed it as a civilian ship. It was big.

"Not a battleship," Vivian said. "It's big, though."

"What is it?" Pete Best asked. "A freight hauler?"

"I don't know," Darius asked. "See if GIGI can identify it."

Captain Darius didn't like depending on the alien artifact too much, yet he couldn't deny he had gotten used to being able to simply ask her questions as if the inorganic life form were just another member of his crew.

"It's moving toward the planet," Pete Best said.

"Any chance it's a troop carrier?" Henry Nash asked.

"It's certainly big enough," Darius replied. "Lieutenant Ramos?"

"It's a slave ship," she said, her voice husky with emotion. "GIGI just sent word."

"Another one?" Henry Nash asked.

"Do you have a lock on it?" Darius asked.

"I do, Captain. Say the word, and it'll be nothing but a cloud of atomic matter."

"Wait," Vivian said. "There could be innocents on board."

"She's right, sir," Henry Nash said.

"Can we disable it from that distance?" Darius asked.

"We can try, sir, but there's no guarantees we won't do more damage than intended," Pete Best said. "I'm just not familiar enough with our weapons or that class of ship."

"We'll leave it to GIGI then. She'll have to use the drones to stop it once it's in atmo."

"Sir, more ships are on the way," Vivian said. "The energy build-up is much bigger than before."

"Alert the Marines. Tell them about the slave ship and our decision to leave it to them."

"Aye, alerting the Marines now," Vivian said.

"Holy crap! They're coming in fast," Pete Best said.

He wasn't lying. The ships were dropping out of hyperspace like raindrops in a hurricane. Some were big; others were smaller. They all bristled with guns.

"Target the troop carriers," Darius said. "Fifty percent power."

"Aye, targeting the troop carriers," Pete Best said.

It was really just a guess at which ships carried troops. There were several large, bulbous-looking ships and Darius hoped they could take them down or at least weaken any ground invasion the aliens had planned.

"Fox one!" Pete Best shouted. There was a flash of light, and one of the fat ships disappeared. "Fox two!"

He fired again, only a smaller ship moved into the path of the shot as the ships began to spread out.

"We're looking at twenty-eight ships," Vivian Ramos said.

"Keep hammering!" Darius ordered. "Nash, prepare to slip us behind the moon."

"Aye, Captain," Henry Nash said.

"Fox three!" Pete Best shouted. "Fox four!"

Two more enemy ships disappeared into clouds of atomic dust.

"Energy build up," Vivian said. "They're preparing to fire."

"Move us," Darius ordered. "Raise the shields!"

"Aye, evasive maneuvers," Nash replied. "Engaging engines."

"Shields at full power," Pete Best said just before multiple flashes of light raced across space toward them. Most lost too much energy over the vast distance to do any damage, but a few sent powerful bursts that might have overwhelmed their shields if they had hit. But the *Renegade* was agile for such a large ship. Her maneuvering thrusters were linked to the engines and with the aid of the dark matter energy conversion; there was plenty of power to go around. The *Renegade* slid sideways and took shelter behind the small moon. More laser flashes lit the space around them, but nothing hit the Arodoni ship.

"Can we isolate those ships with the big guns?" Darius asked.

"I think so," Vivian said. "Four ships are headed toward the planet."

"Bring us out from under the moon," Darius ordered. "Lieutenant, target those ships headed for Casasil."

"Aye, preparing targets," Pete Best said. "Cannons are back at full power."

The ship dipped down under the moon. They hovered there for less than a minute as the *Renegade* fired all four laser cannons before rising back up behind the moon.

"We got two of those ships," Vivian said. "But two of our shots were off target."

"Sorry," Pete Best said.

"The good news is the other ships don't have the power to keep up a steady barrage of shots," Nash pointed out.

"Fighters launching. I've got... too many to count."

Small fighter craft were a problem. They were harder to target and disruptive in a battle. The *Renegade* had to lower her shields to fire the laser cannons. That made them even more vulnerable."

"Range?" Darius asked.

"Nine hundred thousand kilometers and closing."

"We'll deal with the fighters once we've taken out the ships with the big guns. Take us out from behind this moon to starboard."

"Aye, moving us starboard," Nash replied.

"Pete, get your cannons ready."

"Aye, Captain, but the enemy is too spread out. I don't have time to target more than once before they can fire back at us."

"Their energy signature is climbing," Vivian Ramos said.

"We'll pick them off one at a time, if we have to. Target the big guns first."

"Roger that," Pete replied.

The Arodoni ship slid out from behind the moon. More laser fire lit the space between them. The *Renegade* took a glancing blow from one laser. It hit their sonic shielding and bounced away.

"That's too close," Darius said.

"Fox four!" Pete Best shouted.

A flash of light and another ship disappeared.

"Evasive action!" Darius ordered.

"They're down to twenty-three ships, with two of those headed for the planet," Vivian said.

"This is taking too long," Darius said. "Pete, we have the power to be a little less exact with our shots. We're going to dash from the moon to the planet. When we're in the clear, give 'em hell, Lieutenant."

"Aye, Captain," Pete Best said.

"Henry, are you ready?"

"I'm ready, and the ship is ready, sir."

"Good, take us behind the planet at max speed."

"Aye, maximum speed, engaging," Henry Nash said.

The thrusters roared, and the star system seemed to slip sideways as the *Renegade* moved diagonally from the moon to the planet. They were only exposed for a few seconds, and in that time, Pete fired all four cannons. Two more ships disappeared.

"That's nineteen capital ships left that are engaging us," Vivian said.

"How are we looking?" Darius asked.

"We're putting a load on the power supply," Nash said. "But it's keeping up so far. All systems remain in the green."

"Okay, let's gear up for another round," Darius said. "The planet is big enough. They won't know where we're coming out."

"We'll be lucky to get a decent shot at more than one of them before they can target us," Pete said.

"Then we'll take them down one by one," the Captain said. "What's the range on those fighters?"

"Five hundred thousand kilometers, sir," Vivian replied. "They should be in range in about seven minutes."

"That's not enough time," Darius said. "Okay, we're going to slip out, take a shot at one of their long-range ships, then I want to reverse thrust, full power. Can we do that?"

"Aye, Captain," Nash said.

"As soon as you make your shot, Lieutenant Best, raise our shields."

"I still show three long-range vessels," Vivian Ramos said. "And there might be more, I can't be sure."

"We know they need time to charge their weapons," Darius said. "We're faster. Once we're moving, you target the next ship, Lieutenant. Only drop the shields for as long as it takes to fire."

"Aye, Captain."

"Good, let's do this," Darius said. "Make every shot count. Go!"

CHAPTER 19

"TWO SHIPS ARE THROUGH," Remmy said, repeating the information that GIGI had supplied.

The entire platoon and several of the Casian officials, along with Helzo the Dudonus, were gathered to hear the news. There were a few satellites in orbit, but those were pointed down toward the planet. And the Casians had no instruments that could keep track of starships in the system. That left GIGI and the thousand drones she controlled in orbit. Those ships were keeping track of everything going on in the system.

"Two ships," Laila said, shaking her head. "How many soldiers could that be?"

"Impossible to know for sure," Lieutenant Colt said.

"We cannot withstand an army of Ashi warriors," Ernhard said.

"Don't worry, those ships still have to get to the ground intact," Remmy said. "We have a lot of assets in orbit."

"And if they get through the ones in orbit, we've got more on the ground here," Laila pointed out.

"Let's prepare as if they will make it through," Lieutenant Colt said. "Everyone gear up. We'll take two dropships to wherever the enemy lands their troop carriers."

"GIGI is moving to engage," Remmy told the others as they returned to the command tent in full battle rattle.

"Any chance the drones will have much affect on those carriers?" Laila asked.

"Hard to say," Remmy confessed. "They have major armor."

"Hit them in the tailpipe," Tex suggested. "If they can't fly, they can't land."

"Good advice," Remmy said.

GIGI, what's your strategy? Remmy thought.

The Galactic Information & Guidance Instrument responded immediately: *To block their path to the planet, Master Sergeant.*

They're probably expecting a frontal attack, he warned. *Swing around and come at them from the rear. Focus on their engineering section.*

For a moment, there was no response. Remmy had rarely ordered GIGI to do something. The living computer was as much an alien as the Casians or Dudonus. Just because it had allied itself to the humans didn't mean it would follow their commands. If anything, humanity was a lesser-intelligent race. If not for GIGI, they would still be in the Sol system, completely oblivious to what was happening in the greater galaxy.

Affirmative, Master Sergeant. I have analyzed your suggestion and found it to be strategically sound.

Remmy wanted to be sarcastic with the alien artifact, but he held himself. GIGI could read his mind and maybe she already knew what he was thinking, but there was nothing he could do if that was the case.

Can you predict where they might land yet? He asked instead.

Negative, they are too far out to calculate entry windows to the planet.

How long until you engage?

Fourteen minutes to reach the first target vector. The Ashi ships are powering up their weapons.

There was nothing more for Remmy to do. He strapped on his armor and checked his weapons. The first part of the attack would happen in orbit, a long distance out of reach of the Marines on the ground.

Lieutenant Colt came stomping back to the command tent in his full MECH armor. Remmy had never been a fan of the over-powered war suits, but the *Renegade's* computer system had taken the Lieutenant's ideas and made them viable. Of course, the real test would come during combat. The MECH suit had been tested but not yet tried in a combat situation.

"Any change?" The Lieutenant asked.

"Nothing yet, sir," Remmy replied.

"I wish we had radar," Lieutenant Colt complained. "Any updates from the *Renegade?*"

"They aren't squawking," Sergeant McManus said.

"Do we know if they're still alive?"

"Affirmative," Remmy said. "They're still engaged with the armada."

"This was a bad idea," the Lieutenant grumbled over the comlink, where only his own people could hear him complain. "We don't have the manpower to fight a war outside our own solar system."

"We've got the drones," Laila reminded him.

"Eight hundred of them, each one carrying two air-to-ground missiles and guns," Remmy added.

"I'd rather have eight hundred Marines," Lieutenant Colt said.

"Oorah!" McManus exclaimed.

"I think we're doing the right thing," Ricky Thompson said. "Protecting these people sure beats fighting disgruntled miners on Mars or cartels operating off the grid."

"We die here; no one will ever find us," Gunny Rand said.

"I don't care much what happens after I die," Tex replied.

"Who said anything about dying?" Staff Sergeant Laila McPherson spoke up. "You all sound like a bunch of ninnies."

"She's right," Remmy said. "Those ships probably won't even make it to the planet, and if they do, we'll smash them with the drones. All that we'll have to do is mop up the survivors."

"It just seems like we're taking on someone else's fight," Leigh Ann Poh said.

"We are," Laila said. "Look around. We're fighting for those who can't fight for themselves."

"Yeah, don't forget that slave ship," Izzy added. "It had babies on board. They were stealing children from this planet."

"Any government that can be okay with stealing children is bad news in my book," Rip said.

"Besides, they started this fight," Sergeant Jay Thorne pointed out. "Not us."

"Hang on," Remmy said, holding up his free hand. "They just fired at the drones."

"The carriers?" Lieutenant Colt asked.

"Yes, they've got laser cannons. Drones are engaging, too."

"Who's winning?" Tex asked.

"Hard to tell. GIGI's lost half her assets. I can't tell if the attack is getting through the armor of the carrier ships. They're not slowing down or altering course."

"Man, I got a bad feeling about this," Sergeant Dirk Oliver said.

"Down to a third of the drones," Remmy said. "Even spread out, they just don't have the armor to resist the laser fire from the carriers."

"It's not over yet," Laila reminded the platoon. "There's still time."

They collectively held their breath, waiting for Remmy to deliver more news. He couldn't see the battle in his mind's eye, but the information was swirling through his head. Finally, a bit of good news flashed in his mind.

"One's hit!" He exclaimed. "GIGI registered a major explosion in the foremost carrier."

"How many drones are left?" Lieutenant Colt replied.

"Twenty percent," Remmy said.

"That's still two hundred drones," Laila pointed out.

"The foremost ship is drifting around. Venting gas and debris, she's out of the fight. GIGI is using the ship to shield the remaining drones."

"Shield them?" Lieutenant Colt demanded. "They aren't manned craft. She needs to throw everything she's got at that last ship."

"The second carrier is moving ahead," Remmy said. "It's overtaking the damaged vessel, which appears to be in a slow spin."

"She'll pop out behind the other one," Laila said. "Classic flanking maneuver."

"I think you're right," Darius said. "But that ship is about to enter orbit. Hang on."

"Wish I was up there," McManus said. "I hate waiting."

"Patience is a virtue," Izzy said.

"No one ever called him virtuous," Ricky Thompson teased.

"It's a shootout," Remmy said. "GIGI hit that ship with every drone at once, but the carrier is firing back."

They all waited for the outcome. Remmy knew deep down inside it wouldn't be a total victory. The Ashi ship seemed to have too much momentum.

"It made it through," Remmy said. "Damaged, but how badly, I can't say."

"And the drones?" Laila asked.

"Gone," Remmy admitted. "There's less than a hundred total, and that includes those guarding GIGI's ship."

"We knew this was a possibility," Lieutenant Colt said. "Alpha and Bravo teams board the Pegasus. Charlie and Delta teams, you're on the Orion. Remember, we'll be sitting down well away from the carrier. We let the drones do the heavy lifting; then we move forward to mop up. If things go bad, Orion returns to help defend the city. Pegasus will shift to recon duty only. You'll be our eyes and ears, nothing reckless."

"Copy that," Sergeant Thorne said.

Remmy turned to Ernhard and Helzo. "Stay by the communications equipment in this tent," he ordered them. "I'll keep you updated."

"Good luck," Ernhard said.

Helzo lifted a hand. It was a universal gesture of goodwill, and Remmy appreciated it, but there was no time for sentimental good-byes. He jogged toward the dropship designated Orion and walked on board just as the ramp began to close.

"GIGI has a vector on our bogey," Remmy said. "She's transfer-ring the projected flight path to our mapping applications."

He slipped on a battle helmet with a full-face shield and synced it to his armor. The HUD immediately showed a large map of the planet's northern hemisphere. The ship was on course to land over a thousand kilometers south of Kipbur.

"She's coming down in an isolated area," Laila pointed out.

"Thank God for small favors," Izzy said.

"There are mountains to the west of the projected landing zone," Lieutenant Colt pointed out. "Let's rally there."

"Copy that," Remmy said, sending the information to GIGI at the speed of thought.

The carrier is exhibiting erratic flight and may be experiencing technical difficulties due to damage to the vessel's engines.

That's great news, Remmy thought. *Maybe it will just crash and explode.*

Unlikely. But it appears the ship will not be a factor in the engagement. I am shifting my focus to the air-to-ground attack drones—assets launching now.

"Looks like the ship won't crash exactly," Remmy said over the comlink. "But it's disabled. They won't be able to use it once it's down."

"So, they won't be mobile?" Lieutenant Colt said.

"It appears that way, sir," Remmy replied. "I guess we'll have to wait and see what's on that ship."

"Whatever it is, we kill it," McManus said. "Simple as that."

Remmy just hoped it was simple, but he had a feeling they were in for the fight of their lives.

CHAPTER 20

"SIR, I have the last of the long-range ships in my sights," Pete Best announced.

"Fire at will, Lieutenant," Darius said. "Nash, full power on the port thrusters."

"Aye, full power on port thrusters," the chief engineer said.

A flash of laser light dazzled Captain Zeke Darius' eyes for a moment, then another of the Ashi warships disappeared from the plot.

"Got him!" Pete Best shouted.

"Are we out of their range?" Vivian Ramos asked.

"Looks that way," Darius replied.

"They're still coming at us," Vivian said. "Eighteen ships in total... wait a second. Captain, do you see this."

"What?" Darius asked.

"Tango Seven isn't following the other ships," she said.

"Is it headed toward the planet?" Henry Nash inquired.

"No, it's circling the hyperspace portal," she said.

"Mining it," Darius said with a shake of his head. "They're mining the jump point. Trapping us here."

"Is that a bad thing?" Pete Best said. "We can take out their mines easy."

"We don't know what they're doing exactly," Darius said. "We're too far out to get a good look."

"I'm seeing nothing on radar, Captain," Vivian pointed out.

"They might be too small to register, especially at this range."

"Fox three," Pete said, firing at another of the ships. Tango Twelve winked out of existence."

"Ensign Bertoli, see if you can contact the leader of this group," Darius said. "Let's see how they respond to the fact that we've got their Emperor on board."

"Aye, Captain, hailing the enemy now," Jacee Bertoli said.

"They aren't as agile as the *Renegade*," Nash pointed out. "They can't match our turn speed."

"That's good to know," Darius replied. "What about those fighters."

"They're still gaining on us," Vivian said. "I've got two hundred on my scope, sir."

"Lieutenant Best, start targeting the fighters," Darius said. "I want multiple shots in fast succession. Ten percent power should be enough to take them out of this fight."

"Aye, targeting the fighters. They're pretty spread out, Captain."

"Forming a screen between us and their capital ships," Vivian said.

"Get as many as you can," Darius said. "Otherwise, keep our deflector screens up."

It was tense for a few moments. As Darius watched the plot, he could see hundreds of tiny dots closing in. It was a formidable attack force and he had no drones to launch against them. Even if he had the drones, he didn't have pilots for them. He made a mental note to start training the crew to operate the drones so that they could maximize the *Renegade's* resources in combat.

"Firing," Pete Best said.

He pressed a button and the four laser cannons on the *Renegade* flashed in a series of strobing blasts that decimated the enemy fighters. But there were still over a hundred of the tiny ships left when the flashing stopped.

"Excellent work, Lieutenant," Darius said.

"Sir, they're launching something," Pete Best said.

"Shields!"

"Already up, Captain," Pete replied. "Looks like missiles of some kind."

"Can you target them?"

"I doubt I could get them all," Pete said. "But I'll—"

Before he could finish, the projectiles began to flash. And suddenly, everything on the ship went dark.

"What just happened?" Ensign Bertoli said.

"EMPs," Darius said, thankful for the restraints on his chair that held him in place as the artificial gravity went offline.

"We're a sitting duck, sir," Henry Nash said. "Dead in the water."

"Can we get the power back on?" Darius said.

"I think so, but I'll have to get to the *Jericho*."

"Do it. The capital ships are still out there and closing," Darius said. "Have Commander Lee and Ensign Stanislaus go with you. We need every system back up and running ASAP."

"Copy that," Henry said, unfastening from his seat and pushing his floating body toward the Bridge door. It was open and Darius felt a small wave of relief. At least they weren't trapped on the Bridge.

Henry Nash was a big man. He stood six foot, four inches tall, with broad shoulders and long, well-muscled limbs. He remained trim even as he approached his forties and considered himself to be athletic but flailing through the dark corridors of the alien ship, which were much wider and taller than he was accustomed to, made him feel almost helpless. Added to his struggle was the pressure of knowing that with every passing second, enemy ships were gaining on them. The fighter craft had been disabled, like the *Rene-*

gade, but the larger Ashi warships could cruise into effective laser range at any moment. The Arodoni ship had a thick hull and excellent automated maintenance drones, but they had been disabled by the EMP, too. And no ship could survive for long under sustained laser fire.

He found the ramp that led down to the lower command levels and worked his way lower into the ship. When he finally reached the Systems Control Room he called out for help.

"Commander Lee?" He asked.

It was pitch black inside the bowels of the ship. There was no way to know if the other officers were at their posts or if Nash was in the right place.

"I'm here," Lori Lee said. "Is that you, Henry?"

"The one and only. We've got to get to the Jericho."

"Stanislaus is already there," she said. "He left as soon as the ship went dark."

"Captain's orders are for you to follow me. We've got to reset the breakers and get the Arodoni Power Core functioning again."

He was drifting past her. Their voices were the only indication of their proximity. When Henry reached out, he managed to brush her shoulder. She turned and grabbed onto his hand.

"You good Commander?" He asked.

"I'm a little discombobulated."

"Good word," Henry replied. "I like that... discombobulated."

They worked their way toward the corridor that led to the Jericho. Henry's mind was moving much faster than his body. He knew that once they were out of danger, his first priority was to build a set of Faraday cages. He would have them filled with essential supplies, then place them strategically all over the ship.

Getting into the Jericho was harder than he expected. But once they were onboard the smaller, corkscrew-shaped ship, it was easier to navigate. The corridors were smaller, which made them both feel more secure as they moved through the ship. They had just reached the engineering space when they heard movement.

"Alex!" Henry called out.

"I'm here," Stanislaus replied. "But I can't find the circuit breakers for the Arodoni Power Core."

"Stay there," Henry said, while turning to the ship's bank of backup power batteries. He found the junction panel and wrenched it open. The circuit breakers had simple switches. He flipped them all one way, then back the other. Suddenly, the Jericho's emergency lights came on, filling the engineering space with red light. All three officers breathed a little easier, being able to see again.

"I should have thought of that," Stanislaus said.

"The next time you will," Henry said as he pulled himself over to where Stanislaus was braced between the alien power generator and the wall.

Together, they bent over the strange contraption. There were no circuit breakers on the device, but when Henry unplugged it from the ship and then plugged it back in, it began to hum.

"That did something," Alex said.

"Let's hope it's enough," Henry replied.

Bright light came on all over the Jericho, and the life support systems started up. Henry heard the air pumping through the vents.

"It's working," Lori Lee said with relief.

"She should start spinning soon. Once that happens, the power will come on all over the ship again," Henry said. "We should start back. You may have to reboot the ship's computers."

"When will the gravity come back on?" Lori Lee asked.

"Soon," Henry said, hoping it would all be back to normal soon enough. Otherwise, the gravity would be the least of their problems.

CHAPTER 21

FARKA JUEL WAS KNOWN in the Ashi military as a skilled warrior. He was both a pilot and a highly effective fighter. Not that there had been an enemy to test his mettle or martial skill against. But he had been recognized for his skill and bravery during battle simulations and martial contests.

The moment he fired his EMP, he began a mental countdown. Once the device was activated, he would have only twenty minutes of breathable air left in his flight suit, which was electrically powered, just like his fighter.

With the EMP device launched toward the alien vessel, Farka popped the canopy over his cockpit. He had to have that open, or he would be locked inside his ship with no way out once the Electro Magnetic Pulse weapon exploded. He unfastened his safety harness and pulled his feet under him; then, he engaged his ship's thrusters to full power.

The EMPs, several dozen of them, exploded at the same time. He saw the flashes of light and knew his twenty minutes had begun. He also launched himself out of his ship with a powerful jump that sent him flying straight toward the alien ship. It was a difficult and dangerous mission, but just the sort of thing Farka was trained to do. Most warriors in the Ashi military focused only on fighting. None of the planets or intelligent species in the Imperium could mount an attack that would require the kind of infiltration that Farka was attempting. But he felt honored that he had been given the chance to face a true enemy. Nor was he the only Ashi warrior flying through space toward the enemy ship.

Two hundred skilled warriors had been launched against the alien vessel. And thousands of Ashi on the warships had died merely to distract the enemy from the real mission. Emperor Vang wanted the Arodoni ship intact and operational. It was Farka's duty to deliver the prize to his Emperor. Of course, Farka had heard the rumors about Emperor Vang. Perhaps he had been killed on Casasil, as Sheika Kahn suggested. It made no difference to Farka. He would do his duty no matter who was emperor.

It took a full ten minutes of flying through space in just his flight suit to reach the alien ship. When he did, Farka crashed hard into the side. It was only the large magnet with a sturdy handle that allowed him to hang on. The magnet stuck fast to the alien ship just before Farka crashed hard into the unforgiving metal. He gripped the handle hard as his body started to bounce back off into space. It took him a moment to arrest his momentum. He could feel a large bruise forming on his shoulder and another on his hip, but he was alive. Looking around, it was difficult to see much of the ship, but Farka trusted he was not the only Ashi warrior to gain a foothold on the ship. Just as he knew, there were certainly others who had failed to secure themselves and were, at that very moment, hurtling off into deep space with no hope of rescue.

He did not dwell on the dead or dying. Their sacrifice was worthy and his success all the more purposeful because of their fail-ure. He could not move the magnet. It was stuck hard to the ship's hull and pulling it free would probably send him spinning off into space. Instead, he moved hand over hand across the ship. He angled low, crawling toward her belly and the hangers he had been told would be there. It was not a small ship. The alien vessel was three times bigger than the largest Ashi warship. He had seen freight haulers that were bigger than warships, but none were as large as the alien craft. He was nearly out of breathable air when he finally reached the emergency hatch on the hanger. To his relief, he was not the only warrior to reach it and the three who arrived before him nearly had the hatch open wide enough that they could slip inside.

The airlock wasn't big enough for all of them. Farka waited outside the ship, controlling his breathing and focusing on the task at hand. When the hatch opened for him, he was surprised that the vessel had power. But he didn't complain. He went in just as a fifth warrior joined him. The airlock closed, and air was pumped into the room. Farka was starting to feel lightheaded when the inner door opened. He hit the safety latches on his helmet and pulled it over his head.

"Only five," Puka said.

"Five is enough," Zottle said. "Form your weapons."

They each carried the components of a laser rifle. Farka, his mind clearing as he breathed in good, oxygenated air into his lungs, removed the components from the various pouches of his flight suit. He put them together. The last piece was the high-capacity power cell. It was warm to the touch. He slipped it into the grip of his rifle and activated the weapon just as the artificial gravity came back on.

"The enemy is crafty," Puka said. "They restored their systems faster than expected."

"It makes no difference," Coug said. "They will die just the same."

"I had word from Shipmaster Nong," Zottle said. "We have a new mission priority."

"What is it?" Farka asked.

"The Arodoni claim to have Emperor Vang held prisoner on this ship. We are to find him and free him."

"On this ship?" Puka asked. "Finding the emperor on a vessel this size could take days."

"Not if we find one of the Arodoni and make them take us to the emperor," Farka explained.

"Good thinking," Zottle said. "Spread out, begin the search. Set your lasers to the lowest power setting. It will not do to damage the emperor's prize."

The five Ashi warriors spread out and hurried through the empty hanger. The only thing inside the vast space was the shooting range built by the Marine platoon. Soon, they found the gravity lift and were moving up and through the ship.

Puka, Coug, and Barza each left the lift to search a lower level of the ship. Only Farka and Zottle reached the park. They were both stupefied by the sheer size of the open agricultural area.

"This ship is grand," Farka said.

"The Arodoni must be soft to need a place such as this," Zottle said. "I will go toward the stern; you search toward the bow. Find the emperor and kill the aliens on board."

Farka gave a slight bow. Out of two hundred skilled warriors, only five made it into the alien ship. But five Ashi warriors were an army and Farka had no doubt they would prevail.

He didn't see the three beings high above them. Cooper O'Dell had been showing Nurek and Ludus the apartments that over-looked the park when the EMPs went off. They had been stuck in the apartment with only starlight coming through the transparent panels, giving them any light at all. When the power came back on, they stayed where they were, waiting to find out what had happened. When the communications were activated, Connor checked in with Captain Darius and assured him their guests were unharmed. A few moments later, the artificial gravity was restored. The trio was watching the agricultural bots who were helping the animals which had been caught up in zero-gravity. Many had drifted high enough that the fall injured them. Some were dead, others merely injured. Fortunately, it seemed that most had survived unscathed.

That's when they spotted the intruders. Cooper O'Dell had seen video of the Ashi after the initial battle in the Casa system. And, of course, he had studied Emperor Vang with rapt attention. As a civilian, he hated that Captain Darius hadn't immediately returned to the Sol system with the alien ship. But he was so busy learning from the ship and about the aliens themselves that he hardly had time to be angry.

There was no doubt what the trio was seeing as the two Ashi warriors made their way through the park. They were huge, and although they wore full-body flight suits, their heads were uncovered. They also carried laser rifles.

Connor O'Dell activated his comlink and reported the find straight to the captain.

CHAPTER 22

DARIUS FELT a cold sense of fury building inside him. There were still more than a dozen warships in the system closing in on the *Renegade*. Meanwhile, infiltrators had boarded his ship, and he had no Marines on board to protect the crew.

"Activate ship-wide communications," Darius said. "Let's hope everyone has their comlinks on."

It was procedure to keep personal comlinks on and close to hand since the alien ship was so huge. The *Renegade* didn't have an announcement system like human ships. In fact, there was no evidence of any sort of internal communications. The leading theory was that the Arodoni were most likely telepathic beings with no need for ship announcements or comlinks. Humans, on the other hand, needed to always be available. But like every other electrical system on the ship, they would need to be reset after the EMP blast. That meant taking the batteries out and putting them back in. Some of the batteries might have even been damaged by the pulse. And even though Darius had been adamant about the comlink policy, he knew that probably not every member of the crew would follow his order. No one had even considered the possibility that the *Renegade* might be boarded by enemy forces.

"Attention all crew, attention all crew, this is Captain Darius. We are still under red alert after getting power restored to the ship. Be advised a new threat has been spotted. Infiltrators have been seen on board our ship. I repeat, Ashi warriors have infiltrated the *Renegade*. They are armed and dangerous. We are dealing with this threat, but I warn you to keep watch over your stations, and if the enemy appears, stay out of sight. If possible, relay any information about the whereabouts of enemy troops to Commander Lee. That is all."

The Bridge door remained open, and Lieutenant Nash rushed in. He looked worried and angry. Darius felt the same way.

"Have you spoken to your team leaders?" Darius asked.

"Aye, Captain. They'll stay at their stations. No sustainable damage has been reported."

"Thank God for that," Vivian said.

"And Commander Lee?"

"She's gathering as many crew members as she can. The Marines took nearly everything."

"I know, that was my fault," Darius said. "I pretty much made that a direct order."

"You couldn't have known the Ashi would board the ship," Pete Best pointed out.

"I should have considered it. It's my job to consider every scenario," Darius said. "You may all be in the command chair one day. If so, I hope you remember my mistakes and learn from them. Lieutenant Nash power up the ship's engines. Lieutenant Ramos, what is the distance to our closest enemy vessel."

"Just under seven hundred thousand kilometers and closing," Vivian replied.

"Pete, how do the cannons look?"

"They're still in attack formation, Captain," Pete Best replied. "But the power was drained from the EMP attack. I need a few more minutes to reach full power."

"Don't wait," Darius said. "Begin targeting the Ashi ships now. As soon as you hit fifty percent power, I want you to fire on them."

"Their plan didn't pan out," Henry Nash said.

"That's yet to be seen," Darius said. "If their infiltrators sabotage the ship, we could be in a real fix."

Darius hated being caught by surprise. He could tell himself that he was fighting an enemy no human had ever encountered. Not to mention, he was commanding a ship that was built by aliens. There were tactics and strategy at play that were completely foreign to him and yet it seemed like he had fallen for the oldest trick in the book. It was hard to believe that the Ashi would sacrifice so many of their warriors and pilots just to get agents on board the *Renegade*, but that's exactly what they had done ... and no one knew how many Ashi warriors had managed to get inside. But he couldn't worry about them yet. He still had to defeat the armada arrayed against him.

"Sir, I'm picking up new fighters launching from Tango Four and Eight," Vivian said.

"Damn, they're likely to hit us with EMPs again," Darius said. "Ensign Bertoli, go to the supply room and find us some lights just in case."

"Remove the batteries," Nash said. "Dump the tools from one of the metal cases. Not the big ones, the handheld toolboxes."

"Why?" Darius asked.

"They're lined with copper," the chief engineer said. "They'll act as Faraday cages if we get hit with another electromagnetic pulse."

"You understand that, Ensign Bertoli?"

"Aye captain. Flashlights, remove batteries, put them in copper lined tool boxes," she said.

"Close the lid, too," Nash warned.

"And take them to the systems control room ASAP," Darius added. "Stay there and help Alex if we lose power again."

"On my way, Captain," Jacee said as she jogged off the Bridge.

"Laser power is forty percent," Pete Best announced. "Preparing to fire."

"Fire at will, Lieutenant. Nash, get us moving the moment he makes his shots."

"Roger that, Captain," Nash said.

"Fox one!" Pete said.

A flash lit the Bridge. Darius had to push the infiltrators from his mind, which was no easy task, and focus on the plot. There had been seventeen enemy warships. One disappeared.

"That's a hit," Pete said. "Fox two!"

Another flash, another ship disappeared. Darius brought up the energy readings on his command chair's screen. Human lasers required massive amounts of electrical power, which was usually produced by combustible fuel sources. They could be deadly, but without enough energy, they could be worthless. It was one of the reasons that the SDF relied heavily on traditional weapons. Most human ships had missiles, torpedoes and kinetic weapon launchers. A two-ton tungsten rod hurled by a rail gun at over a thousand kilometers per hour would punch through the hull of any ship in the fleet. But the Renegade didn't have traditional weapons. It relied solely on the four massive laser cannons. Each one of which utilized more power than an entire space station would consume in a week. And yet the Arodoni dark energy Power Core could produce such massive amounts of energy that the lasers were quick to recharge.

"Fox three!" Pete Best shouted.

His targeting was spot on. It helped that the laser blasts moved at the speed of light. Still, Pete was hitting targets that were moving fast through space, and the Renegade was moving, too. Everything was in motion. Marksmanship in space battles was not an easy skill to master. But his name said it all: Lieutenant Pete Best was an excellent gunner.

"Fox Four," Pete said, firing the fourth cannon.

"All engines, reverse thrust," Darius ordered. "Fifty percent power."

"Aye, Captain, all engines reverse, fifty percent power."

The ship was moving again. Their enemies noted the change

and began to change course. None could hope to outrun the *Renegade,* and none were in range with their smaller, less powerful lasers. Instead, they began to spread out.

"They're running," Nash said.

"Giving up already," Pete Best said.

"They aren't giving up," Darius pointed out. "Just prolonging the fight and giving their infiltrators time to work."

"Permission to help Commander Lee," Nash asked.

"Denied. You're too valuable to me here," Darius said. He pressed the transmit button on his comlink. "Ensign Stanislaus, do you read me?"

"Aye, Captain," Alex replied from the systems command room.

"Any chance you figured out how to lock down the Command section of the ship?"

"Not yet, sir, but I can change the gravity in the ring. I can even increase it above Earth standard. And the Bridge can be locked down too."

"Alright, we'll lock down here. You make sure that Commander Lee doesn't need that gravity ring, then dial up the pressure."

"Aye, Captain."

"We've got more fighters pursuing us, Alex. That probably means more EMPs. I'm sending Ensign Jacee Bertoli to you with flashlights in a makeshift Faraday cage. If we get hit with another pulse, I'm trusting the two of you to get everything back up and running ASAP."

"Roger that, Captain. I know what to do now, sir."

"Very good. Let's pray that Commander Lee can take down the infiltrators. Otherwise, we're all in very big trouble."

CHAPTER 23

THE ORION WAS HOVERING low in the valley between two mountain peaks. Charlie Team and Delta Team consisted of Sergeant Jay Thorn, Corporal Al "Rip" Van Winkle, Sergeant Dirk Oliver, Corporal Ricky Thompson, and Corporal Tyler "Tex" Fry. They were all crowded into the cockpit of the dropship so that they could see.

"That thing is coming in fast," Tex said.

"They must have lost their thrusters," Dirk added. "They've got no way to slow down."

"Any chance they'll all be killed on impact?" Ricky Thompson asked.

"Don't count on it," Master Sergeant Remmy Steel replied.

The alien ship was massive. It looked like a huge disk with engines sticking out of the rear. It was over a hundred kilometers away and dropping fast toward the wide prairie below the mountain range.

"Master Sergeant, you copy?" Lieutenant Micky Colt asked.

"Five by five, sir," Remmy replied.

"What's the status of our drones?"

"In the air and moving this way, sir. GIGI has them in groups of twenty. Half will stay to the north of the prairie and half are going to circle around to the south. The plan is to hit whatever comes out of the alien ship in successive waves."

"Copy that," Colt said. "I hope they leave a few for us to clean up."

Remmy understood that the Lieutenant in his MECH armor wanted to test his creation. But the Ashi warriors were giants that made comic book superheroes look like pipsqueaks. Remmy knew they could be taken down; they had proved as much on Planet Casasil already, but he didn't want to risk any more of the Marines getting hurt or killed. He would be more than happy to let the drones do all the fighting.

"Here it comes," Rip said.

The alien ship plowed into the ground at speed. To Remmy's disappointment, it didn't break up. Instead, it held together, and the ground gave way. When it finally stopped, the alien vessel was half buried, with the back part of the spherical craft sticking up. Gases vented from ports near the engines.

"Now we wait and see," Sergeant Thorne said.

"They hit pretty hard," Dirk Oliver replied. "It had to take a toll."

Remmy increased his helmet's telephoto digital imaging. It had a 200x zoom capacity, with image stabilization. He could see the ship clearly and watched as hatches on either side of the engine section opened.

"It's opening," he said softly. "They'll be coming out."

"Not if they all died on impact," Ricky Thompson pointed out.

"Someone must be alive if they opened the door, genius," Rip teased.

"Maybe that's automated," Ricky argued.

"And maybe they had artificial gravity that negated any kinetic energy from the crash," Sergeant Thorne suggested.

"What?" Ricky asked.

"They're alive," Tex told him. "Never doubt it.

As if on cue, the Ashi warriors emerged. But they weren't

anything like what Remmy expected. The first army he had seen was like savage warriors. They wore boots kilts, and carried laser rifles. Their chests had been bare and they wore no armor. The warriors emerging from the ship were different. They were just as big and savage-looking, but they wore what looked like armor and rode on hovering platforms that reminded Remmy of chariots, only without the wheels and horses.

"Damn," Ricky Thompson said.

Tex added a few curses to Ricky's. Remmy couldn't blame them. The enemy was coming from the ship in large numbers. At least twenty on each hovercraft, and they were sailing out of the crashed ship one after another on each side of the engine section.

"Two by two," Sergeant Thorne said. "Unreal."

Remmy's comlink conveyed Lieutenant Colt's voice as if the officer were standing right next to his master sergeant.

"Should we hit the ship with the drones?" Colt asked. "Maybe stop them before they can get out and fight?"

"Not likely, sir," Remmy said. "That ship looks unscathed from the crash. I doubt the drone bombs would make a dent. We'd just be wasting ammo, and the aliens could wait safely inside. Better to hit them in the open."

"They aren't waiting around for a welcoming party," the Lieutenant said.

He was right. One group moved steadily to the north, the other south. They were like a long snake, with each hovercraft following directly behind the one in front of it.

"Say the word and we'll unleash the drones," Remmy said.

"Do it," Lieutenant Colt said. "If they get out of the prairie, they'll be able to take cover. Hit them in the open, Master Sergeant."

Artillery had been a component of human warfare for centuries. From catapults and trebuchets to cannons and, eventually, air raids, the idea of hitting an enemy force from a distance with heavy munitions was a sound strategy. GIGI's computing power was incredible. The alien artifact controlled eight hundred

drones simultaneously. The squads spread out into chevron formations, flying fast and low. The first drones appeared from the north
and raced toward the snaking line of enemy hovercraft. To
Remmy's horror, the Ashi had large weapons. They were mounted
on mechanical arms that connected to their body armor. They
operated the weapons with both hands and fired what looked like
large caliber bullets up toward the approaching drones. At the same
time, the hovercraft began evading.

It was war. The skies grew dark with hundreds of drones, some
from the north, others from the south. Bullets flew and bombs
dropped. Some of the hovercraft were hit directly, killing everyone
on board. Others were rocked by the shockwaves of near misses,
sometimes dumping some of the passengers. A few even flipped
over. But, despite the carnage, it seemed that very few of the alien
fighters were being killed. On the other hand, the drones were
taking heavy losses.

Climb! Remmy ordered.

Munitions will be less accurate from altitude, GIGI responded.

*The Ashi return fire won't be able to reach you. Get to fifteen
hundred meters. We can't risk losing the drones too quickly.*

The alien artifact did as Remmy ordered. Some of the hovercraft rose up nearly a hundred meters but couldn't stay in range of
the drones. Bombs fell like rain. The aliens turned their aim toward
the bombs so that nearly half of the heavy munitions exploded in
midair. Those that hit the ground caused damage but not always
directly affecting the armored aliens.

"This isn't going to be the slaughter we hoped for," Lieutenant
Colt said. "Orion, head north back toward Kipbur. Find a good
place to dig in and hold the enemy back."

"Copy that, Lieutenant," Remmy said. "Good luck, Perseus."

"You too, Orion. Give 'em hell," Laila said.

"You know it, Staff Sergeant!" Rip said.

The dropships moved out of the mountains on a wide, curving
arc. Remmy had no doubt where the aliens moving north would be
going. Kipbur was the obvious target. Fortunately, it was far enough

away that they could hit the enemy several times, leapfrogging back toward the city. Remmy stayed focused on GIGI, which had a mountain of data rushing through its sensors. Nearly half of the drones were either down or out of bombs. And there were still hundreds of aliens on the ground.

"There," Sergeant Jay Thorne said, pointing to a ridge.

"Good eye, Sarge," Remmy said.

GIGI immediately took the drop ship down for a landing behind the ridge.

"What's the plan, Master Sergeant?" Dirk Oliver asked.

"We'll see what we can do from the ridge. Defensive positions should give a slight advantage. Once the enemy gets too close for comfort, GIGI will hit them from behind, hopefully giving us time to get back to the dropship. Then we'll find a new spot and do it all over again."

"Sounds like a party," Rip replied.

"You think their armor will stop our bullets?" Tex asked.

"Only one way to find out," Remmy said as the hatch opened at the rear of the dropship. "Everyone find good cover and wait for my signal. And keep your grenades handy, too. We'll use them right before we run for the ship."

"Maybe we won't have to run," Thompson said. "Maybe we'll hold them off."

"Yeah, that's probably what the Spartans said at Thermopylae," Sergeant Thorne said.

"If we gotta go out, that's one hell of a legacy to follow," Tex said.

"We aren't going out," Remmy said. "Not here. That's an order. No heroics. We will fight the enemy as many times as we can until we reach Kipbur. If we have to die, that's where we do it."

"Roger that, Master Sergeant," Dirk Oliver said.

The others nodded in agreement.

"Good," Remmy said. "Now, let's show these ogres what humans are made of."

CHAPTER 24

FARKA WAS NEARLY OVERWHELMED by the alien ship. Only his battle discipline kept him focused. He moved quickly through the park. To say that it was stunning to the Ashi warrior was an understatement. Farka was used to harsh environments. No Ashi ship, even the luxury cruisers used by the royal family, had such lavishness. The open space alone was hard to grasp. He didn't feel like he was on a spaceship. It was like he had been transported to another world.

But it wasn't just the elegance of design or the vast space of the *Renegade* that surprised him. It was the emptiness. He couldn't understand how such a massive ship could seem so empty. There should have been thousands of Arodoni on the vessel. He fully expected alarms to sound as his fellow warriors cut down the unsuspecting aliens on the lower decks. But as he jogged across the grassy landscape, no alarms sounded, and no people of any race appeared.

Farka did see robots. The Ashi warrior recognized them. Certain planets and species used robotics, mainly in manufacturing. But, slaves were cheaper and easier to maintain than robots. Normally, Farka didn't think much about politics or morals, but he felt a rising wave of disdain for the Arodoni. They appeared to be wasteful. Why build a massive ship and not fill it with people? He couldn't wrap his mind around the emptiness. Perhaps the occupants of the giant ship did know that Ashi warriors were aboard. Perhaps they had run to protective chambers, fearing for their lives. The excessive luxury of the ship pointed to a race of soft, pampered beings, not hardened warriors willing to do whatever was required to achieve victory.

When Farka reached the end of the park, he went immediately through the open doorway into the commercial section of the ship. Again, he was aghast at the emptiness. Not only were there no people, but nothing in the rooms on either side of the wide glistening walkway. It occurred to him that perhaps the ship was fully automated. Perhaps there were no living beings other than the herds of prey animals he saw in the park. That didn't explain how Emperor Vang had been captured. Farka wasn't privy to the supreme commanders who were leading the attack, but if Emperor Vang were on the planet Casasil, then surely he would have contacted the shipmasters soon after the armada arrived in the system. Word had been transmitted to his fighter that the Arodoni claimed to have the Emperor in their possession. Surely, his superiors would not have passed that information along if they were in contact with Emperor Vang. So, there must be some living creatures on the ship! It could even be argued that they were surely valiant fighters if they were able to destroy the Emperor's invasion force and take him hostage.

Farka kept his rifle against his broad, meaty shoulder but moved swiftly through the open corridors. Eventually, he came to a room that was occupied. Through the broad windows Farka saw technical equipment. It was radically different from anything he had seen before in the Arodoni ship. It was bulkier, almost clunky looking. There was none of the sleek design he saw everywhere else on the ship.

There were beds, too. Short, narrow platforms with padded mattresses and rails on the sides. He saw no people of any species ...

except one. Right in the middle of the room, on a wide industrial platform, Emperor Vang was strapped down.

Farka entered the room expecting a trap. Every cell in his massive body was screaming for him to move back, but he could not deny his duty. Farka had never met the Emperor before, but he had served under Vang's father and remembered the murderous coup when the elder Ashi's son slayed him and took the throne. Vang's image was quickly raised everywhere, from statues on distant worlds to massive banners in military starships. Recognizing his sovereign ruler was not a chore despite the wounds that Vang had suffered.

The emperor lay on his crimson cape. One shoulder plate was intact and adorned with the curved Runic horn that only the Imperium rulers wore. The other had been shattered. That same side of Vang's face was swollen. There were white, gauzy patches on his face, too, many with dark spots from body fluid that were seeping into them. The Emperor's left arm was in some sort of molding that Farka didn't recognize and his limbs were held down by thick cargo straps.

When no trap was sprung as he entered the space, which he assumed was some sort of medical ward, he moved to the Emperor's side. Still, no aliens appeared. The Arodoni were nowhere to be found.

"My liege? Can you hear me?" Farka asked.

Vang's narrow eyes fluttered, then opened slowly.

"My Emperor," Farka said, crossing his arms over his chest and bowing at the waist.

"Whazz happenin' to me?" Vang said, his voice a hoarse whisper and his words slurred.

"I have come to rescue you, my lord," Farka said.

He drew a long, curved knife from a sheath strapped to his left thigh. The blade was razor sharp, yet when he tried to cut the straps away, they would not yield.

"Sorcery," he hissed.

"Where am I?" Vang asked.

"On the Arodoni ship," Farka said. "You were taken prisoner."

"Ahhh," Vang said, as his memories came back to him. "The Arodoni... they don't fight fair. I feel strange."

"They must have poisoned you," Farka said, putting his knife away and looking at the ratchets that held the straps in place. "Hold still while I free you."

His hands were big, with three wide fingers and one thumb; it took him a full minute to figure out how to release the ratchet. Once the tension was out of the straps, Farka flung them away. Emperor Vang, leader of the Ashi Imperium and ruler of the galactic core, tried to sit up and failed.

"What have they done to you, my liege?" Farka said.

"Their sorcery has robbed me of strength," Vang said, his words more clear than before.

"Let me help you."

Farka pulled Vang into a sitting position and helped him rotate around so that his feet touched the floor. The emperor still wore his boots and kilt but had no weapons.

"The room is spinning," he complained.

"Wait for a moment; maybe the sensation will pass," Farka suggested.

"Is there gravity on this vessel?"

"Yes, Lord Emperor. Good gravity... good air."

"I think I can stand," Vang said.

Farka wrapped the Emperor's good arm over his thick shoulders. Vang gripped Farka's flight suit tight and then stood up. He swayed for a moment, and his legs felt incredibly weak, but he didn't fall.

"I'm okay," he proclaimed. "I can walk."

"The Arodoni ship is vast," Farka said. "But I have seen no sign of the aliens."

"They aren't big," Vang said. "Maybe half our size. They have very effective weapons and use drones in combat."

Farka cleared his throat and spit on the deck. "Cowards."

"We must be careful," Vang said.

"I will protect you with my life, Lord Emperor."

"And you will be rewarded. Lead the way, valiant warrior."

Farka bowed slightly, then turned to the door. He once more raised his rifle to his shoulder. Vang still held tightly to the skilled warrior's shoulder and followed him out of the medical facility.

CHAPTER 25

"WE NEED WEAPONS," Commander Lori Lee said. "But the Marines took everything."

"I doubt that," Culinary Specialist Eli Johnson said.

"I know there are weapons on the *Jericho*," Donny Elgersma said.

"He was a weapons specialist," Eli said. "He would know."

"No need for a weapons specialist on a ship that only shoots lasers," Donny grumbled.

He was an unhappy man. The long cruise was bad enough and only made worse when Staff Sergeant McPherson embarrassed him in front of his friends. She had beaten him bloody, but he was drunk at the time. Part of him wanted a rematch, but the other part of him just wanted her back. Not that they had been especially close. She liked to move slow and he didn't mind giving her the time she needed to realize what an awesome guy he was. Especially since they were on a long cruise. And the *Jericho* was like a luxury spaceliner compared to the rest of the fleet. There was plenty to keep Donny occupied.

But he hadn't expected her to change her mind without notice. She didn't even give him a chance to convince her that she should stay with him. Of course, there was another guy; there had to be, even though she denied it. What other reason could she have for dumping him like she had?

"Specialist! Where's your head at?" Commander Lori Lee demanded.

"What?" Donny asked.

"Get your head out of your backside and focus. There are alien warriors on this ship. We need weapons and you said you knew where they were."

"I do," he said. "Yeah, on the *Jericho*. There were lockers in the munitions compartment and engineering that had emergency supplies, including shotguns with rubber pellets."

"I doubt rubber bullets will do us much good against the Ashi. They're thirteen feet tall," Lori Lee complained.

"We get the guns from the *Jericho*," Eli said. "I'm betting we find some real bullets down in the Marine armory. They may have taken most of their weapons, but they can only carry so many bullets."

"He's got a point," Donny said.

"Alright, we get weapons, find better ammo, and recruit more help along the way," Commander Lee said. "Let's move."

They were in the Command section of the ship, which occupied the forward and upper decks of what looked like the head of the fish-shaped ship. The *Renegade* was a huge vessel that resembled a fish with an open mouth. They hurried down to the middle of the open mouth, where the *Jericho* slowly turned and supplied the larger ship with power.

It took time to get on board and even longer to collect enough weapons from the various places. There were no more than two inside the emergency lockers. They left the *Jericho* with eight shotguns and hurried toward the gravity ring.

"How many boarders are on the ship?" Eli asked.

"Unknown," Lori Lee said.

"What do you think they want?" Donny asked.

"They aren't here to invite us to a party," Commander Lee snapped.

"I know, I'm just saying," Donny said, realizing he sounded like an idiot and scrambling to come up with a reason for his question, "do you think they want to kill us or just rescue the prisoner?"

"Their Emperor, if that's really who he is," Lee said, considering the question. "My gut says they're here for more than a rescue mission. If they can sabotage the ship, the other vessels in the system can hunt us down and kill us all."

"Or maybe they will," Eli said. "I'm a cook, not a soldier."

"You're in the Space Defense Force," Lee argued. "Fighting is what we do."

"But if they're hunting for their Emperor," Donny said. "Maybe we can wait for them outside sickbay and ambush them when they try to free him."

"That's not a bad idea, but we need more people," she said. "Three isn't enough. We could be outnumbered by the enemy, who are already more than a match for us."

"You make it sound hopeless," Eli said. "I knew we should'a gone back home instead of fighting in some crazy war."

"We didn't really have a choice," Donny said.

"You can complain about Captain Darius all you want," Lee said. "Just don't let me hear you."

"He got us into a real jam," Eli said.

"And he'll get us out," she said. "Now, let's get to the armory and stop talking."

They had to call back to Alex Stanislaus to dial down the gravity in the ring around the fish head on the alien ship. Then they drifted down to Epsilon deck and found the Marine armory. It was mostly empty, just a bunch of lockers, suits of space armor and some big crates filled with all sorts of ammunition. Most of it was for other types of guns, but it didn't take long to find shells for their shotguns.

"What are buzzers?" Eli asked.

"Steel blades instead of pellets," she said. "They cut through flesh like a buzz saw."

"Damn," Eli said.

"Might not have the stopping power we're looking for, though," Donny said. "I think these soft alloy slugs are a better option."

"Load up," Lori Lee said. "Every minute we waste gets the enemy closer to their goals."

"Been thinking on that," Eli said. "Bet you a hundred creds they're heading for engineering."

"Sabotage the ship?" Donny asked.

"Yeah, that makes the most sense to me," Eli said. "If they can knock out our engines, we'll be dead in the water."

"There is no water in space," Lee snapped.

"You know what I mean, Commander," Eli argued. "Fighting us, they run the risk of getting killed before they accomplish their mission. Take out the engines first, then the people."

"Engineering is clear on the other end of the ship," Donny said.

"More importantly, we need to recruit more help."

"Should be four specialists in the kitchen. It's two floors up," Eli said.

"Most of the weapons specialists are serving as backup to the engineers and machinist mates. I was only up here because I forgot my comlink."

"You're supposed to keep it on you at all times," Lee sighed.

"I know, but I forgot it. It was an honest mistake, commander."

Lori Lee wasn't angry at Donny Elgersma. In fact, she was glad he had forgotten his comlink. He was one of the biggest members of her crew, and she was glad he had been available to help her. Lori Lee had performed dozens of simulations against boarders and pirates, but there was a huge difference between a training exercise where no one was supposed to get hurt and being boarded by hostile aliens. She felt small and weak. Not that she was either one of those things. She was actually athletic and taller than most female officers, but she was still small compared to most men, and for all her strength, she couldn't compete with their muscle mass and bone density. Not that she was afraid because she was a woman. Her gender didn't matter. She had seen the prisoner close up. Emperor Vang was the biggest, scariest being she had ever laid eyes on. She had seen uglier, and she had seen aliens that looked less human, but she had never seen such a powerful-looking organism.

The Ashi were thirteen feet tall and packed with bulging muscles. Their green skin and wide jaws reminded her of orcs from a fantasy video game. But the Ashi were real. They carried laser rifles and could obviously snap her neck easily with their incredible strength. She didn't want to be anywhere near them, and yet her duty called on her to hunt the invaders down and kill them. She felt better with eight powerful slugs loaded into her tactical shotgun. The firearm was a semi-automatic weapon. All she had to do was pull the charging lever to load the first shell into the breech and flip off the safety.

"Red is dead," Commander Lori Lee said. "Keep your safety on until we see the enemy. And keep in mind these slugs could potentially breach the hull."

"There's a lot of mass between us and the hull," Donny pointed out.

"Just be careful what you shoot," she insisted. "Now, let's find some help and track the enemy down."

They went back up two floors using the long ramps instead of the gravity ring. The *Renegade* had no stairs. The Arodoni preferred ramps, and from the statue of the wide-bodied aliens on the main deck, she understood why. In the kitchen three more culinary specialists were huddled together talking. Lori went straight to them with the extra shotguns.

"We need your help," she said.

"Commander, we ain't no soldiers," LeRoy Washington said.

"We don't have a choice," Lori told him. "There are aliens on board the ship and the Marines aren't here."

"It's a big ship," Sasha Minsk said. She was tall and very thin, her skin pale. Her hands shook as she took the shotgun that was offered to her. "Maybe they'll leave us alone."

"Wishful thinking," Roby Toto said.

"If we don't find them," Lori said. "We'll all die. We can't hide from this, Spaceman Minsk."

"You know, I just joined the SDF to get money for school. The recruiter said I could be a culinary assistant, and I wouldn't have to fight."

"We all have to fight sometimes," Lori said. "But we'll do it together. Come on."

They set out together and, along the way, ran into two more crew members, Munitions assistant Carma Ramis and Machinist Mate Leon Gesa. They heard them before they saw the couple, and from their flirtatious banter, it was clear they were fraternizing together.

"Specialist Elgersma, catch up to those idiots and have them stand by... silently," Lori ordered.

She felt like she was in the middle of a bad dream. There had been times upon being promoted to Commander that she dreamed of being on board a ship that was crashing; only everyone she met was oblivious to the danger. In her dreams, she could never convince them that the ship was going down. Fortunately, she always woke up before the inevitable crash occurred. But she wasn't sleeping and the only relief from the nightmare she was in would be to fight the enemy and win.

When she caught up with the couple, she gave them her coldest glare.

"Explain yourselves," she snapped.

"We weren't doing anything wrong?" Carmen said.

"Just having a little fun is all, Commander," Leon Gesa said. "We're both off duty."

"The ship is under attack, you fools. Where are your comlinks?"

They both looked down.

"Apparently," Lori Lee said in a quiet but furious tone, "you are both idiots. I won't be forgetting this slip of protocol. But for now, you're with me. Take these."

She handed the couple the last two shotguns.

"What's going on?" Carmen asked.

"Aliens got on board," Sasha explained.

"That's impossible," Leon insisted.

"Don't be a fool," Lori Lee snapped. "There are Ashi warriors on this ship, and we're going to stop them."

"Stop them from what?" Roby Toto asked.

"Whatever it is they have planned," she responded. "Now we move quiet. Keep your head on a swivel. And keep your guns on safety until we see the enemy."

"Aren't the Marines supposed to be doing this sort of thing?" Leon argued.

"Man, where you been, bro?" LeRoy Washington said. "They done went down to the planet to fight."

"Should'a stayed on board," Eli Johnson said in a sulky voice.

"For now, we're the Marines," Commander Lee said. "You do what I tell you when I tell you and we'll all go home alive."

It was obviously a promise she couldn't keep. It buoyed up a few, but it was obvious that most of the people didn't believe her. But there were no other options immediately available. She had to do something to save the *Renegade*. Everyone was depending on her and she was determined not to fail.

CHAPTER 26

THE RIDGE WAS STEEPER on the backside but not as deep. Fortunately, between the ridge and the low, forested hills beyond was enough space to hide the dropship. They left it powered on with the back hatch down, ready for a speedy retreat.

"Alright, Marines, spread out," Remmy ordered. "But don't get too far from the drop ship. When I give the order, drop two grenades down the hill and run for the ship."

"It's good ground," Jay Thorne said, looking around. "We'll have the advantage."

"Their hovercraft may negate the climb," Dirk Oliver said.

"Or they may just swing wide and go around us," Ricky Thompson pointed out.

"I doubt that," Remmy said. "They're fighters. Once we open up, they'll come right at us."

"But that's suicide," Rip pointed out.

"Not necessarily," Sergeant Thorne argued. "There are only six of us. How many of the enemy do you suppose are left, Master Sergeant?"

"GIGI's drone attack was successful by any metric. She traded half her drones for half their fighters."

"Half? So, there's about five hundred left?" Dirk asked.

"That would be my guess," Remmy said. "Plenty of meany greenies for us to kill."

"Meany greenies!" Tex said, barking with laughter.

"We'll start with Tex shooting the long gun," Remmy said. "His goal is to take down as many of the hovercraft as possible. If we can slow their advance, that gives us another advantage."

"They aren't built for long marches, not fast ones anyway," Sergeant Thorne added.

"Exactly. We can jump back ten or twenty klicks and let them wear themselves out on the long march, then hit them again. Maybe at night, if we get lucky."

"Who says they can't see at night?" Ricky Thompson asked. "Maybe they've got cat eyes."

"Maybe, or maybe we'll catch them sleeping and drop some more explosive ordinance on them. But whatever the case, it all starts here. Tex, you shoot the hovercraft. They may not even know you're doing it until their platforms stop flying."

"Wouldn't that be something," he said. "Cut 'em down at the knees."

"One last thing," Remmy said. "Conserve your ammo. We've got a little more on Orion, but not enough to be careless. Make every shot count."

"What if we can't penetrate their armor?" Sergeant Thorn asked.

"Then we aim for where they don't have armor. Head or feet, it don't matter which," Remmy said. "I doubt they'll be able to use their heavy guns if they can't stand up."

They deployed in a line across the ridge top. Remmy had a good spot between two boulders. It didn't give him the widest field of fire, but the cover was excellent. The Marines were left to wait nearly half an hour before the aliens came into view. Once more, Remmy activated his helmet's telephoto zoom capabilities. His tactical app listed the lead skiff at over six kilometers distant. The

Ashi war party was still traveling in a single file line. Remmy wished he had field artillery. He could just line it up with aliens and blast away, knocking them down like a line of dominoes.

"Tex, you got eyes?" Remmy asked.

"Sure do, Master Sergeant. The lead skiff is nearly in effective range."

"Good luck, Marine. Everyone else, lock and load. It's go time."

"Oorah!" Rip said.

"What about our air support?" Dirk Oliver asked.

"Holding steady at two thousand meters altitude and approximately ten klicks back from the line," Remmy said. "On my order, they will begin strafing runs."

"It's not a bad plan," Ricky Thompson said. "But I wouldn't complain if we had another battalion of space marines backing us up."

Tex fired the first shot. The laser from his sniper rifle was invisible to the naked eye. And the aliens either didn't see it or didn't think it was a threat. They just kept flying straight forward, making the Hemlock Stinger an effective weapon. The laser burned through the housing around the repulsor lifts. Remmy had no idea what sort of technology the aliens were using but the laser brought it down. The skiff suddenly dropped to the ground, sliding forward over the grassy plain while most of the warriors lost their footing and fell off.

"Nice shootin' Tex!" Rip called out.

"Pour it on," Sergeant Thorne said.

The aliens weren't sure what was happening at first. They must have chalked the skiff's sudden failure up to a technical difficulty. The following units swerved around the leader and kept going. Tex took a second skiff, and the aliens realized they were under attack. The closest unit was still over four klicks out, too far for regular arms. The following skiffs spread out. Tex shot them down as fast as he could, but just as Remmy expected, they charged forward with increasing speed to join the fray.

"Wait for it," Remmy cautioned his Marines. "Don't waste ammo until they're in range."

"There goes another one," Ricky Thompson said.

The enemy opened fire as soon as they cleared two kilometers distance. Their big weapons roared. They even had tracer rounds so that Remmy could see the bullets coming. Most fell short, pounding harmlessly into the dirt of the hillside, but some were aimed high and came arcing down closer to the Marines.

"Incoming," Sergeant Dirk Oliver called out.

"Get small," Remmy said. "Don't start shooting yet."

"Six skiffs down," Tex announced. "I'm changing batteries."

"When we retreat, you leave the spent batteries, Tex," Remmy said. "Don't let anything slow you down."

"Roger that, Sarge."

"They're crossing a thousand meters," Sergeant Thorne said.

"Almost in range," Ricky said.

"Tex, switch to regular arms," Remmy ordered.

"Copy," Tex replied.

"Now!" Remmy ordered. "Fire at will."

He already had his rifle trained on a skiff full of alien warriors. He fired a three-round burst. The Nelson LTX's explosive rounds crossed the distance in less than a second and hit one of the aliens just below the arm of the heavy weapon it was firing. The impact knocked the Ashi warrior backward. He fell into another of his compatriots and both toppled from the skiff. Remmy fired again and again in quick succession. The bullets weren't penetrating, but the kinetic energy, combined with the moving skiff under their feet and perhaps even the heavy weapon they were balancing on the mechanical arm connected to their armor, knocked the Ashi warriors down.

Remmy managed to clear one skiff of warriors before having to reload his rifle. But it was quickly becoming a dangerous maelstrom. The aliens were firing large caliber rounds and while the Marines made small targets, the entire ridge was hammered.

"That's enough," Remmy shouted. "Grenades!"

He rolled slightly down the ridge onto his back to get clear of the incoming fire. Then he pulled the pin on two of his thermobaric grenades and tossed them high over the ridge.

"Retreat to the drop ship!" he ordered. "Go! Go! Go!"

The Marines all scrambled down the steep backside of the ridge. Remmy slid more than ran as the ground shook from the grenade detonations and waves of fire spread thick black smoke in all directions.

GIGI, fire with all drones, Remmy ordered.

The drones dove toward the battleground and opened up with their machine guns. The narrow projectiles didn't penetrate armor, but they got the confused warriors turning in all directions. Remmy jumped on the loading ramp and waved the others in.

We're on board, he thought. *Get us out of here.*

The engines on the drop ship roared to life and the craft rose several meters, then raced down the valley between the ridge and the forested hills. Once they were several kilometers from the battle site where the Ashi warriors were still blasting away at the ridge, completely unaware that the Marines weren't still there, GIGI closed the rear hatch and rose up into the air. At five thousand meters, the dropship circled back to the battlefield.

"We caused some mayhem," Dirk said. "But I can't tell how many are down."

"Some," Remmy said. "That's progress. We're all still alive."

"How many drones did we lose?" Sergeant Thorne asked.

"Thirty-eight," Remmy replied. "I think we gave them more than they could handle."

"Their weapons are heavy duty," Tex said. "Way more reach than I thought."

"Looks like we took down almost half their skiffs," Remmy said. "GIGI has better intel than what my eyes can see through the smoke."

"How many dead?" Rip asked.

"Not as many as we would like. They're already reloading the skiffs. I'd guess maybe twenty-five killed or wounded."

"Twenty-five?" Thorne said. "We hit them with everything we've got."

"Their armor is stout," Tex said. "Big boys got big toys."

"From the front," Remmy said. "Let's find a place to lay low, let them fly past us, then hit them from the rear."

"Good plan, but if they turn around and attack us, we'll be cooked," Thorne said. "There's no way to hide the drop ship."

"So we don't hide it," Remmy suggested. "Once we hit the back ranks, GIGI flies in and picks us up. We coordinate it right, and we'll be gone by the time they turn around."

"You're in command," Tex said. "Sounds good to me."

"If it works," Sergeant Jay Thorne said.

"That's a big if," Sergeant Dirk Oliver said.

"You're right," Remmy said. "We'll improve our odds if only half are in on the ambush. I'll go, any other volunteers?"

"Count me in, Master Sergeant. I'm ready."

"Me too," Tex said.

"It might be better if you snipe at them from a distance," Thorne said. "We can calculate how far to place him, say on the right flank."

"Once they get moving again, my guess is they'll fly due north, just like before," Remmy said.

"I'll join you," Sergeant Thorne said. "Dirk and Ricky can stay on board."

"Ricky can help me hump the batteries for the Stinger," Tex said.

"Oorah," Ricky added.

"Well, I'm not sitting it out," Dirk complained. "Let Master Sergeant Remmy watch from a safe distance. That's what officers are supposed to do anyway."

"That's a hell of a thing for you to say to me, Sarge. I work for a living," Remmy said with a smile.

"But he's right about one thing," Thorne interjected. "You're the only one with a connection to air support."

"Fine," Remmy said. "I'll watch from above. We'll swing down, pick you boys up, then swing over to collect Tex and Ricky."

"It's a good plan. Now we just need the right place to spring the trap," Dirk said.

"Let's go find it," Remmy said.

The drop ship turned and raced off over the ridge and past the forested hills toward Kipbur.

CHAPTER 27

THE BATTLE to the south was a different story. The mountain chain widened and the course the aliens set was straight through the rugged peaks. Lieutenant Colt ordered the Pegasus down on a plateau overlooking the pass the aliens were traveling through. With his MECH suit, he was able to fly himself over to the opposite side of the pass.

"Once I'm there," he said, "we'll rain down fire on the enemy from both sides."

Staff Sergeant Laila McPherson had been in enough battles to understand the benefits and risks. The high vantage point gave the Marines an advantage, but they were less than three hundred meters above the floor of the pass. She had no doubt that the alien weapons would reach them on the plateau. And while the flat space offered some cover from those down below, to be effective the Marines would have to lean out and shoot down, putting them directly in the line of fire.

But it wasn't her place to argue. In fact, Gunnery Sergeant Chad Rand was the senior non-commissioned officer. He should have pointed out the dangers of the Lieutenant's plan, but he remained silent. Laila didn't think it was good to speak up and cause doubts just before the battle. What she did instead was pick very specific stations for her team and help them dig in.

There were no rocks of sufficient size to fight behind. There were, however, some rocky outcroppings that would give an additional layer of covering. Laila set Izzy Berry above one bulging section of rock and Jack Fortnoy was above another. Jack had been quiet since getting stunned on the slave ship. The energy blast had been absorbed by his suit and had only rendered him unconscious for a short time, but he seemed to have fallen into a deep melancholy ever since. Laila had seen it before. Some Marines fought in dozens of battles without ever facing their own mortality. Others were wounded in the fighting or nearly killed; some even saw their friends die right before their eyes and it changed them. Jack seemed to have grown dark and while Laila did her best to encourage him, she knew there was ultimately nothing she could do to pull him out of the malaise he was stuck in.

She found her own spot and waited. But her sense of foreboding about the battle didn't get better when Lieutenant Colt fired his rockets and flew across the expanse. It was obvious right from the start that he wasn't quite steady. He shot up fast, then nearly crashed as he worked to correct his course.

"Rocket man!" Hugo McManus cheered.

"He's going to kill himself," Izzy declared.

"He can hear you, Corporal," Gunny Rand reminded her.

But if he did hear the Marines he didn't respond. Laila watched him streak across the valley and go down on the far side.

"That did not look good," Hugo said.

"Did he crash?" Laila asked.

"I can't see him," Gunny Rand said. "He went down on the far side of that peak."

"Lieutenant Colt? Do you read me? Over," Laila said.

There was no reply.

"That's not good," Izzy said.

"Could be interference," Leigh Ann Poh suggested. "These

mountains could have a high iron content that would block radio signals."

Laila called for the lieutenant again but there was still no answer.

"Should we go and search for him?" Gunny Rand asked.

"We go and there won't be an ambush," Hugo pointed out. "We'll have to push on and try again."

"I say we wait, hit the enemy, then circle back to look for the LT," Laila said. "If he's having a com issue, he won't be happy that we let the enemy off the hook."

"Agreed," Gunny Rand said. "We stay put, finish the job, then we comb the woods for the LT."

Half an hour later, there was still no word from Lieutenant Colt and Laila's sense of impending doom was so thick she felt like she could taste it. The mountains were cold. It was hard to stay hidden without getting too cold. Her battle armor would stop a laser blast, but it did little to insulate her from the frigid mountain air.

Snow was falling by the time the aliens appeared. They flew along on their skiffs in a long serpentine line that followed the valley between the mountains. Laila didn't know what the capabilities of the hovercraft were, but it seemed unlikely that the occupants could handle steep inclines without falling off the open platform.

"Here they come," Gunny Rand said, taking charge. "Wait for my signal."

Laila and the other Marines held their weapons in hands that ached with the cold. Her heart rate increased. She felt exposed on the plateau. Even at a distance, she could see the big weapons the enemy carried. The Ashi warriors were huge, and for them, having weapons that needed mechanical assistance seemed especially daunting.

"To those of us about to die," Jack Fortnoy said quietly. "We salute you."

"The only ones dying today are the enemy," McManus said. "Get your head in the game, Jack."

"Stay cool," Laila said. "We hit the enemy here, then pull back. No heroics. This is a marathon, not a sprint."

"Alright, platoon, get ready to fire on my mark," Gunny Rand said. "Three, two, one ... mark!"

Six fully automatic weapons opened fire. Laila was focused on just one skiff and poured nearly half of her 85-round magazine down on the enemy. As it turned out, the vertical angle was a good one since the enemy wore no armor on their heads. Those that were hit went down. Laila killed nearly half the warriors on the skiff she had targeted, but there were dozens more and the enemy quickly began to return fire. Their large automatic weapons spewed heavy caliber bullets straight up the mountainside. Rocks and dirt flew out as Laila moved away from the edge of the plateau.

"This isn't working," McManus said.

"Where's the Lieutenant?" Izzy asked.

There didn't seem to be any crossfire from the far side of the valley. Nor did it appear that the return fire from the Ashi warriors was divided. The plateau thundered with the pounding from down below.

"Gunny! What's your orders?" Laila asked.

Rand didn't reply.

"Is he hit?" Izzy asked.

"Negative, negative," Leigh Ann Poh said. "We're fine."

"Orders!" Laila shouted, only to be met once more with silence.

She realized two things in that instance. The first was that Gunny Rand was no longer fit for service. All the signs of his mental breakdown had been there. He tried to cover it, to laugh things off, but he had admitted his struggles to her and Remmy. Laila had hoped that getting back into action would shake him out of the struggles he had since their operation on Lawash. Unfortunately, the opposite had happened.

"Hugo, get him out of there!" Laila ordered.

The second thing that was obvious to her was that if they tried to fight on, they would be wounded or killed.

"Retreat to the ship!" She continued giving orders. "Alpha Team, Bravo Team, pull back. GIGI, get the dropship ready to fly."

"Engaging all systems," came the computerized voice through Laila's comlink. "Dust off in sixty seconds."

"You heard her," Laila continued issuing orders. "Move, move, move! We are getting off this rock right now."

Laila had been in bad situations before, but nothing seemed to compare to the blaze of enemy fire on the plateau. So many rounds were pounding the edge of the plateau that it began to crumble. Laila looked for Hugo. He had Gunny Rand by one arm and was dragging the NCO back to the ship which was parked forty paces from the edge of the plateau.

"This place is coming apart," Izzy declared as she ran for the ship.

"We can't keep pace with their guns," Leigh Ann Poh added.

Laila agreed. They needed heavier munitions, but a Special Operations platoon was known for speed and stealth, not heavy fighting. They were usually sent into tight windows across harsh environments that required them to operate with light armor and weapons. The only guns that could come close to what the Ashi were firing were platform-based. Laila knew they needed a different strategy altogether. Fortunately, as she ran for the dropship, a new idea was forming in her mind.

She reached the ramp at the same time as Hugo. The big Marine hauled Gunny Rand inside easily. Izzy and Poh were already on the ship.

"Fifteen seconds to launch," GIGI announced.

Laila's duty as Staff Sergeant was to keep her people together and safe. Everyone was accounted for except Jack Fortnoy. She turned around to find him, expecting to see him running toward her. Instead, he stood dangerously close to the edge of the plateau.

"Fortnoy! Get over here. We are leaving, Marine!"

"It's no good," he said softly. Laila struggled to understand him over the roar of the dropship's engines and the thunder of gunfire from the valley below.

Jack dropped his rifle and pulled two grenades from his belt.

"Corporal Fortnoy, get to the dropship now! That's an order!" Laila shouted.

"It's no good," Jack said again.

Then, to her horror, he pulled the pins from the grenades and dove off the edge of the plateau.

"No!" Laila screamed.

She didn't even realize what had happened when Hugo grabbed the handle on the back of her battle armor and pulled her onto the ship just before it lifted off. An explosion sounded in the valley below. The shooting decreased for a moment. Laila felt an ache in her gut as the ramp of the dropship closed. Her premonition had been right, and everything about the operation from the moment the platoon split up had been wrong.

"What happened?" Izzy asked.

"Where's Jack?" Leigh Ann added.

Laila couldn't form the words. She just shook her head. Jack was gone. It was a reality of war. They all knew it. They had all experienced losses in battle before. But Laila felt a heavy sense of guilt. His death wasn't her fault and yet she hadn't done what he needed either. She had to ask herself if her obsession with Remmy had clouded her judgment. She was no headshrinker, but she had been around enough Marines struggling with PTSD to recognize the signs. She should have pulled Jack's ticket. But the odds against them were so overwhelming that she hadn't even considered scrubbing him from her team.

And Jack wasn't the only casualty of the failed ambush. Hugo had Gunnery Sergeant Chad Rand strapped into a jump seat with a five-point harness, but gunney sat slumped, not moving or speaking. Without Lieutenant Colt and separated from Remmy, the decisions for Alpha and Bravo teams fell to her.

"How's gunny?" She managed to ask.

"He's not hurt," Leigh Ann said. "But he's not responding."

"Mental break," Hugo said. "Just like Jack."

"At least we didn't lose them both," Izzy said.

"What do we do now, Staff Sergeant?" Hugo asked.

She couldn't see his eyes because of the face shield on his helmet, but she could feel them boring into her.

"We circle around, search for the LT," she said.

"What if we can't find him?" Leigh Ann asked.

"Yeah, he might have crashed his new suit and died," Izzy said.

"Then we press on," Laila said. "Continue the fight."

"The mountains ain't such a good place to do it," Hugo said. "We need a way to neutralize their guns."

"I've got an idea about that," Laila said. "Let's find the LT, then we make a new plan."

"Can't be as bad as the last one," Hugo said.

"No, it's time we used the enemy's strength against them," she declared.

CHAPTER 28

COMMANDER LORI LEE wanted to curse but she couldn't let her frustration show in front of her small band of fighters. They were on the verge of falling apart just at the idea of fighting the enemy warriors who had boarded the ship. The discovery that their prisoner had escaped didn't help matters.

"They must have found him," Donny Elgermsa said. "Ain't no way that thing got out of those restraints without help."

"Agreed," Lori Lee said. "Which means they probably have a way off this ship."

"How's that?" LeRoy Washington asked.

"Either they have some sort of vessel so close we missed it on radar," Commander Lee said. "Or..."

"They're headed for the hanger," Donny said.

"I thought all the ships were launched for the invasion," Carmen Ramis said.

"All the attack drones and some of the dropships, but not all of them."

"Can they fly our ships?" Eli Johnson asked.

"We should assume they can," Lori Lee said as she tapped the transmit button on her comlink. "Captain Darius?"

"I read you, Commander. What's the sitrep?"

"The infiltrators have found our prisoner," she said. "I have an eight-person team in the commercial section of the ship. We're going to head for the flight deck."

"Copy that, Commander Lee. Be careful. We have word from the engineering spaces. The crew there is on high alert. We'll inform you if the enemy is spotted."

"Roger that, Captain, and thanks. Lee out."

"What now?" Donny asked.

"We know where we're going," Commander Lee said. "The aliens probably don't. Let's move as fast as we can and try to cut them off."

She led the way. Commander Lori Lee wasn't the type of officer who used her position of authority to avoid doing things she didn't like. Nor was she like many officers who stopped training the moment they completed boot camp. Lori Lee still did some type of cardio work five days a week. She liked to mix it up, using the exercise equipment on the *Jericho* and actually jogging through the park since taking over the *Renegade*. She wasn't in the best shape of her life. Age was taking a toll, especially on her joints, but she was still young enough to make a five-kilometer run through the ship to the drone hanger.

Unfortunately, not everyone else was in as good a shape as Commander Lee. Exercise was strongly encouraged on Fleet vessels. And usually, there weren't a lot of recreational options on the small spaceships. Most of the crew put some time into the gym, but not all. Eli Johnson, Sasha Minsk and Leon Gesa struggled to keep up.

By the time they were halfway through the park, the stragglers had simply given up. Commander Lee ordered them to keep moving, even if it was just at a walking pace, but she didn't wait for them either. Donny was the largest of her team. He was sweating freely and breathing hard but not complaining as they reached the gravity shaft that led down to the hanger bay.

"No sign of them," he said. "You think they might have some type of camouflage?"

"There's no way to know for sure," Commander Lee said. "It could be camouflage or maybe just a small number of infiltrators."

"We don't know how many there are?" Roby Toto asked.

"Two for certain ... could be more," Lori said. "Only two were spotted."

"Who saw them?" Donny asked.

"Connor O'Dell."

"That guy?" LeRoy Washington exclaimed. "He ain't no spaceman."

"He's a lurker," Carmen Ramis said. "I've seen him watching people."

"Can we trust him?" Donny asked.

"We have no reason to believe he lied," Commander Lee said. "And I would add that the missing prisoner is proof."

"So, what now?" LeRoy asked.

"We go down to the hanger," Lori said. "Make sure to switch off the safety on your rifle once we're out of the lift."

"Will these weapons even stop those things?" Roby asked. "I mean, they're huge."

"Hit them low in the stomach," Commander Lee said. "That's where they're most vulnerable. Keep in mind you've only got eight shots before you need to reload."

"I've never worked one of these," Carmen said.

"It's easy," Donny told her. "Go ahead and pull the charging lever."

She did. Releasing it, the lever made a reassuring ~*ka-chunk!*~ sound when it rammed the first shell into the firing chamber.

"Now, all you need to do is point and shoot," Donny said. "But don't switch off the safety until we're on the flight deck and don't point it at anything you don't want to kill."

"This makes me really nervous," Carmen said.

"It's okay," Roby told her. "Stay beside me."

"We did this in basic training," Donny said.

"Not with shotguns," Carmen complained.

"Don't worry, you probably won't even need to use it," LeRoy said.

"Enough talk," Commander Lee said. "Let's move."

She led the way once again, stepping into the zero-gravity shaft and pushing off the padded ceiling that covered the opening. As she drifted down she wondered if any of the animals in the park ever got caught inside the lift. They would make a real mess bouncing up and down for who knew how long. Commander Lee was grateful the *Renegade* had a small army of maintenance robots that did all the cleaning and upkeep on the ship.

Her heart rate was already elevated from the run through the ship. Sweat made her short hair cling to her scalp and she couldn't keep her hands from trembling slightly. Lori Lee was the type of person who did things that needed done no matter how she felt about it. Fear wasn't going to stop her, but the moment she reached the bottom of the lift and grabbed onto a railing just inside the doorway that led to the flight deck, she heard the enemy.

Turning to look up at the others she placed a finger across her lips for silence, then slipped out of the gravity lift. The sudden sense of gravity weighed her down for a moment. She could hear quiet grunting and muffled sounds like a barking dog might make. There were still forty shuttles in the hangar. Most of the other drones were gone, but she saw that some were being replaced already. The *Renegade's* manufacturing plant could print, machine, refine, and assemble anything the ship's computer designed. Not that the system in itself was necessarily ground-breaking. Humans had built manufacturing plants that took in raw materials on one end and rolled out finished products on the other as far back as the nineteen sixties. Lori Lee was a vehicle enthusiast who enjoyed reading about cars back when land-based travel was done on roads instead of hover lanes.

Of course, those production plants were massive structures and utilized hundreds of employees to operate the machinery within. The manufacturing plant inside the *Renegade* was much smaller and utilized robotics, including the drones that moved finished goods to various parts of the ship.

As soon as Donny and Roby joined her, Commander Lee stepped out from behind the shuttle nearest the lift. Down the open deck were two hulking aliens. One was clearly their former prisoner. He still had one arm wrapped in bandages with a temporary splint wrapped around it. His face also had bandages and there were blood stains on his side and kilt.

The other alien was obviously more robust. He also carried what looked like a laser rifle, but it was the first time Lori Lee had seen one and couldn't be sure. She silently chastised herself for not reviewing the reports from the Marine platoon more carefully. Surely, she thought, there was helmet video that would show the aliens using their weapons. But there hadn't really been time to review everything in detail. And if Lori was being honest, she didn't think it was her responsibility. The Marine platoon should have been doing what she was doing at that moment, only there weren't any Marines on board the ship.

Lori stepped back behind the shuttle and tapped out a text message on her comlink to Captain Darius.

Two intruders spotted; one was our prisoner—request permission to engage.

Granted, was the Captain's reply, which meant he would be monitoring the flight deck and ensuring that it could be sealed off if the hull was compromised.

"What are they doing?" Donny whispered as LeRoy and Carmen caught up to them.

"Looking for a way off the ship," Lee whispered back. "We show them no quarter."

"Hell yeah," Donny said.

"This is crazy," Roby added.

"Follow my lead," the commander whispered. "Donny, take position right at the nose of the ship. The rest of you stay hidden unless we go down. Then come out guns blazing."

"Is that an order?" LeRoy asked. "Guns blazing?"

"Yes," was the sharp answer he got from Commander Lee.

It took all of her considerable courage to move forward, but she dashed out from the safety of the shuttle to create distance between herself and the others. The last thing she could afford to do was have them all gunned down at once because they were huddling together. Her steps on the deck made noise and the two aliens turned. At the same time, she raised her shogun and fired at the alien with the weapon in his hand. The slug hit him in the middle of his chest and caused him to stagger backward. The bullet broke the skin but didn't penetrate the bone plate that covered his vital organs.

As it staggered back, it raised its own weapon and fired. The laser blast was close enough that Lori felt the heat from it. The side of her face felt immediately as though she had been out in the sun too long without protection.

From the shuttle where he was waiting, Donny fired. His shot hit the alien in the middle of his stomach. It was wearing a flight suit of some sort, not unlike the coveralls that human fighter pilots wore. The slug tore through the suit and into the alien's unprotected abdomen. Blood instantly soaked the front of his suit as he dropped to his knees.

As the alien swung his weapon toward Donny, Lori Lee fired again. This time, her shot hit the side of the alien's head. Blood erupted in a shower from the wound, along with broken teeth. The alien's jaw was broken and it toppled sideways, firing a string of laser blasts that hit the wide airlock door. Alarms suddenly blared to life. Around them, maintenance droids appeared, rushing toward the damage. Lori looked at the door. It was huge, like the hanger door on an airport building. There were scorch marks and cracks in the smooth metal finish but no holes that she could see. The hull didn't appear to be compromised.

When she looked back, the former prisoner was pulling the injured alien between two of the shuttles and out of her line of sight.

"Specialist?" Lori called out.

"I'm good," Donny replied.

"All right, let's finish this," Lori Lee said.

She moved forward. In her mind, she kept thinking, *six shots left, six shots*. She fully expected to see the former prisoner helping the wounded alien. Emperor or not, the alien was loose on her ship and she couldn't have that. She was prepared to gun it down, only it wasn't there.

"Where is it?" She said.

The wounded alien in the flight suit lay bleeding to death on the deck. It twitched and might already be dead. Lori couldn't be sure, but the former prisoner, the alien with the broken arm, wasn't there.

Donny moved out from his position, followed by Roby and Carmen. LeRoy took Donny's spot. They spread out along the deck, moving down the line of ships, searching for the missing alien. No one saw or heard the two intruders who came silently out of the gravity lift. LeRoy Washington died when one of the newcomers ran a long, curved knife through his back. LeRoy screamed and the second alien began shooting.

Roby was hit and killed instantly. Carmen turned with her rifle across her body held in two hands, almost as if she were using it to ward off the danger. The alien's second shot hit the gun and sent her tumbling across the deck.

Donny fired back. His shot hit the alien in the shoulder and caused it to drop the laser rifle. Unfazed by the bullet wound, which had crippled its right arm, the alien charged forward.

Lori saw the second alien stepping out from behind the first. She fired at it but missed, her bullet ricocheting off the shuttle and then deck before smashing into one of the overhead light panels. The light in the damaged panel went dark and the alien rolled back behind the ship for cover.

Donny meanwhile fired again at the alien charging him. The bullet hit the alien in his upper thigh. It staggered but kept coming. Donny fired again. The third shot, his fourth overall, half of his supply, hit the alien in the gut. It seemed to absorb the gunshots and just kept going. Lori aimed at the alien just as it reached Donny and fired. Her shot hit the wounded shoulder and sent the alien spinning to the ground. Donny finished it with a shot straight into the alien's face.

"There's another one!" Lori shouted as she reversed course back across the flight deck.

She didn't see Eli, Leon and Sasha arrive. But the alien must have. It fired at the trio, killing Leon. Sasha and Eli fired back. One hit the alien in the center of his chest, knocking him back into the shuttle; the other hit its knee. The alien fell to the deck and Sasha fired two more times. The thick slugs tore into the alien's guts and left it trembling in its death throes.

"It's down!" Eli shouted. "We got one."

"Good to see you," Donny proclaimed.

"Leon's down," Sasha said.

"No!" Carmen screamed.

"Look out!" Donny shouted as he dove toward Lori.

The laser blast was too fast to see. It was like unseen lightning that lit the sky. Lori saw the flash and felt Donny's body crash into her. They fell to the deck. She was alive, unscathed, but Donny was staring at her with unseeing eyes.

"Specialist?" Lori said.

His body was heavy on top of her. It didn't move.

"Donny Elgermsa!"

He still didn't move. He wasn't even breathing. The wounded alien who had been a prisoner on board the *Renegade* suddenly loomed over her. She didn't remember having lost her grip on her rifle, but it wasn't in her hands, which she grabbed and raised to cover his face as the towering alien pointed his weapon at her. But before it could fire, a hail of bullets tore into him. Eli and Sasha were firing at the same time, two fast shots each. The bullets impacted the already injured Ashi alien high on his body and knocked him off his feet.

Lori rolled Donny to the side and scrambled up. She kicked the wounded Ashi leader's weapon away from him. The impact of kicking the heavy weapon broke her toe and caused her to sprain her ankle.

"Oh!" She shouted in surprise, nearly falling as she hopped on her good foot to keep the pressure off.

"Is it dead?" Sasha asked.

"No," Lori replied. "But it's hurt pretty bad."

"Are there more of them?" Eli asked.

"There might be," Lori said. "Eli, cover the gravity lift. If you see green, you kill it."

"Aye, Commander," he said. Lori took notice that there was a little more confidence in the Culinary Specialist's voice.

"Sasha, check on the others."

Sasha turned and knelt by Leon. When she turned back to Lori, she shook her head. Looking around her, Lori felt lucky to be alive. Leon was dead. Donny had died saving her. Roby and LeRoy had been gunned down, too. Carmen was weeping across the deck. Lori didn't know if she was hurt or just grieving, probably both.

With trembling hands, she raised her comlink and pressed the transmit button.

"Captain Darius, this is Commander Lee."

"Go ahead, Commander. What's your status."

"Four casualties," she reported. "One more injured. I think I sprained my damn ankle, too."

"Can you walk, Commander?"

"Aye, Captain. We killed three intruders and wounded the prisoner. I don't know if he'll make it or not."

"Stay where you are," Darius ordered. "I'm sending Doctor Lanski and his med techs to your location. I'm glad you're going to be okay, Commander."

"Me too," Lori said, even though she felt terrible saying it. "Munition Specialist Donny Elgersma sacrificed himself to save me, Captain. And crewmen Eli Johnson and Sasha Minsk shot the prisoner before he could shoot me, sir. We're in pretty sad shape."

"Don't worry, Commander. We'll get you patched up in no

time. And every crewman's heroic actions will be recorded and recognized both on the ship and when we get back home."

It was the only thing they could do, and yet the gesture felt completely hollow to Lori. Tears stung her eyes, but she held them back. There would be a time to let her emotions loose. It wasn't that time yet.

"Aye, Captain. Thank you, sir."

"Thank you, Commander. Darius out."

Across the hanger Sasha was helping Carmen to her feet. She had burns on her hands, and the shotgun she had been holding was ruined on the deck, but she was alive.

"Help is on the way," Lori said. "Let's just hang on a little longer."

"We stopped them," Eli said. "Dirty sons-a—

Before he could finish, another alarm sounded.

"What's that?" Sasha asked.

"I don't know," Lori Lee said, pulling more slugs from the loop on the shotgun's stock and loading them into the breech. "I guess we're not out of the woods yet. Let's make sure we're ready."

"For what?" Eli asked, a bit of his fear coming out once more.

"For whatever comes our way."

CHAPTER 29

AT FIRST, Lieutenant Micky Colt couldn't move. He had simulated flying in his MECH suit many times, but the real thing was different. The suit's propulsion system was much more powerful than he expected and the winds high above the mountains were strong. Yet he had managed to regain control after initially losing it. Everything should have been fine, but there was no flat place to land on the far mountain. The plateau on one side of the valley seemed like the perfect ambush space, but he hadn't bothered to recon the far side. When he came down, his feet slid on loose rock. The MECH had turned suddenly and slammed down hard on its head. The unexpected blow left Micky unsteady. When he tried to get up, things only got worse.

Not far below him was a deep crevice. In no time at all, Micky slid down, rotating into a head-down position and toppled into the crack in the side of the mountain. He fell down into a narrow spot where the MECH suit lodged between the rocky sides. Lieutenant Colt, already reeling from his crash landing, suddenly found the blood rushing to his head. He passed out cold.

When he woke, everything hurt. He was in a dark space, even

though there was enough light somewhere to convince him that it wasn't nighttime.

"Alpha Team," he said slowly in a thick, pain-laced voice, "do you read me? Over."

There was no reply.

"Bravo Team... come in."

Still nothing. He tried to move but couldn't. He had to take a slow, stuttering breath as a wave of fear threatened to throw him into full-blown panic. Then he realized he wasn't as helpless as it seemed.

"Run diagnostic," he said, activating the MECH's voice controls.

"Suit integrity ninety-two percent. Weapons undamaged. Propulsion fifty-eight percent. Communications off-line."

That was the real issue. He had been afraid that maybe he had missed the battle completely. What if Alpha and Bravo teams had been slaughtered and he wasn't there to help them? That was a horrifying thought. He breathed a little easier and focused on his situation. He needed to move, but he couldn't; at least, it seemed that he couldn't. One arm was pinned across his chest, but his other arm and legs could move.

He had to feel around until he could find a place to hold onto. Then, using his suit's powerful hydraulic strength, he pushed himself upward with one hand. Outside the suit, it would have been impossible. Micky Colt was no weakling, but he wasn't strong enough to lift his entire body weight with one hand. The suit, however, was more than capable of such a feat.

Inch by inch, he pushed himself up and out of the bind he had been in. Then, using his legs to brace himself, he managed to free his pinned arm. It felt good to move. And it felt even better when he managed to turn himself upright in the crevice. He let himself rest after that. The blood drained from his aching head, relieving a lot of the pressure in his skull. Once his head cleared and his vision returned to normal, he looked up. He was nearly a hundred meters down the crevice, but he could see up the uneven sides and knew it would be possible to climb out.

He could also use his suit's propulsion system, but just the thought of attempting to fly again made him feel queasy. That was the problem with Mechanized battle suits; there was a fine line between how much of the many systems should be computer augmented. Too much and the pilot was restricted ... too little and the suit became too difficult to control. He would make improvements, but he had to survive first.

Climbing out of the crevice got his blood pumping. Not that the weight of even his own body was on him with the suit doing the actual work, but the constant movement made his heart rate increase and the blood flowing through his arms and legs helped loosen the muscles and joints. At the top of the crevice, he crawled out and slowly made his way around the mountain peak, expecting to see his fellow Marines across the valley. But the plateau was empty. Smoke hung in the air. He hadn't noticed it before and his suit's respiration system filtered it out, so he hadn't smelled it, but it hung like a pall of doom between the two mountains.

Down below him, he saw carnage—four wrecked and abandoned skiffs. Two more had been hit with explosives of some kind. And there were bodies. Not as many as he expected after the ambush he had envisioned, but then again, he had planned to hit the enemy from both sides of the valley. Looking across the expanse, he could see the pockmarks where bullets had chewed up the edge of the plateau. To his relief, there were no bodies lying dead on the mountain. His people had escaped. He would need to join them soon, but he couldn't deny the fact that the thought of flying made him nervous.

Micky Colt was an officer in the SDF Space Marines. It pained him to admit that he felt nervous or afraid of anything. And yet, he had never been able to lie to himself. He had gone to the esteemed Lunar Military Academy, where he graduated eighteenth in a class of forty-two. It was respectable but not impressive. From there he had gone right into Officer Training, which included physical training and weapons. His focus was on Special Operations and he had run three successful missions before being assigned to the *Jericho*. It had never occurred to him that he wasn't as good at his job as he thought. He was a perpetually positive person, but the crash had rattled him. And missing the ambush he had planned made him angry. The Marines had been counting on him and he had failed them. That was something he would have to make up for, however he could. The first priority was returning to his teams.

It made sense to fly high. From altitude, he could see farther and potentially reach the Pegasus more quickly. But remembering the winds and considering his propulsion system was down to half power, he didn't like the idea of being high in the air if the system stopped. He decided instead to stay low. There was plenty of space on the trail to land safely if he needed to. And if he fell from a low altitude, he was more likely to survive.

The hardest part was activating the system and stepping off the cliff that overlooked the valley. He fell but the propulsion system slowed his descent. He activated the motion stabilizers and focused on keeping himself balanced. Soon, he landed safely on the ground amidst the carnage of the battle. He counted forty-two dead Ashi. It was, strictly from an analytics perspective, a victory for the Marines. But he had hoped to vanquish the Ashi force entirely. He had no connection to GIGI, with his communication system ruined. He reached up and touched the side of the suit's head that had slammed into the ground. He could feel the damage there. Without a connection to the alien artifact, which was their eye in the sky and controlled the drone fighters, he had no way of knowing how many of the enemy were left.

He set off at a jog. The suit gave him a long stride that had no problem making good time along the path. He could fly, and it would be faster, but as long as the path before him was smooth, he decided he would stay on the ground.

He hadn't gone far when he rounded a turn in the path and

came upon a group of Ashi traveling on foot. Most were wounded or injured, but a few were whole. They turned, and for a moment, the group stared at Lieutenant Colt in the MECH suit. Then he raised his arm and fired a series of mini-missiles. All but two of the Ashi were caught in the explosions. The small rockets were designed for high impact. In fact, Colt felt the shockwave and staggered back. The aliens, however, were torn to pieces by the series of blasts.

The two who jumped away in time were flattened by the shockwave but recovered quickly. As they rose to their feet, Micky rushed to meet them. He wasn't sure what had happened to his large machine gun, but it was no longer in his possession after the crash. Instead, he extended a long, doubled-edged blade from his right forearm. It stuck well out over his fist and he used it to knock aside the first alien's weapon. Micky followed that with a hydraulic-powered punch that landed hard on the Ashi warrior's wide jaw. The tusk was shattered under the MECH's iron fist and the alien was sent sprawling on the ground.

When the second alien saw that Micky wasn't using a firearm, it hit a release on its armor that caused the mechanized arm to go slack. Then he shrugged off his armor, drew a long curved knife and growled menacingly.

"You want a piece of this?" Micky said with a chuckle. "Come get some!"

They rushed at each other. Micky had studied various martial arts, from Krav Maga to Brazilian Ju Jitsu. He could fight with his hands and with traditional weapons. But moving in the MECH suit was not as fast or smooth as without it. He tried to duck under the alien's high slash but lost his balance and nearly fell on his face.

The alien rammed a knee into what would have been Micky's face. They were roughly the same size, but the suit protected the pilot just as it was meant to and instead of sending his opponent reeling, the alien had merely helped arrest Micky's forward momentum. He raised up and grabbed the alien's wrist. It was the same hand he held the knife with. The Ashi warrior managed to hack the blade into the MECH's shoulder, but the blade did not damage the thick armor.

Meanwhile, the powered grip of the suit began to cause the alien pain. He tried to pull free but couldn't. The bones started to give way. The alien wailed in pain as it dropped the knife. It reared back, then swung forward in a vicious headbutt that should have dropped Micky. But once again, the alien's blows onto the MECH suit did not have the intended consequence. The alien only managed to pulverize its own nose and rip the skin around its eyes.

With the Ashi warrior wounded and dazed, he had no problems ramming his own blade into the alien's stomach. The narrow alien eyes widened in pain. The Heads Up Display inside the suit gave Micky a full one-hundred-and-eighty-degree view. He saw the other alien wrestling its big gun around. Micky turned, still holding the dying alien, just as his companion fired. The bullets tore into the Ashi warrior, killing him instantly. Many even punched clean through and pounded onto the MECH armor. But even at close range, after going through the dead alien's body, the bullets had lost enough momentum that they failed to cause anything but cosmetic damage.

Still, the Ashi warrior was back on his feet with his big gun in hand. It might have spelled doom for the Marine Lieutenant, but suddenly, the high-powered, mechanical weapon jammed. Micky had seen guns jam plenty of times. It was one of the reasons the Marines preferred to carry their weapons of choice into combat. A tried and true, high-quality firearm could be counted on not to jam.

Recognizing the opportunity, Micky flung the alien aside and rushed toward his attacker. The big rifle on the mechanized arm was a powerful weapon when it worked and a cumbersome distraction when it didn't. The alien tried to raise the rifle to deflect Micky's blade, but the lieutenant caught the rifle with his free hand. Using the MECH suit's powered servos, he was even stronger than the hulking alien. He held the gun down long enough to slash the blade mounted to his right forearm across the alien's throat. The blade bit so deep it nearly decapitated the alien, who fell to the ground dead.

Micky looked around and decided the suit was a smashing success. Then he set off again, more determined than ever to find and join his lost platoon mates.

CHAPTER 30

DARIUS FELT a cold lump of fury and guilt form in his stomach. Crew members were dead. It was always a risk. They were part of the Space Defense Force, after all, and defense always involved risk. Not to mention the fact that space was not a safe environment for humans. There were countless ways to get hurt or killed in space. But it wasn't space that had killed his crew members. They died defending the ship and Darius felt that loss was a failure on his part. His had made a mistake in underestimating what the Ashi were capable of and it had cost crew people their lives. It was a haunting burden that he couldn't just shake off.

"Captain!" Henry Nash said suddenly. "The starboard engine just went off-line."

"What? Why?"

"Unknown, I... I can't tell what's happened. It just stopped," Nash said, immediately activating his comlink and requesting information from his engineers in that section of the ship.

"Sabotage," Pete Best said.

"What are your people saying?" Darius asked.

"They aren't, sir," Nash said, turning to look at Darius with fury in his eyes. "No response from that area of the ship."

An alarm sounded. Darius sprang to his feet. He wasn't sending anyone else into harm's way.

"Lieutenant Ramos, you have the con," he said.

"Captain?" Vivian asked, clearly not liking what she saw Darius about to do.

"I'm going," he said. "I won't let these devils wreck our ship. And I'm not sending anyone else to die for me today."

"Sir, let me go," Pete Best volunteered.

"Negative, you're all too valuable at your jobs to risk losing," Darius said. "I'll escort the med staff to the flight deck, then push on to engineering."

He hurried from the Bridge to his private quarters, calling for Dr. Vivik Lanski to gather his medical technicians and supplies as he went. In his quarters, Darius opened a narrow case. Every ship Captain in the fleet had one. Inside was a gun belt with a small laser pistol, and beside it was a Weston Tactical Rifle. It was a laser weapon, too, with several high-capacity battery units. The weapons were expensive and used for just such an occasion. They could be powered up or down, depending on the need. At full power, they could cut through steel panels and locks. At the lower settings they would wound without blowing holes in the ship. Knowing the enemy he faced, Darius would have preferred a high-power assault rifle, but he didn't have one. Nor did he have time to seek one out.

Strapping the gun belt around his waist and slinging the rifle's strap over his shoulder, he met Dr. Lanski in the hallway with four medical techs.

"What is happening?" Lanski asked.

"We're under attack," Darius said. "Try to keep up."

He wasn't in a talkative mood and fortunately for the ship surgeon, he picked up on his superior's state of mind. They hurried through the ship, stopping in the med bay for just a few minutes to allow Dr Lanski to retrieve supplies and the cargo hover sled.

It took them longer than Darius wanted to reach the flight deck. Fortunately, in that time, nothing else had been sabotaged, which led him to believe there was only a small number of Ashi infiltrators on the ship. As soon as he reached the flight deck, he found Commander Lori Lee waiting for him.

"Captain," she said. "You shouldn't be down here."

"If anyone else dies today, it's going to be me," Darius said.

"That's ridiculous, sir," she snapped. "I think you know that."

"We've got more infiltrators on the ship," Darius said. "Starboard engines are down."

"My team can handle it," Lori Lee said.

Darius looked around. Most of her team were dead. Two female crew members were consoling one another, while the only male left was guarding the gravity lift.

"You've done your part," Darius said. "Now let me do mine."

"Fine," Lori Lee said. "If that's what you want, but we're coming with you."

"I need you to escort the doctor back to sick bay."

"Specialists Johnson and Minsk can do that. I'm going with you. And you're going to need something more substantial than your laser weapons to stop the Ashi."

She picked up one of the shotguns. It had been the one Donny Elgersma carried. She reloaded the shotgun and handed it to Darius. He swung his laser rifle to his back and checked the safety on the shotgun.

"Starboard engineering, that's as good as any place to start looking," Commander Lee said. "Let's go."

They left the medical team struggling to get Emperor Vang's wounded body back onto the cargo sled. The massive alien was still alive, but there were no guarantees that he would last much longer. The blood loss was substantial.

Like he had done on the *Jericho*, Captain Darius often walked the ship in his downtime. It was both a cathartic exercise and also a good way to get a sense of the ship. He knew the lower levels below the park were reserved as cargo and engineering spaces. There were highly technical workshops complete with exotic tools and materials which had yet to be identified. More importantly, Darius knew that two floors up from the drone hanger where Lori Lee's battle had taken place was a corridor that led straight to the engineering section for the starboard engine.

Darius led the way. He liked the feel of the shotgun. It had a weight to it that felt dangerous and the barrel was much larger than that of his laser rifle. When they reached the engineering section for the starboard engine, the first thing they discovered was two dead crew members laying on the deck..

"Damn," Darius said.

"Laser blasts," Lori Lee said as she bent over them. "It's Petty Officers Ramerez and Stoltz."

"We'll come back for them," Darius said.

They continued into the corridor. Like everything else on the Arodoni ship there was elegance to the design of the engines and support machinery. And the corridors were wide, not cramped like the engineering spaces on a human ship.

They hadn't gone far when they discovered several maintenance drones lying haphazardly on the deck. They had been hit with laser fire, too.

"I'm getting the feeling whoever sabotaged the engine is just sitting back somewhere sniping at whoever gets close," Lori Lee said.

Darius wasn't as familiar with the engine compartment as he wished at the moment. "What are you suggesting? We have to find them and stop them."

"But maybe we don't go straight at them, Captain," she said. "We could circle back and come at them from above."

"That's a good suggestion," Darius said. "You do that, I'll distract them here."

"Don't be so reckless," she chided. "I've never known you to act like this."

"I've never lost crew members on my watch because I made a mistake," Darius argued, his temper flaring. "Six people that we know of are dead because of my failure to prepare and anticipate the enemy."

"That   makes   you   human," Lori   Lee   argued. "Not incompetent."

"I want to make these murderous aliens pay," he said.

"You have and you will," she said. "But not if you throw your life away."

He wanted to argue. He wanted to charge hard and fast down the hallway and fight. But he knew she was right. It was her job to be his sounding board, just as it was her job to tell him when he was being a fool.

"You're right," Darius said. "I... I guess I just got carried away."

"Me too," Lori Lee said. "I did the same thing on the flight deck. If Specialist Elgersma hadn't dove on top of me, it would be me in a body bag instead of him."

"I don't want any more crew members to die," Darius said.

"Then let's go finish these green-skinned monsters off, before they do some more damage."

CHAPTER 31

THEY HAD FOUND the perfect ground for their second ambush of the day. Everyone was in place, including Remmy, who was still in the dropship monitoring from a distance.

"They're almost on you," Remmy said over the comlink.

"Copy that," Sergeant Thorne said from where he lay in thick grass not far from where the Ashi hover skiffs were about to pass by.

"I've got eyes," Tex added. "They're coming out of the forest."

"Drones are inbound," Remmy said. "We'll hit them in sixty seconds."

Sergeants Dirk Oliver and Jay Thorne were hidden in the grass along with Corporal Rip Van Winkle. A few kilometers away on a hilltop lay Corporals Tex Fry and Ricky Thompson. The plan was simple. The drones would drop ordinance on the lead alien skiff. Hopefully, that would lead to the aliens spreading out. They normally moved in a single file line, but Remmy's plan was to get them spread out so that the three Marines hidden in the grass could spring up behind them and mow them down.

Once the shooting started, Tex would knock out as many of the skiffs as he could. Long-range lasers had proven useful for that. Remmy would then send in more drones from the front, catching

the aliens in a crossfire, and also allow him to swoop in and evacuate Thorne, Oliver and Van Winkle.

But, of course, all the best planning could fall apart the moment
things got violent. It was just the nature of war. Fighting made
people do unpredictable things. Fear, rage, pain, panic ... could all
wreck a perfect plan, and that's why Remmy was in the dropship
and not on the ground with his Marines. If things went sour, it was
up to him to order the air support and find a way to rescue his
people.

"They're passing us," Sergeant Dirk Oliver said in a low voice.

"I've got their attention," Remmy said.

It wasn't actually the master sergeant, but at times he was so
tuned in to GIGI that he forgot what was his doing and what was
hers. A squadron of drones, twenty in total, were in plain sight of
the aliens, who immediately began to fire at them. GIGI had calculated the effective range of the Ashi machine guns and kept the
drones just high enough to thwart their counterfire. Bombs were
released. Twenty small warheads, not much bigger than a hand
grenade, yet packed with enough high explosives to be incredibly
lethal. Of the twenty dropped, only two made it to the ground
before the aliens detonated them in midair with counterfire. Those
two both hit the lead skiff in quick succession. The hovercraft was
blown apart. The aliens on board the hovercraft, thirty in total,
were wounded or killed in the explosion.

As the drones circled for another attack, the aliens did exactly
as Remmy expected them to do. They spread out, flying in a V-
shaped staggered formation. There were sixteen of the hovercrafts
in total after the lead ship was destroyed by the drone bombers.

"Ground team is go!" Remmy ordered.

The three Marines hidden in the grass popped up and opened
fire. Bullets hammered the last three skiffs. They tore into the unar-
mored legs of the aliens, rending flesh and shattering bones. Dozens
fell off the back of the skiffs. The mechanical arms connected to
their armor didn't survive the impact as the wounded warriors
rolled and bounced along the ground. It was a good attack, and

perhaps if the entire platoon had been hidden in the grass, they might have struck a decisive blow. But there were only three Marines and they didn't even manage to kill all the aliens on the skiffs they targeted before the floating platforms were out of range.

"Get me down there," Remmy ordered GIGI.

He didn't often speak out loud when communicating with the alien artifact that controlled the drones and the dropships, but he was focused entirely on the battle below.

Commencing controlled dive now, GIGI replied.

Remmy grabbed an overhead pipe and braced himself as the dropship turned sharply and dove toward the planet.

"They're coming around," Tex said. "Permission to fire?"

"Granted," Remmy said. "Take down as many as you can."

Tex, perched on the hilltop with his Hemlock Stinger and with Ricky Thompson spotting for him, shot the first of the hovercraft that turned. They were not agile vehicles and probably couldn't be with passengers on the open platform. Tex knew that shooting directly into the front of the hovercraft caused catastrophic damage. He waited for the angle to be perfect. The beauty of the laser rifle was that he could hit anything he aimed at. There was no waiting for a projectile to cross the distance between sniper and target. The laser traveled at the speed of light and was unaffected by wind, gravity or the rotation of the planet. All he had to do was see the target and hit the target.

But there was a downside, too. The Hemlock Stinger was a semi-automatic weapon that required heavy, external battery packs. Each battery gave Tex eight shots. And as powerful as the lasers were, they didn't always penetrate through armor with a single shot. It took three or four blasts to bring down the skiffs. He could do it in two if they were flying straight toward him. Tex could group his shots incredibly close, but the hovercrafts were turning, which required greater impact from the lasers.

"One down," Tex said. "Ricky, get the next battery ready."

"On it," Ricky Thompson replied.

The targeted skiff didn't explode. Instead, it just dove into the ground. The occupants were thrown but not killed. Tex didn't have time to watch them. He was already lining up his next target.

"Twelve left," Remmy said. "Ground team, prepare for evacuation."

"Stay low," Thorne warned.

The skiffs turned slow, but the aliens were faster. Some turned around and fired back at the Marines on the grassy plain. Remmy couldn't see the gunfire, yet he didn't have to. He had been on the receiving end of all sorts of weapons, from laser rifles to artillery shells. He could imagine what his friends on the ground were going through.

"GIGI, release the dogs of war," Remmy said.

Bombs were dropped from fifteen thousand meters overhead, and four, twenty-drone squadrons rose up from the grassy plain, one at each corner of the battlefield. They raced forward, flying low and opening up with their light machine guns the instant they came into range. Most of their thin, finger-length bullets merely bounced off the alien armor, and what found flesh was more irritating than debilitating, but their role was to buy the Marines a little more time.

And time was at a premium on the battlefield. The ground team was in the open with no cover as the world turned to fire and steel all around them. The bombs dropped from fifteen thousand meters fell at approximately ninety-six meters per second. Which meant from the time they were released to the time they would reach the surface was just over two and a half minutes. That was how much time Remmy had to rescue the ground team and dust off.

The dropship roared in with the rear hatch already down. It settled just forty meters from where the three Marines were ducking enemy fire. Remmy had traded his Nelson LTX for an Ambrose Hill XOR. It was a dual-purpose gun that packed a heavy punch. The lower section was a grenade launcher with an eight-round revolving cylinder. The upper was a machine gun that fired Shock Wave kinetic rounds from an elevated straight magazine containing forty of the heavy rounds. He didn't bother aiming and just blasted away with the grenade launcher. He fired five rounds before the first one detonated. The grenades didn't have the range needed to hit the aliens, but they threw up clods of dirt and clouds of dust and smoke. After emptying the grenade cylinder, Remmy switched to the machine gun and blasted away in short bursts as the trio of Marines raced toward them.

Still, the aliens fired in their direction. The tracers were visible in the air as they streaked through the smoke and toward the Marines. The dropship was an easy target. It suddenly sounded like hail was falling on the aircraft as the bullets impacted and some even penetrated the ship.

"Hurry!" Remmy screamed.

But he wasn't the only person shouting. Rip was hit. The bullet impacted his right elbow, which was bent and sticking out slightly behind him as he ran. He grunted, fell, then screamed in pain.

Remmy started down the ramp, but Sergeant Thorne waved him back.

"I've got him!" Thorne shouted.

Dirk Oliver dropped to his knees and began shooting to give his comrades cover. Remmy stayed on the ship and joined in the fray. Sergeant Jay Thorne was thirty years old. He should have been a senior NCO but had missed promotion twice by sheer luck when his platoons completed missions without contacting the enemy. That meant he had the experience but not the combat to earn him a steady rise through the ranks. But he was no stranger to war. He had fought in the Caldee Rebellion before joining the special forces and saw combat on two recon operations on Mars. He turned toward Rip, letting his rifle dangle free on his harness and using both hands to drag Corporal Al "Rip" Van Winkle to his feet.

"We have to move, Marine!" He snarled.

Rip was in shock; the pain from his shattered elbow was nearly overwhelming. The large caliber bullet had nearly torn his arm off. The elbow was gone, and only a few blood vessels and tendons held his forearm to his upper arm. He held it like a newborn baby and staggered toward the dropship. Thorne wrapped his arm around Rip's waist and helped him hurry forward.

They were just at the bottom of the ramp when Thorne pushed Rip forward. They should have come together, but Jay Thorne turned, taking hold of his rifle with both hands and firing away. Dirk needed no order to understand the cover his friend was laying down so he could evacuate the battlefield. He sprinted to the ship, racing past Thorne and right up the ramp into the passenger compartment.

Thirty seconds to ignition, GIGI warned.

"We're leaving!" Remmy screamed as he stepped inside the compartment and hit the switch to close the ramp.

Thorne stepped onto it. He was still shooting and shuffling sideways when a series of tracers ripped him in half. Remmy knew that Sergeant Jay Thorne was dead. He died before the separate halves of his body hit the ramp. There was nothing anyone could do for him, but Remmy dove forward anyway. He landed hard on the metal, the heavy XOR bruising his chest, and grabbed hold of Thorne. With his right hand, he snagged the Sergeant's arm, and with his left hand, he latched onto Thorne's leg. Blood was everywhere. The scream of the engines and the pounding of bullets on the ship were joined with the alarms from the ship's systems, which had taken a beating from the alien onslaught. Altogether, they drowned out Remmy's bellow of disbelief.

The ship raced away from the scene just seconds before the bombs fell. Unlike before, the drones that dropped them had been so high overhead they were out of sight. And the Ashi warriors were so busy engaging the various threats around them they never bothered looking up. Most of the bombs fell and exploded without injuring anyone or doing any real damage, but others dropped among the enemy fighters and their skiffs. Fire, smoke, body parts and debris filled the air.

"Tex, Thompson, get out of there," Remmy managed to order as the dropship crashed.

It hadn't been very high and just slid over the grassy field a few kilometers from the fighting. The hatch hadn't even managed to close. Remmy got to his feet, looked at his slain friend and knew that it was a sight he would never forget. Then he dropped the XOR and snatched up his Nelson large bore automatic from the rack by his jump seat and waved for the others to follow him.

"We can't stay here," he said. "Let's move out."

The battle was over, although there were still some aliens with fight left in them. But there was so much dust and smoke around the aliens that all they could do was fire blind. Remmy and Sergeant Dirk Oliver took up positions on either side of Rip and led him toward the hill that Tex and Ricky Thompson were retreating from.

GIGI, we need another ship. Orion is down.

I have a shuttle inbound, GIGI replied. *ETA, forty-seven minutes.*

The time crunch had shifted from too little to too much. Remmy didn't know if he could keep everyone alive for nearly an hour. They hustled to the bottom of the hill and went to their knees in the tall grass.

"He needs a tourniquet," Dirk said.

"Get it done," Remmy replied. "I've got another ship coming, but it won't be here for an hour."

"Hurts so bad," Rip lamented.

Remmy opened his own trauma kit and pulled out a morphine vial. It was the timeless antidote to traumatic pain. The small vial had a needle on one end. Remmy pressed it into Rip's good shoulder and squeezed the plastic vial to inject the medicine into his body.

"This'll help," Remmy said.

Dirk pulled the latches on the strap that held Rip's gun to his body. Then, he used the strap to restrict the blood flow to his lower arm. Remmy handed over the roll of bandages from his trauma kit. Dirk added it to his own and secured Rip's lower arm to his body, so that it would not be torn off as they moved.

"What happened?" Tex said as he and Ricky Thompson ran toward Remmy and Dirk.

"Rip's hit," Remmy said. "Sergeant Thorne's gone. Tex, I need eyes on the enemy."

"Copy that," the rangy Marine said.

He hurried up the hillside.

"We need egress fast," Thompson said.

"It ain't coming," Remmy said. "Not fast enough anyway."

"Looks like there are still nearly a hundred aliens on their feet," Tex said over the comlink. "It's hard to tell through all the smoke. They're trying to get their bearings."

"How many skiffs?"

"Just one or two that aren't damaged," Tex said.

"If they get just one operational, we're in for it. We couldn't outrun those things even if Rip wasn't hurt. Alright, people, let's move while we can."

"Where to?" Dirk asked.

"Back toward the forest," Remmy said. "That's the only decent cover we're likely to get."

"And if they follow us?" Ricky Thompson asked.

"Then we kill them," Remmy said. "That part of the plan hasn't changed."

"For Sergeant Thorne," Dirk said.

"Sergeant Thorne," Ricky echoed.

"Yes," Remmy said. "We'll get some payback for Jay. Tex, we're moving out."

"On my way, Master Sergeant."

"Get Rip on his feet," Remmy ordered. "You two keep him moving. Tex and I will cover our retreat. Stay away from the dropship. It's going to attract the enemy."

"What about Sergeant Thorne's body?" Ricky asked.

"They can't hurt him now," Remmy said; the image of Jay's body torn in two by enemy fire flashed in his mind again unbidden and the tired Master Sergeant nearly threw up. "Go!"

And, just like that, the chase began.

CHAPTER 32

CAPTAIN DARIUS and Commander Lee retraced their steps. At the gravity shaft they floated up the park, then went into the starboard side residential complex. They had both explored the area before. It was like a luxury hotel with wide corridors. The floors were made of slabs, what appeared to be a marble or alabaster that was highly polished. There were chrome accents on the walls and the lighting was both soft yet completely illuminating. Despite having been unoccupied for hundreds of years, there was not a speck of dust anywhere to be seen.

Unlike a human-designed structure, there were almost no hard angles. The corridor had an arched roof and was curved instead of straight. The apartments, likewise, weren't boxy or uniform. Every dwelling was unique. Many had doorways on the opposite side of the corridor from the park, then on the inside, they rose up or dove under the corridor so that every single apartment had a view of the park with its walking paths, streams, bridges, flowering shrubs, green meadows, floating pavilions, and herds of exotic animals.

But Darius wasn't interested in the residential area or the architecture of the dwellings. His entire focus was on finding and stopping the invaders. They made it through the residential area and into the research section of the ship. No one knew if the labs had been for education or the development of new technologies. There were wide rooms that were part workshop, part educational areas where either the Arodoni had taught or worked together. No one could say for sure. Each one was filled with tools and equipment, much of it so alien that it hadn't been identified yet. Nash's engineers had taken a pass through that section of the ship, but their main focus had been on the engine rooms beyond.

Just before Darius and Lori Lee reached the massive compartments that were built around sections of the even more gargantuan engines, they ran into Connor O'Dell and his two alien companions.

"Captain!" Connor called out.

"I don't have time right now, Mr. O'Dell," Darius said.

"But you're hunting the Ashi warriors who boarded the ship, yes?"

"We are," Darius said.

"They're in that compartment," he said. "Two of them. They're armed with laser rifles."

"You're sure?"

Nurek stepped forward, holding the small translation device. "We have observed them through the viewports."

"Show me," Darius ordered.

Connor O'Dell and the alien Dudonus weren't part of his crew, and yet they hurried to one of the lab rooms and pointed toward a long, wide transparent wall that overlooked the engine compartment. There were no lights on in the workshop, but bright light was clearly visible through the transparent wall.

"This must have been some sort of observation lab," Connor said. "I think they may even have computer controls for the engines in here, but it's clearly designed to allow you to see into the engine compartment."

"Why?" Lori Lee asked.

"I have no idea," Connor admitted.

Nurek had an idea that he ventured forth. "It might be possible to flood the engine compartment with gas," he ventured.

"The engines are all electric," Darius said. "They don't run on fuel."

The alien's eyes grew wide. It was obvious he had never heard of a starship that was purely electric.

Producing that amount of energy without the Arodoni Power Core would be impossible. Even ships with fusion reactors used to produce electrical power needed fuel to feed into the fusion core. Humanity had tried to build efficient fusion engines, but they were notoriously hard to maintain and often had disastrous meltdowns.

"But there are canisters of heavy gases here," Nurek said, pointing to the tall, metal containers. They were all labeled in the strange, flowing script of the Arodoni.

"Sir," Lori Lee said. "It might be possible to release some of that gas into the engine compartment."

"It could damage the engine," Darius said. "And we have no idea if it would even stop the Ashi."

"Nitrogen Dioxide is lethal to the Ashi," Nurek said. "The hemocyanin in their blood cannot process it."

"It's lethal to humans also," Connor said.

"Humans?" Nurek asked.

Darius quickly changed the subject. "Do we have Nitrogen Dioxide?"

"Yeah, the gases have symbols that our guests identified."

"Show me," Darius said.

He followed Connor to the row of large gas canisters. They were as tall as he was and nearly as wide. The torpedo-shaped containers had valves at the top.

"This one," Connor told Darius before dropping his voice and whispering. "I think they know we aren't Arodoni."

"You told them?" Darius whispered back.

"No, but the fact that we know so little about the ship and can't read the writing on the containers here is a pretty good indication that we aren't the original builders of this ship."

"Fine, I'll deal with it, once we're out of danger," Darius said.

Beside the large gas canisters were smaller containers that appeared to be made of glass. It didn't take a leap to recognize the lid on the small bottles was designed to fit on the valve atop the larger gas canisters. Darius picked one up and attached it to the valve on the Nitrogen Dioxide container. For a few seconds, there was the sound of air under pressure passing through a narrow opening. When it quit, Darius removed the glass container.

"Commander Lee, do you know the way into that engineering compartment?" Darius asked.

"I do, sir," Lori Lee replied.

"Take me there."

They walked past the two aliens. Nurek watched with a knowing eye while his companion, Ludus, seemed confused. Darius heard them speaking softly in their own melodic language. He didn't know if it was going to be a problem for the Dudonus that he and the crew were not Arodoni. In fact, he guessed it wasn't really an issue that they were human but that they hadn't shared the truth with their guests.

His speculation about the aliens would have to wait. There was a battle raging in the Casa system. And if Darius didn't find a way to eliminate the Ashi infiltration team, the *Renegade's* crew would be in serious trouble.

"What's the plan, sir?" Lori Lee asked.

"If we go in guns blazing we might get them, might not," he said.

"We might also damage the engines."

"Agreed, so you're going to open the hatch, I'm going throw in this container of Nitrogen Oxide, and we're going to hope that it breaks."

"Releasing the gas and killing the bad guys."

"Is that too much to ask for?"

"Maybe, maybe not. What about the engine?" Lori pointed out. "How do we fix that if there's toxic gas in that compartment."

"We don't," Darius said. "We send in the droids and hope they can repair it."

"Are you sure that gas isn't flammable?" Lori asked.

"I don't think so."

"What's it used for?"

"I'm no chemical engineer, but I'm pretty sure it's used to help make rocket fuel and explosives."

"Sounds flammable to me," Lori Lee pressed.

"It's been a long time since I took chemistry, but I'm fairly certain it's an oxidizing agent. It helps things that burn to burn hotter and faster, but it doesn't burn by itself."

"You're call then," she said. "We can use the gas or I'll lead the charge."

"The gas," Darius said. "Open the hatch."

The controls on the hatch, like those throughout the ship, were designed for the Arodoni. In certain places, such as the command section, those controls had been swapped for human hands. But the hatch that opened the engineering compartment was still Arodoni. Fortunately, Henry Nash had small keys printed up that mimicked the tiny, three-prong fingers of the Arodoni. Commander Lee put hers into the control panel and turned it.

The hatch swung open and Darius threw in the canister. He heard it shatter just as Commander Lee closed the hatch again. The pair of them hurried back to the lab that overlooked the compartment.

"Did it work?" Darius asked.

"Nothing yet," Connor said.

The Ashi were massive. Both of the intruders in the compartment had on flight suits but no helmets or breathing masks. They had laser rifles in hand. One was facing the long corridor Darius and Lori Lee had started down before turning back after finding the bodies of the slain crew members. The other faced the door that they had just tossed the canister through.

"We don't even know for certain that there was anything in that canister," Darius said.

"Or how fast it might work even if there was Nitrogen Dioxide in it," Lori Lee said.

Nurek made a purring noise. The translator supplied the expression in English.

"It will only take a tiny amount," he said. "It is on the list of toxic substances and outlawed in the Imperium."

"Look!" Connor said.

The Ashi were starting to sway as if they were dizzy. One went to his knees and used his rifle like a crutch. The other toppled over face down. The final Ashi warrior roared a deep-throated bellow of rage, then collapsed on the floor.

"Are they dead?" Connor asked.

"Looks like it," Lori Lee said. "You want to go in there and check?"

"That would be foolish in the extreme," Connor replied.

Lori chuckled.

"She was teasing, Mr. O'Dell. Commander Lee is going to stay here and keep tabs on the aliens. I'll have Ensign Stanislaus see if he can get more maintenance droids down here to repair the damage the aliens caused. Remember, keep your comlinks on."

"Aye, Captain," Lori Lee said.

"We're not out of the woods here. There could be more of them on the ship," Darius said. "Until we do a complete sweep, we can't be sure."

The only problem was the fact that there weren't enough humans on the *Renegade* to do a thorough sweep. But they would have to do their best.

"I'm returning to the Bridge," Darius continued. "Until we've finished dealing with the Ashi, I'm going to ask our guests to wait for the answers to their questions. Now is not the time for a lengthy discussion."

As the translation device transferred his words into the Dudonus language, Nurek and Ludus bowed.

"Be careful, Captain," Lori Lee said.

"Always," he told her, even though it wasn't true. Sometimes, he threw caution to the wind. He was human, after all, and there were times when his emotions got the best of him.

As he set off jogging back through the park, a shotgun in his hands, his laser rifle slung across his back, and his mind weighed down with the fear that there might be more saboteurs on the ship, he forced himself to consider the possibility that Nurek or Ludus, perhaps even both of them, were behind the Ashi gaining entrance to the *Renegade*. They could be enemy spies pretending to be victims. He would have to be careful what he revealed about himself to them.

Pushing all his doubts and fears aside, he focused on his breathing and hoped there wouldn't be any more surprises in store for the crew of the *Renegade*.

CHAPTER 33

RUNNING for his life wasn't fun. Remmy and the survivors from the Orion had just reached the trees of the forest when the Ashi began to fire in their direction.

"Take cover!" Tex shouted.

Fortunately, the trees were very good cover. The high-caliber bullets fired by the enemy's mechanically assisted rifles chewed into the wood but didn't pass completely through. Remmy slid down behind a large tree.

"They're still shooting high," Dirk said.

"We'll crawl if we have to," Ricky said.

There were limbs falling and bits of wood from the bullet impacts, making the space around them feel dense and dangerous.

"How many do you count, Tex?" Remmy asked.

"Fifty, sixty, maybe," he replied.

Remmy could see through the trees. They hadn't gone far into the forest and the aliens were coming out of the dust cloud. He took aim with his LTX, made sure the firing indicator was on burst mode, and started shooting. The armor the aliens wore covered their bodies, but their legs were vulnerable. The explosive rounds from Remmy's rifle punched into the thick muscle and sent bullet fragments tearing even deeper. Bones were shattered and arteries severed, but the warriors' return fire was getting dangerous.

Tex had discarded the long-range laser rifle and was shooting back with his M88. The depleted uranium bullets were so hard they passed right through the unarmed parts of the aliens but couldn't penetrate their armor.

"Fall back," Remmy said. "Stay low."

Sergeant Dirk Oliver and Ricky Thomson were already on the move with the wounded Rip Van Winkle between them. Remmy and Tex followed, crawling at first, then as they got into a thicker part of the forest, they got to their feet and ran.

It didn't take long for the shooting behind them to stop. Remmy sent Tex up a tree to see if he could make out what the enemy was up to.

"They're loading up," he said. "Looks like they've got a couple of skiffs still working."

"Head back down here," Remmy told him. "We'll wait to see where they go."

"Can't see 'em down there, Sarge," Tex pointed out.

"Don't worry, GIGI can," Remmy said. "Maybe we'll get lucky and they'll push on to the north."

"You think they'll still try?" Dirk asked. "They're down from a thousand to less than a hundred. What could they possibly accomplish?"

"Destruction, mayhem, maybe even revenge for us taking their leader," Remmy said. "How's Rip?"

"Hurting," Ricky Thompson said. "The morphine is wearing off."

Master Sergeant Steel, the Ashi warriors are taking their skiffs south into the forest, GIGI warned.

"Heads up, people, the Ashi are coming this way," Remmy said.

"What do we do now?" Tex asked. "Can't outrun those skiffs on foot."

"How long until a drop-ship arrives to get us?" Dirk asked.

"Thirty-three minutes," Remmy said.

"That's too long," Ricky Thompson complained.

"If we can't run, we've only got two options," Tex said. "Hide or fight."

"I'm not hiding," Remmy said. "As long as we stay in the thick part of the forest, they'll have to abandon their skiff to get to us."

"They don't have to get close with those cannons they're carrying," Dirk said.

Remmy's mind was racing. So far, the aliens had been predictable. They were lethal fighters but not adept at strategy and tactics. The Marines had gotten the edge on their enemy time and again, but it felt like their luck was running out.

"What about the drones?" Tex asked.

"They're useless as long as the enemy is in the forest," Remmy said. "The best we can hope for is that they manage to keep tabs on them."

"Probably not likely in this canopy," Dirk said.

The trees on the alien world were thick and tall. Unlike trees on Earth, they didn't appear straight and didn't have a single trunk. Instead, from one root, a central tree started, then branched out in opposite directions over and over again. Fifty feet up, branches began to grow with broad, crimson leaves that blocked out the light from above.

"We'll circle," Remmy suggested. "They'll be coming in straight and won't expect us to swing around and engage them from behind."

"Why fight them at all?" Ricky Thompson said. "Why not just stall for a while until our dropship reaches the LZ?"

"That's not our job," Remmy said.

"Live to fight another day," Ricky argued. "We engage in this forest and we could all be killed."

"And if we don't, the enemy might reach the locals," Remmy said.

Ricky shrugged. Remmy didn't blame him for wanting to do whatever it took to survive the battle. And if the locals couldn't defend themselves after what the Marines had done, was that really something the humans should worry about? Perhaps not, Remmy admitted to himself, but he didn't like the idea of just running away.

"I won't force anyone to join me," Remmy said. "But I won't just leave now. Our mission is to wipe the Ashi off this world completely. I won't rest until we've done that."

"I'm with you, Master Sergeant," Tex said.

"It's going to be hard to fight and keep Rip alive," Dirk said. "I'll keep Ricky with me, and we'll get Rip to safety."

"Sounds like a plan," Remmy said. "But watch your six. There's no guarantee the aliens didn't split up."

They all stayed together at first. Remmy used the compass in his helmet's mapping app to guide them through the dark forest. Despite the danger, they moved quickly. Remmy took point while Ricky, Dirk and Rip stayed together, helping the wounded Marine to keep up. Tex brought up the rear. It was standard formation, but they were moving through alien territory and the Marines were all acutely aware of the fact that they were outnumbered more than ten to one.

Five minutes passed quickly with no sign of the enemy. Another five minutes and they were back into the section of the forest that had been chewed up by the heavy fire of the enemy. Remmy raised his hand in a fist to stop his companions. They weren't wearing sealed helmets that would allow them to talk without being heard ... with no idea where the enemy might be hiding, it was better to proceed with caution.

Remmy turned, pointed at Dirk, and then motioned for him to move off to his left. He then pointed at himself and Tex, then held up two fingers, followed by three fingers, indicating that he would join the trio in twenty-three minutes.

Dirk gave a thumbs-up and then moved off with Ricky and Rip. Tex closed in on Remmy, but they didn't stay close together. That would make them an easy target. Instead, they stayed just in sight of one another and moved around to a wider trail through the trees. The hovercraft left no tracks and didn't disturb the ground, but it was a big vehicle that required space to maneuver through the trees. Remmy followed the trail, and soon, the skiff was in sight. The hovercraft had stopped, and most of the enemy warriors had spread out in search of the Marines. Only a few remained at the skiff.

It would have been best to be able to communicate with Tex, but they didn't want to risk being heard. They actually knew very little about the Ashi. How well they could hear or see was a mystery. Maybe it was as good as a human, or maybe better. Compared to most species on Earth, humans heard very poorly. So, instead of talking, Remmy motioned with his hands. He pointed at Tex and then held up his hand in the universal signal to stop. Then he put his flat hand over his fist to communicate that he wanted Tex to cover him.

They both turned and looked down the trail. They were hidden by a tree that was surrounded by thick shrubs. Around the skiff were four aliens that they could see. But Remmy knew there might be more. He moved carefully through the trees, angling around to come at the skiff from the side. Time was ticking by, but that played into their hands. Soon, the dropship would arrive to rescue them. In the air, they were faster than their enemy and with greater mobility.

Remmy looked hard, trying to see if he could spot more of the aliens. It wasn't the four guards around the skiff that he was worried about, but the aliens nearby that he couldn't see. The Ashi were too big to take out quietly. His combat knife would surely cut their throat, but he couldn't reach it. The Ashi warriors were thirteen feet tall. He would need to use his weapon to take them down, and that would make noise sure to draw the enemy's attention. But if he could take the guards out quickly enough, it might be possible to steal their hovercraft. He watched for several moments until he was certain that he had located the controls of the skiff. They were two simple foot pedals with no handles, control stick, or switches. There was no guarantee that Remmy could operate the skiff, but he intended to try.

With one final glance around, he raised his rifle and took aim. It wasn't good enough to wound the guards. A wounded enemy might be able to take a shot at him. He needed killshots and he needed to make them fast. He aimed for the nearest guard's head, selected semi-auto on his rifle and pulled the trigger. The alien's head snapped to the side as the bullet punched into his skull, then detonated inside, turning his brain into soup. But the shot also alerted the other three guards, who turned.

Remmy had one advantage. In the thick foliage, the enemy couldn't locate him immediately. Their big machine guns, linked to their armor by thick mechanical arms, weren't simple to move. They were designed to give the shooter support for the powerful weapon, but they couldn't be swung around as easily as Remmy handled his LTX.

Before the enemy could locate him, Remmy killed the second guard. The last two opened up with their machine guns. Remmy was kneeling, both for cover and stability, with his rifle. The Ashi were essentially shooting from the hip, which was as tall as Remmy was. The bullets ripped through the trees above him. Remmy was about to shoot the third guard but Tex beat him to it. The guard's face seemed to cave inward under the impact of the depleted uranium bullet. The last guard, hearing the report of Tex's rifle, turned to fire in that direction. Remmy's shot was a bit too high. The bullet hit the thick upper section of the alien's skull and ricocheted away. The guard staggered and then fell.

There was no time for a follow-up shot. Remmy charged out of the trees and dove onto the skiff. He slid across the surface, got to his knees and lunged for the controls. From the ground, the wounded guard tried to crawl up onto the skiff. He was dazed but so big and strong that he managed to pull himself up just as Remmy rotated the vehicle around. He could hear large bodies crashing through the trees. Remmy leaned his weight forward on the pedals and the hovercraft moved back down the trail.

The two pedals were like directional levers. The skiff raced forward. Remmy barely managed to slow down for Tex to jump on.

By then, the dazed guard was rising to his feet. When Remmy accelerated again, he nearly lost control and crashed into the side of a tree. The impact crumpled the edge of the vehicle's flat surface and knocked the two Marines off their feet. Fortunately, they weren't thrown from the skiff, but the wounded guard was not so lucky. He fell backward and flipped off the platform.

"Go! Tex shouted as a group of enemy fighters raced out of the trees and onto the trail.

Remmy slid toward the controls and used his hands on the pedals. The skiff shot forward again. Remmy stayed on his stomach with only his head raised as he guided the hovercraft back through the forest. They weren't going exceptionally fast, but the aliens on foot were even slower. They fired at the Marines, but the trail wasn't straight and they were soon out of the enemy's line of fire.

In less than a minute, they were out of the forest and back onto the plain where the battle had taken place. Remmy rose up on his knees just as another group around a second skiff turned. The aliens had been seeing to the wounded, using large knives to put them out of their misery.

"This ain't good," Tex said.

The aliens, startled but quickly realizing what had happened, turned their weapons toward Remmy. He quickly pressed down on the right pedal, causing the platform to turn. Tex meanwhile fired on the aliens. The closest two went down from the kinetic energy of the depleted uranium smashing into their body armor. They weren't dead, but they were knocked off their feet. The others returned fire, forcing Remmy to zig and zag as they raced for the hill Tex had been on during the battle. It would have been all over for the two Marines if more gunfire from the edge of the forest hadn't saved them.

Unlike the group of aliens who had ridden into the forest on the skiff that Remmy had stolen, the other group only consisted of eight Ashi Warriors, and two of them were down from Tex's quick action. At the edge of the trees, Ricky Thompson and Dirk Oliver were waiting with Rip. They saw the skiff with Remmy and Tex come flying out of the trees, and when the aliens turned to fight, Dirk and Ricky mowed them down. The aliens had no cover. Dirk was shooting a Higgins Auto Repeater. It fired rapidly, ripping through the unprotected legs of the aliens. Ricky's rifle was a Sterner M88 Classic. The two Marines made quick work of the aliens and Remmy turned the skiff back toward the forest.

"Hot damn, that's what I'm talking about," Tex said as they slowed down near their friends.

"Nice ride," Ricky Thompson said. "Can I drive?"

"Next time," Remmy said. "How's Rip?"

"Still breathing," Dirk replied.

Tex helped pull the wounded man onto the skiff. Once he was secure, the other two hopped on, and Remmy took off. Unknown to the humans, the aliens were closing in. They opened fire from inside the forest. Fortunately, the trees blocked clear shots. Remmy pressed both pedals down as far as they would go, coaxing the hovercraft to full speed.

"Too late, you green bast—"

A series of shots hit the platform. They weren't close enough to endanger the Marines, but one blasted a chunk of metal straight into Ricky Thompson's knee. He screamed as he fell. Dirk covered his body in a protective gesture as the firing behind them faded.

"How bad is it?" Remmy shouted as they raced over the open terrain.

"Shrapnel," Tex said.

"He'll need medical attention," Dirk said. "It's best if we don't remove it."

"We're safe now, though," Tex said. "The Ashi can't catch us."

It was true, but even as the group breathed a sigh of relief, Ricky Thompson, groaning in pain as he lay on his back, pointed up. In a shaky voice, he asked, "What's that?"

Remmy was already slowing down. There was nothing in front of them to harm the skiff. He looked up and saw dark shapes tracing across the sky, trailing smoke. He knew instantly what he was seeing. It made him feel weak in the knees.

"Is that bombs?" Tex asked.

"Not bombs," Remmy said. "Escape pods."

"What?" Dirk asked.

"The second carrier ship," Remmy said. "It was disabled, knocked off course, but not destroyed."

"It's more of them?" Tex asked.

"Can't GIGI just use the drones to take them out?" Dirk asked.

"They're built to withstand reentry and even crash landings," Remmy said. "Nothing the drones carry can stop them."

"Things just went from bad to worse," Tex said. "I'm beginning to hate this world."

"We need to link back up with the Pegasus," Remmy said. "And figure out a whole new plan."

CHAPTER 34

"ARE YOU FINISHED?" Laila asked, her voice carried across the canyon by her comlink.

"Just got the last one set," Hugo McManus said.

"That's good, 'cause here they come," Leigh Ann Poh said.

What remained of Alpha and Bravo teams were positioned on a mountain overlooking what was the narrowest canyon on the trail through the mountains. Using their jump ship they had raced ahead of the alien horde and put Staff Sergeant Laila McPherson's plan into place.

"Good, now get the hell out of there, Sergeant," Laila ordered.

She had used all of their grenades, syncing them to a single detonator, which she held in one hand. The grenades could be thrown to detonate, but they also had tiny receivers which could be activated and synced to remote detonators for just such an occasion as the Marines found themselves in.

With their armor and heavy weapons, the group of aliens, around four hundred strong, were too well equipped to be ambushed by the handful of Marines.

"I'm clear," Hugo said after scurrying through a gap near the top of the canyon and reaching the Pegasus on the far side.

"Dust off," Laila ordered. "But stay out of sight."

"Roger that," Izzy replied.

Laila was on a tall peak directly ahead of the canyon. It was freezing cold and windy, but she had a great view of the canyon. At the far end of the narrow gorge was another set of high cliffs. Corporal Leigh Ann Poh was there serving as their lookout.

"You too, Corporal Poh. Head to the rally point."

"Copy that, Staff Sergeant. I'm moving out."

Just then, the dull sunlight broke through the clouds and the aliens on the skiffs came sailing up the trail and into view. They were packed onto the open platform hovercrafts. Each of the towering thirteen-foot-tall behemoths had a huge machine gun, the kind that humans could only attach to vehicles or on the sides of ships. The guns were attached to the aliens' armor, which made them even more difficult to kill. But improvisation was a virtue that the Space Marines embraced. There was no obstacle they couldn't adapt to or overcome.

The aliens came into the narrow valley by single file. The terrain made that necessary, but it was how the Ashi warriors had moved since coming out of their carrier ship several hundred kilometers to the north. There were nearly twenty of the skiffs, each with at least twenty warriors on board and ready to fight. Fortunately, the narrow gorge was long. It took patience to wait for the last of the hovercraft to come around the bend and into the narrow space. She could see the warriors studying the hilltops in expectation of an attack. But it wasn't Marines with guns that were waiting for them.

Fear and excitement made her hands tremble slightly as she lifted up the detonator. It was time to see if her plan was actionable. The tall sides of the canyon seemed perfect. They were craggy and thick with loose rock.

"Time to die," she said softly as she pressed the button on the detonator.

Instantly, forty separate explosions blasted rocks and debris from the sides of the canyon. The grenades broke sections loose and sent them tumbling down, but it wasn't just the rock knocked loose by the blasts. The chain reaction had weakened both sides of the canyon. As the rocks tumbled and fell, they knocked more loose. Within seconds of detonating the grenades there were landslides on both canyon walls. The dropship rose higher in the air to give the Marines a better view.

Laila watched, hardly breathing, as her plan came together even better than she had hoped. Clouds of dirt and dust billowed from the landslide and blocked her view of the bottom of the gorge where the aliens were, but not the sides of the canyon. She could see more and more of the rock and debris shifting, sliding, and tumbling down toward the bottom.

"Instant burial," McManus said. "That is beautiful."

"Nothing could live through that," Izzy added.

"We don't know that for sure," Laila said. "Pick up Leigh Ann, then keep circling. We stay here until we're certain."

"Copy that, Staff Sergeant," Izzy replied.

"Great plan, Staff Sergeant," Hugo added. "Seriously, one of the best tactical ideas I've seen in combat."

"Thanks, Hugo," Laila said.

She didn't let the praise go to her head, but she did agree that it seemed to have worked perfectly. Of course, it wouldn't have if the terrain hadn't been so well suited for the landslides, including the narrow valley below. They really had no idea how much of the rock and dirt had fallen on the aliens. It needed to be substantial to stop them, and she would have to wait for the dust to clear before they could know for certain.

"Staff Sergeant," Izzy said. "I have movement to the north."

"More Ashi?" Laila asked as fear blew its icy breath across the back of her neck.

If there were more they would have to fight in a more traditional means, which meant more risk to her platoon. They really needed to resupply before trying to take on another group of the hulking aliens ... but could they afford to wait? She didn't know. It was frustrating to think that they hadn't gotten all the Ashi warriors in their trap. What if the rockslide didn't incapacitate them? She simply didn't know what else to do.

"Negative, it's not the aliens. Looks like a lone figure. Big though," Izzy said. "It's hard to get a good look because of the mountains."

"Get closer, but stay out of rifle range," Laila said. "I'll wait here to see if any of the aliens survived."

"Can't imagine anyone surviving that," Hugo said.

"Agreed," Leigh Ann added. "They might still be alive, but not for long."

Laila felt the same as her platoon mates, but she feared that the big aliens had recognized the danger and found a way to negate it. They were twice the size of a human and incredibly strong. Anything was possible. It was hard to hope for the best while planning for the worst outcome.

"Staff Sergeant!" Izzy said. "I think it's the Lieutenant!"

"What?"

"Yeah, looks like his MECH suit," Izzy said. "I still can't raise him on comms, though."

"We should fly down, let him see us," Hugo suggested.

"Agreed. Confirm it's the Lieutenant and make contact one way or another," Laila said. "He might need medical assistance."

"Copy that," Izzy said. "GIGI is taking us down now."

All Laila could do was wait and that wasn't her strong suit. She was a woman who preferred taking action. It was a trait that served her well in combat, but it could drive her crazy, too, especially when a plan of action required her to wait on others.

She zoomed her HUD in on the ground of the canyon. It was still too dusty to see anything. And in the confined space it might take hours for the dust to clear. She was aware of the need to wait, but it was cold and she was impatient.

"It's him," Izzy said. "We're landing to pick him up."

"That's excellent news," Laila said, feeling relieved.

She didn't mind taking charge when she needed to. That was a Staff Sergeant's job. Most regular Marine platoons only had a Staff or Gunnery Sergeant whose job was to ensure that said platoon carried out their lieutenant's orders. And in battle, it was not unusual for a platoon or group of Marines to get cut off from their commanding officer. In that instance, the senior NCO took charge, which was exactly what Laila had done when Lieutenant Colt went missing. But she had felt his absence, too. Alpha and Bravo teams had lost too many members. Corporal Jack Fortnoy was dead and Gunny Rand was incapacitated. They had the Gunnery Sergeant strapped into the dropship. He was conscious but uncommunicative. Laila hated seeing injuries and death, even to the Marines she wasn't close to. And with their limited numbers, everyone they lost was a significant loss.

"Staff Sergeant McPherson, what's our sitrep?"

"It's good to hear your voice, Lieutenant. We tried to find you, sir, after the initial assault."

"It's no surprise you couldn't. We can discuss my misadventures later. What's going on with the enemy?"

"We set grenades into the mountains, sir, just inside a narrow gorge," Laila explained. "When the enemy entered, we blew the charges, creating landslides that we hope have buried the Ashi warriors completely."

"I see," Lieutenant Colt said. "Good work. We'll continue circling and watching for enemy movement."

It took over an hour. Laila felt like a human icicle, but she survived the wait. When the dust finally settled, there was no movement in the valley and no sign of the enemy.

"Lieutenant, the entire trail is covered," Laila happily reported. "No movement, no sign of the enemy."

"Looks like a total victory," Colt said. "I just got word from GIGI that Master Sergeant Steel is coordinating an attack to the north. I say we pick you up and head that way. We'll leave drones here to keep an eye on things. They can notify us if the enemy manages to dig their way out."

Laila didn't see how that could be possible. Perhaps if rescuers rushed to the gorge and worked tirelessly they might be able to save a few of the Ashi warriors, but she didn't think they could find a way out on their own. And no one was going to help the Imperial warriors. Her plan had worked; she only wished she had thought of it sooner. Perhaps then, Jack Fortnoy would still be alive.

CHAPTER 35

"CAPTAIN ON THE BRIDGE!" Pete Best announced as Darius finally returned.

His run back through the ship from the engineering section had taken twenty minutes. He was breathing hard and sweating as he dropped into his Captain's chair.

"Report," he said.

"Sir, we've taken out two more of the Ashi battleships," Vivian Ramos said. "And devastated the fighter squadrons before they could get close enough to use more EMPs."

"Outstanding," Darius said. "Any word from the planet?"

"No sir," Vivian said. "GIGI reported that one of the carrier ships made it to the surface intact and that the Marines were preparing to engage. We've heard nothing since then."

"I want to start moving back toward Casasil," Darius said as he looked at the holographic plot. "They're all running away."

"Can't see where they hoped to go," Nash said. "There are no other habitable worlds in this system. No space platforms either."

"And only one hyperspace portal?" Darius asked.

"That we know of," Vivian said. "And it's been seeded with something. We're still too far out to get a decent scan."

"So, swing us around wide of the portal but close enough to get your scan," Darius said. "Lieutenant Ramos can set the course. Lieutenant Nash, what's the status on the engines?"

"Still down to the port engine, sir. I'm not as familiar with the technology as I should be, Captain. I know what's wrong, but I can't say exactly what it means or how to fix it."

"We can't get in there anyway," Darius said. "We opened a canister of Nitrogen Dioxide in the engine compartment to deal with the infiltrators who were holding that area. It worked, but we'll need to find a way to vent that area before sending our people inside. What's our mobility with just one engine?"

"Everything you could want, sir," Nash said. "The Port engine has enough power to operate all directional thrusters and enough output to give you fifty-five percent thrust. We won't reach the top speed that the *Renegade* is capable of normally, but it's still much faster than we've needed so far, Captain. Even enough to make the jump into hyperspace."

"That's excellent news," Darius said as he pressed the button to activate the comlink that was built into his chair. "Dr. Lanski, any word on your patient?"

There was a slight pause, and then the ship's surgeon spoke up. "It's touch and go, Captain. He's alive for now and that's all I can say. There was major blood loss. If he was human, we could give a transfusion, but..."

"Do all you can, doctor; that's all anyone can ask."

"The good news is that while the gunshots were significant, they aren't in and of themselves life-threatening," Lanski continued. "Scans show all vital organs intact and functioning. There's no internal bleeding. Brain waves are active. I don't really have a baseline to compare it to, but it's not dead. So, blood loss is the most pressing issue. I took the chance and started an IV drip. It's just saline, but I'm hopeful it's enough to keep his hearts beating."

"Sounds like you've got things under control. What about Spaceman Ramis?"

"First and second-degree burns on her hands," Lanski said.

"Nothing that can't be treated and fixed. She's also got a minor concussion, so I'm keeping her here under observation, but scans all came back normal."

"Very good," Darius asked. He wanted to ask about the bodies of the crew members who were killed, but he decided not to do that on an open channel in front of the officers on the Bridge. That information could wait for a more discrete moment of inquiry.

Darius hit a different button that connected him to the Systems Control room. "Ensign Stanislaus, report."

"Aye, Captain, all systems are in the green with the lone exception of the starboard engine," Alex said. "Maintenance systems are active. The engineering droids should be down in the engine compartment soon."

"Very good. Any luck on the security concerns we discussed?"

"Negative, sir. The Arodoni had no such systems in place. No surveillance either. It seems they valued privacy and weren't concerned about internal security on the ship. There's plenty of computing power, though, sir. I think we could pull components from the *Jericho* or have the manufacturing section print up some security cameras. It wouldn't take more than a few days to get everything we need set up and running."

"Plan to do that once we're clear of the Ashi in this system," Darius ordered. "I want eyes and ears in all three hanger bays, plus any other ways into the ship."

"Aye, Captain, I'll start writing the code now, sir."

Darius felt a little better, but he wanted his Marines back on board. He wanted a full sweep of the entire ship, along with an active security system and contingencies for both boarding parties and EMP attacks. The problem was the lack of manpower. He simply didn't have enough personnel to do everything the ship really needed ... and after losing six crew members to the Ashi boarding party, his crew would be stretched even thinner.

"Course set to bring us around the portal and back into orbit around Casasil," Vivian announced.

"Lieutenant Nash, I want maximum speed, but keep an eye on our systems. I don't want to push us too hard."

"Aye, maximum speed, Captain. Engaging port engine now, fifty percent power."

"Lieutenant Best, can we still target the enemy?" Darius said.

"I'll have to factor in our speed, but it shouldn't be a problem, sir, as long as we're oriented in the right direction."

"Very good. Let's clean this place up. Make your first target and fire at will."

"Aye, Captain, targeting Tango Four now."

It took six hours, but by the time they cruised past the hyperspace portal, there were only three enemy ships left in the system.

"Sir, I'm picking up some strange readings," Vivian Ramos reported.

"From the portal?"

"Negative, sir, from one of the carriers."

"I thought it was disabled and out of the fight?" Darius said, getting up from his seat and moving to where she was hunched over a screen in her console.

"Look," she said, tapping the screen with one finger. "It looks like escape pods."

"They're abandoning ship," Darius said, turning to Ensign Bertoli. "Any communication from those pods?"

"Negative, Captain. I'm not picking up anything. No chatter between the Ashi ships. The system is quiet."

"Alright, I know you're all tired. It's been a very long day," Darius said. "But we've still got people down on the surface of Casasil. Let's stay alert and make sure we don't miss anything here."

Darius tapped out an order to the culinary staff to have coffee and refreshments brought to the Bridge. It wasn't the rest they all needed, but it would have to do until they were certain there was no more danger to the ship or the Marines on the ground.

"What about the portal, Lieutenant Ramos? Any idea what Tango Seven dropped there?"

"Some sort of mines, I think," Vivian said. "All I'm getting is magnetic readings."

"Lieutenant Best, launch the drone," Darius ordered.

"Aye, Captain, launching Victor One now, sir."

They all waited and watched. The drone wasn't very big, about the size of a family hovercar. It flew from the *Renegade* straight toward the portal.

"ETA?" Darius asked.

"We're ninety thousand kilometers out," Vivian said.

"Drone speed is a thousand KPH and climbing."

"Alright, what about the escape pods?" Darius asked.

"Only a third are anywhere near the planet," Vivian said.

"We gonna rescue the aliens?" Henry Nash asked.

It was a reasonable question. In the Sol system, an escape pod had to be rescued no matter where it originated from or who might be in it. That was a law respected and obeyed by everyone. But they weren't in the Sol system and as much as Darius would have liked to think that he cared about life no matter what the species or race, he knew that bringing Ashi warriors onto the *Renegade* was a terrible idea. The ship had no brig. They might be able to rig up a holding cell, but there was no guarantee the giant aliens couldn't find a way to thwart it. And just five infiltrators had already wreaked havoc on the ship. Darius had no desire to give his enemy another chance to harm his ship or his crew.

"Not this time," Darius said. "I'll put it in the log. This is my decision. I'll own it and ensure it does not reflect on any of you."

"I doubt anyone here would disagree with that decision," Vivian said.

"You think a third of the pods will land on the planet?" Darius asked.

"No, more like a quarter of them. Some will bounce off the atmosphere, and some will make it through but land in the ocean or some other inhospitable environment."

"How many is a quarter?" Pete Best asked.

"Around four hundred pods," Vivian said.

"And how many warriors to a pod?" Henry asked.

"That's impossible to know," Vivian said. "Based on the side of the pods and the anatomy of the Ashi, I'd guess eight to ten."

"As many as four thousand enemy fighters," Pete Best said. "That's outrageous."

"From what I can see, the pods have no flight controls," Vivian said. "They aren't being guided toward the planet. They could come down all over. Four thousand enemy combatants spread across several continents in both hemispheres."

"They don't give up easily," Darius said.

"What about the other pods?" Nash asked.

"If they get picked up, they'll be okay, but I don't see any of the other ships moving toward them. The Ashi battleships are still running for the edge of the heliosphere."

"Ensign Bertoli, prepare to send a message to the other ships in the system," Darius ordered.

"Aye, Captain, go ahead."

"It has come to our attention that the disabled carrier ship near Casasil has ejected their emergency escape pods," Darius said in a clear voice. "As Captain of the *SDF Renegade,* I hereby pledge to allow any ship willing to pick up the pods free and safe travel to do so. I repeat any ship willing to pick up the escape pods can do so without fear of being fired on by us. That is all."

He waved a hand, and Jacee Bertoli nodded. "It's sent."

"Think you'll have any takers, sir?" Henry asked.

"I'm curious to see," Darius replied.

"I don't understand," Pete Best said. "We showed no mercy to the ships we were fighting earlier. We must have killed thousands on those vessels. So, why offer the enemy a chance to rescue the escape pods?"

"It's been a tradition in human warfare for thousands of years," Darius said. "The enemy doesn't know us. I want to show them we are formidable but not without mercy."

The coffee arrived, along with snacks that were high in protein and fat but low in carbohydrates, that might make the crew members even more sleepy. Darius skipped the food. He was hungry but he settled for a large mug of coffee. The bitter, hot brew warmed him from the inside out and the caffeine gave him a jolt of energy that helped him to focus.

Victor One never reached the portal. Halfway through its journey, some of the devices that were seeded around the hyperspace link began to move. They suddenly raced through space straight toward the drone. Pete did his best to evade, but the devices followed. The moment they made contact, they exploded.

"Mines," Henry said. "Looks like we may be here a while."

"No one can come through, either," Vivian said. "That seems extreme."

"The Ashi want us here," Darius said. "If they can't defeat us, they can trap us in the system."

"Actually, sir, I can take those mines out with our lasers," Pete Best said.

"We know that," Darius said. "The enemy doesn't. If this were a standard Fleet ship, we wouldn't have the power to destroy all those mines."

"Not without refueling," Nash said. "And since we're not a Casasil ship either, there's no guarantee that we can get what we need here."

"Desperate," Vivian said. "But I suppose it makes sense. Would the Imperium really just write off an entire star system?"

"Who can say what they might do," Darius said. "They've thrown a lot of ships and manpower at us. Did you get any readings when the mines went active?"

"Negative, sir," Vivian said. "My guess is they're magnetically drawn to approaching vessels. No electronics, nothing fancy, just basic space mines with magnetic triggers."

"They want to drain our resources one way or another," Darius said. "Any response from our message?"

"None," Ensign Bertoli said. "They're still running, too."

"Cowards," Pete Best said.

"They don't think they can trust us," Henry Nash said.

"Can't blame them for that," Darius said.

"Should we take out the mines, sir?" Pete asked.

"Not yet," Darius replied. "They're keeping any more hostiles out of the system. Let's focus on what we can do to help the Marines; then we'll figure out our next step."

Everyone on the Bridge looked at him. Some nodded encouragingly. Others were clearly full of doubt. The one thing on everyone's mind was clear to Captain Darius. They all wanted to know when they could go home.

CHAPTER 36

A DROPSHIP LOWERED to the ground close to where the Marines were gathered together beside the alien skiff. Corporal Rip Van Winkle had been given another dose of morphine and Sergeant Dirk Oliver had the wound in Ricky Thompson's knee bandaged up. Together, the group of wounded and weary Marines boarded the ship and took off.

"What's the ETA for Kipbur?" Dirk asked.

"Forty-eight minutes direct flight," Remmy said. "But we need to touch base with the Perseus first."

"I wouldn't mind sticking around long enough to see what the Ashi do as well," Tex said.

"You disabled the skiff?"

"Yeah, it's toast," Tex said.

"Then they won't go far," Dirk said. "Master Sergeant, these men need medical attention. Let's drop them off at base and go back for the other ship."

"And what if that hour and a half is the difference between life and death to Alpha and Bravo teams?" Remmy asked. "We can't take the chance."

He could tell that Dirk disagreed. The truth was, they were all spun out over Sergeant Jay Thorne's death. Remmy knew a loss like that could wreck a platoon. Grief was like a wedge driving between them. He wanted to ensure that Ricky Thompson and Rip got the help they needed, but he couldn't just ignore his duty to get it.

"This entire mission is coming apart, Master Sergeant," Dirk said. "Good men are dying for people we don't even know."

"That's not true," Remmy said. "We may be in a foreign system, but we are still serving mankind."

"I don't see it that way. I think we should take the *Renegade* and go home."

"We can't take the risk that the Ashi Empire might follow us there," Remmy pointed out.

"Maybe they wouldn't have if we hadn't slaughtered their people," Dirk said. "I'm just saying what we're all thinking, Master Sergeant. Maybe this op was a mistake."

"They always feel like a mistake when someone dies," Remmy said softly.

"Only this time, who do I look at and say, my best friend died for you? I can't. The people here aren't just strangers. They're aliens ... and they should be defending themselves."

"They can't," Remmy said.

"Then maybe they deserve whatever they get."

"You don't mean that," Tex interjected."

"It's better than our own people dying," Dirk said.

"Sergeant Thorne didn't die for nothing," Remmy said. "And he didn't die for the Casians either. He fought for you and me, the Marine on his left and right. That's what we all fight for, Sergeant. And if we die, that's what we die for, so you can go home, so Tex can keep fighting. That's a sacrifice we can understand and support."

"Nah, I don't support it," Dirk said. "Not me. Not anymore. This was all a mistake. We never should have been here."

Remmy leaned his head back. He didn't even disagree with Dirk Oliver. He wished they had never left the Sol system, but he had agreed with the Captain's decision when Darius made it. And whether any of them liked it or not, it was the Captain's call. Their duty required only that they make the most of whatever terrible circumstances they found themselves in. Giving up was never an option.

The comlink sounded in Remmy's ear, shaking him from his own morbid thoughts.

"Orion, this is Perseus. Do you read? Over."

"I read you, Perseus. It's good to hear from you, sir," Remmy said, recognizing Lieutenant Colt's voice.

"We are headed north to your location," Colt said. "What's your sitrep, Master Sergeant?"

"Three casualties, sir. Corporals Thompson and Van Winkle are wounded. Sergeant Thorne was KIA."

There was a pause as Remmy collected himself and took a breath. "We've taken out the Ashi mobile platforms. There are still about fifty enemy troops below us. With your permission sir, I'd like to send Sergeant Oliver back to Kipbur while Corporal Fry and myself stay here and fight."

"Why not just use the drones, Master Sergeant? There's no need to put anyone else in harm's way."

"GIGI has tasked the drones with following and recording the escape pods," Remmy said. "I'm sure you saw them coming down, sir."

"Escape pods? This is the first I'm hearing of it."

"The carrier that was disabled jettisoned escape pods. GIGI was able to identify and track nearly three hundred and fifty pods that entered the atmosphere with good odds to survive the landing."

"That could be hundreds of Ashi combatants," Lieutenant Colt said.

"Or several thousand, depending on how many made it to the pods and survived the drop," Remmy said. "The fighting here isn't over, sir. I'm sorry to be the bearer of bad news but we aren't out of the woods yet."

"Agreed," Lieutenant Colt said with an obvious note of disappointment in his voice. "We're almost to your location. Wait for us. Gunny Rand is suffering some kind of mental breakdown. We'll transfer him to your ship and join you in the hunt for the final Ashi warriors you have left to kill."

"Roger that, sir. We'll land and start making a plan of attack."

The transfer was quick. Remmy only glanced at Gunny Rand once. Chad's face was slack, his eyes open but not looking at anything. He had to be supported to walk. Remmy felt terrible for his friend, but he wasn't surprised. The attack by the worm creature on Lawash had taken a toll on Gunny Rand. Despite his training and years of service, there were things that the mind just could no longer tolerate.

"You lost Jay," Laila said as she approached. "I'm so sorry, Remmy."

"Morale is pretty low," Remmy admitted. "What happened to Corporal Fortnoy?"

"He gave himself up," she said. "I should have seen it coming, but I missed it."

"Damn, we can't afford to be losing so many people."

"I said I didn't see it coming," she snapped at him. "Are you really laying this at my feet?"

"No," Remmy said, putting a hand on her shoulder. "I didn't mean that."

"What the hell did you mean, Master Sergeant?"

He knew that whenever Laila used his rank, he was in trouble. "What I meant," he said slowly, "is that people are starting to really feel the strain. Sergeant Oliver was openly questioning my orders just before you guys caught up with us."

"It's hard not to feel like we shouldn't be here," Laila said, a little calmer than before.

"Exactly," Remmy said. "I'm sorry I was careless with my words. I never meant that you were to blame."

"I'm sorry, too," Laila replied. "I guess I'm a little sensitive about it."

"And I should have expected that," Remmy said. "It's not your fault."

"He was my team member. It's my job to notice when people aren't acting right."

"We're in a new environment doing things no one has ever done before. Who's to say what 'normal' is anymore?"

The rest of the platoon formed up around Lieutenant Colt. They were down to just six enlisted Marines. Along with Remmy and Laila, there was Tex, Hugo McManus, Izzy Berry, and Leigh Ann Poh. Everyone was armed with their favorite rifles, as well as long-range laser weapons.

"What do you think, Master Sergeant?" Lieutenant Colt asked.

"The enemy is still in the forest," Remmy said. "Tex has had luck sniping at them with the Stinger. My suggestion would be to position ourselves on the hilltops and wait for the enemy to show themselves."

"What's the range on their machine guns?" Laila said.

"Five hundred meters effective range," Remmy said. "But they're still deadly a thousand meters out if you get hit by their high-caliber ammo."

"Armor don't stop it, that's for sure," Tex said.

"So, we stay out, what ... two and a half klicks?" Laila said.

"Yeah, we start that far and go farther. If the enemy presses forward, we leapfrog back," Remmy said.

"What if they outrun us?" Izzy asked.

"That won't happen," Remmy said. "They're slower than we are without the armor and heavy guns. With them, we won't have any trouble staying out of their range."

"It'll be dark soon," Lieutenant Colt said. "Let's make sure we're all ready to move quickly. Check your helmets for night vision. They may be planning to slip away in the dark."

"Or maybe they've given up," Leigh Ann Poh suggested.

"Wouldn't that be nice," Tex said.

"Remmy takes point," Lieutenant Colt said. "Corporal Fry is the best shot; he can take up position farthest out. I'll cover your retreats in my MECH armor. Plus, I've got a few long-range missiles that can do some damage if the enemy comes out together."

"And your comlink?" Laila asked.

"I'll have to use the one from a battle helmet, but otherwise, I'm all systems go," Colt said. "Let's get into position."

Remmy wanted more time with Laila. It was a fact of life. He had found the woman that he deeply cared for and despite his sense of duty and his love of combat, he simply couldn't get enough time with Laila. He switched over to a private frequency and pinged her to get her attention.

"Did you just ping me, mister?"

"I did," Remmy said as he started climbing up the nearest hill. "I missed you."

"Oh, so now you're flirting with me?" Laila teased. "Just like a man to totally misread the situation. Your timing needs work."

"Not you," Remmy said with a chuckle. "You're right on track."

"It's not easy being this good, but I manage," Laila said before shifting to a more serious tone. "Tell me you're okay, Master Sergeant. I don't think I can handle it if you break down on me."

"So far, so good," Remmy assured her. "I kinda feel like I was made for this."

"I was thinking the same thing, like everything in my career was leading up to these moments."

"Do you believe in a higher power?"

"I believe in God," Laila said. "Always have."

"And discovering what we have about other species in the galaxy and all, that doesn't shake your faith?"

"Nope, not one bit. I believe in a God who made the entire universe. It's not surprising to me that he made other beings on other worlds."

"I had the same thought," Remmy said, "But it's all a little blurry to me. I'm a pretty simple kind of guy. I like to know who the enemy is and where he is, so I can fight him straight up."

Laila laughed. "You are one of a kind, Remmy Steel. A true Marine grunt if ever there was one."

"I take that as a compliment."

"You should. It's the highest one I can think of."

Remmy reached the crest of the small hill. He didn't need to be extremely high. The edge of the forest was just over two kilometers away, and he had a clear line of sight. The sun was setting. Everything about the alien world looked strange and beautiful. He could see the Orion and the bodies of the Ashi they had fought and killed in their second ambush of the day. There was no guarantee that the aliens would come out of the forest. And if they did, it wasn't very likely that they would come out right where they had gone in. But, if so, he was watching and waiting. He had only one battery pack for the Hemlock Stinger. He unslung the heavy power cell and set it beside him. Should the enemy show up, he planned to make eight fast shots and leave the weapon behind. He didn't want the heavy battery to slow him down.

"I'm in position," he said over the main channel of his comlink.

"Copy that, Master Sergeant. Any signs of movement?" Lieutenant Colt asked.

"Negative, sir, it's quiet," Remmy said.

Nor did he mind that. It was better if the Marines were all in place, with weapons ready when the enemy arrived. It was possible that they had been watching from the forest. If so, they could have noted that two ships landed and only one took off again. They might know the Marines were waiting for them. Or it might be a long uneventful night. Remmy reached down and felt the cargo pocket on his left thigh. Inside, it had a few dissolvable caffeine pills that would help him stay awake. The cold would help with that, too. There was no snow, but as the sun went down, so did the temperature.

"Staff Sergeant McPherson is in place," Laila said.

"Copy that, Staff Sergeant," Micky Colt replied.

Eventually, as the sun set, they all radioed in. Six snipers spread across the plain. Remmy felt sure that even if the enemy fighters tried to sneak around them, there was too much open ground to cover for them to get a jump on the Marines.

"Any word from GIGI?" Colt asked.

"Not lately," Remmy said. "She's not here to give me intel, so I haven't checked in."

"Let's make sure the *Renegade* isn't trying to raise us on comms," Colt said. "I don't like being cut off from the ship."

"Me, either," Remmy said.

Checking in with GIGI took only a few seconds. The alien artifact was hundreds of kilometers away and yet he could speak to her as simply as he could form thoughts in his mind.

Any word from the Renegade?

Negative, Master Sergeant Steel. Should I ascend into orbit to ensure the Arodoni ship is still there?

If it wouldn't put too much stress on you while you track the escape pods.

All pods are down—three hundred and seventy-four of them. So far, eighty percent have had at least one occupant that has emerged. Total number of Ashi combatants from the pods is one thousand, four hundred, and eighty-six.

Are they all armed like the others?

Negative. Some carry only bladed weapons, but the majority have standard-issue laser rifles.

That's good news, Remmy said, already formulating a plan to go after the newcomers.

He related the details that GIGI had given him to Lieutenant Colt on the main channel of the comlink, so the rest of the platoon heard the update as well.

"Fifteen hundred of them," Colt grumbled. "And spread all over the place. It's going to take forever to wrap this up."

"Not necessarily," Remmy said. "The drones will shave that number down. What's left the locals can take care of."

"They're not fighters; you said so yourself," Laila pointed out.

"True, they are not. But if we can teach them to fly the dropships, we could mount some guns and let them take down the Ashi from the air. Their laser rifles only have an effective range of a few hundred meters."

"Interesting idea," Colt said. "We'll have to see what the locals think."

"Give a man a fish and he'll eat for a day, but teach a man to fish ..." Izzy said.

"And he'll need a boat, new tackle and lots of time on the lake," Tex joined in.

It was an old joke but everyone chuckled. Remmy liked anything that reminded him he was a human with a rich culture and fine traditions. It had never meant anything to him before, but since leaving the Sol system, he held tight to anything from his old life.

"Spoken like a man with experience," Leigh Ann Poh said.

"Oh, yeah," Tex said. "My daddy lived on the lake every weekend in the summertime. There weren't many fish to be caught and he released every one he hooked, but that was his happy place. I spent many a fine weekend out on the water, yes, sir!"

"I prefer a spa," Leigh Ann said. "Facials, mani-pedis and bottomless cocktails. Maybe even a massage."

"You paint a lovely picture," Izzy said. "I'll take a nice restaurant and good shopping."

"Movies," Hugo said. "I used to spend the entire day at the movies when I had liberty. What about you, Master Sergeant?"

"Oh, I don't know. I enjoy a good bookstore."

"Now you're talking," Laila said. "Some good coffee and a comfortable chair."

"And nowhere you need to be," Remmy added.

"How old are you, Master Sergeant?" Tex asked.

"Yeah, do you need a cardigan?" Izzy teased.

"Very funny," Remmy replied. "Hilarious."

"Can't you get any book you want right on your tablet?" Leigh Ann Poh said. "Why pay more for a book on paper?"

"It's not the same," Laila spoke up. "There's a feeling you get browsing the aisles."

"And holding a real book in your hand," Remmy added. "It's

different. Don't get me wrong, I still read on my tablet, but there's nothing quite like turning actual pages."

"Does the Marine Corps have a retirement home?" Tex asked. "Cause sounds like you could be the director, Master Sergeant."

"What's your idea of a good night out, Lieutenant?" Laila asked.

It was a reasonable question, but Remmy suspected that Laila only asked it to change the subject. He felt a surge of affection for her. Not that he minded being teased. He understood the way humor relieved tension before a battle and, at times, he had encouraged it. Still, he found it endearing that Laila shifted the conversation away from him.

"An aged bourbon and a good cigar are hard to beat," he said.

"Spoken like a bachelor," Izzy said. "Cigars are nasty."

"No one wants to kiss an ashtray, LT," Leigh Ann Poh remarked.

Remmy was enjoying the banter, but GIGI broke through his thoughts with a message from Kipbur.

Master Sergeant, there are enemy forces near the capital.

What? Remmy asked.

Several pods came down around the city. I have been monitoring them for enemy movement. The occupants waited until dark to egress from their emergency escape vehicles. I regret to say there are more than my resources can stop unless I pull units from monitoring other groups.

How much time do we have?

Perhaps an hour before the enemy troops reach Kipbur.

Remmy dropped his laser rifle and jumped to his feet.

"Lieutenant, we have a problem," he said as he sprinted down the hillside. "Enemy forces are converging on the city."

"What city?" Colt asked.

"Kipbur," Remmy said. "Several hundred of them. GIGI can't stop them all."

"What about the Ashi in the forest?" Tex asked.

"Can't worry about them," Remmy said. "On foot, they won't be able to reach the city for days."

"I still don't want to lose track of them," Lieutenant Colt said. "I'll stay here and keep eyes on the enemy force in the woods. The rest of you go back and help defend the city."

Remmy would normally have argued, but Lieutenant Colt had resources in his MECH suit that none of the rest of the platoon had.

"Can't the locals defend their own city?" Leigh Ann Poh said.

"It's not just the city that's at stake," Remmy said. "Rip, Gunny Rand and Ricky Thompson are there, along with our med techs. There's too many Ashi converging on the city for Sergeant Dirk to fight alone."

"We're on our way, Sarge," Tex said.

"Lieutenant, do you want backup?" Laila asked.

"Negative. I can move pretty fast in this thing. Plus, I've got some long-range munitions that should prove effective. I won't put myself in harm's way."

"We'll be back as soon as the city is safe," Remmy said. "Don't be a hero, sir."

"Right back at you, Master Sergeant. I don't want to lose anyone else on this op."

"Agreed," Remmy said. "Good luck, sir."

"And to you, Master Sergeant."

The dropship was already rumbling to life. Remmy ran up the ramp and waved the others on. Time was short. It would take nearly an hour just to reach the city. By then, the enemy might already be attacking. He felt the tension like a strap around his chest that was slowly tightening. The Marines had done an outstanding job of stopping the Ashi forces, which, if left unchecked, would have taken control of the entire planet. Remmy didn't like to think of what the death toll could have been. From the stories he had heard, the Ashi didn't have any qualms about killing innocent civilians. And Master Sergeant Steel was not about to stand by and let that happen on his watch.

CHAPTER 37

COMMANDER LORI LEE had waited until the droids entered the engine compartment. They moved the bodies of the Ashi infiltrators before beginning their repair work. She was only too happy to see that they were dead and wouldn't be happy until their bodies were jettisoned from the ship, but she felt safe leaving the engineering section of the ship.

Maybe she should have hurried back to the command section, but instead, she took her time walking through the park. Despite the danger the ship was in, the herds of animals seemed completely at ease. She wondered how they managed to survive the sudden loss of gravity. Some had to have been hurt or killed. Yet those that survived seemed completely calm.

The air in the park was rich with fresh oxygen, the scent of flowers, and she could even smell the soil beneath her feet. It was unlike air on any human ship or space station. The air she had breathed for so long in her career was sterile. It passed through filters that removed the carbon dioxide and left the air completely void of any smells. Not that there was nothing to smell inside a warship. Metal, cooking food, sweat, body odor, and stringent cleaning chemicals gave warships a very unique environment. It was the polar opposite of the freshness and vibrancy of the air in the park.

At one point, her eyes watered. She was an officer in the SDF. Never had she fraternized with a crew member on board one of her ships. Her dedication to the job had been recognized. She learned from every section and specialty as she prepared to one day take the Captain's seat. But in all that time, she had never seen crew members die in the line of duty. And she had certainly never had anyone sacrifice themselves for her. The reality of what had happened with Donny Elgersma sat heavy on her conscious. She felt survivor's guilt … and fear. She had been seconds away from death and it was the first time she had ever come face to face with her own mortality.

There had been accidents on board her ships before. There had been casualties in the fighting on planets and space stations. Marines from her ships had fought and died, just never in her presence. She found herself struggling emotionally with the heavy toll the battle on the flight deck was costing her. At one point in her walk through the park, she stopped and cried. She even fell to her knees and prayed for the first time in her life.

Commander Lee was a practical woman. She had always been able to focus on the tasks before her and wasn't much for hypotheticals or philosophy. She knew that many people believed in God, but she didn't count herself as one of them. Yet, with the guilt and fear nearly crushing her, she couldn't help crying out, "I'm sorry. I'm sorry."

In truth, she wasn't sure if she was apologizing to God or to Donny. In the moment, she just needed to say it. She needed to be heard by someone who could hear it and accept the apology. When her emotions settled somewhat, she got back to her feet and kept walking. Movement was good. She was tired. Exhausted, really, but there was no rest for the weary during battle. But she hadn't reached out to Captain Darius since his return to the Bridge. For the first time in her career, she wanted a break. She wanted to go back to Earth and let someone else carry the weight of an entire ship on their shoulders.

Trying to sort her feelings out, she realized that from a technical perspective, she had won the battle with the infiltrators on the ship. So why did it feel so terrible, she wondered. Why did it seem more like a loss? Was it because she cared for the crew? She did care; there was no doubt about that. Or was it more personal? Donny Elgersma had died to save her. She couldn't wrap her mind around that fact. What she knew of the weapons specialist was that he had a big personality. Some people liked him; some hated him. She had never known him to be kind or generous. He was often bombastic, crude, and sometimes intimidating, the classic bully under the right circumstances. Donny did his job well enough, though with no real ambition. Weapons specialists on Fleet vessels essentially moved and stored missiles, torpedos, and bombs. They were trained to handle dangerous objects and during a battle, supply them to the appropriate sections of the ship where they could be utilized. In times of peace, their job was to store, catalog, clean and train for battle. There was nothing in the job description or in Donny's behavior on board the *Jericho* or the *Renegade* that would have made her think he would sacrifice himself for someone else. Yet that's exactly what he had done. So why did Lee feel so terrible about it? She couldn't say.

Leaving the park, she made her way through what the crew was calling the commerce section of the ship. Most of the space was empty, but it did look like commercial space. There was room in just that one section of the ship for hundreds of stores. Five decks rose above her and there were storage compartments and space for workshops and production facilities below. The empty space gave her a strange feeling. It was like walking through a ghost town.

In what was thought of as the middle of the commerce section was the big statue and fountain. Commander Lee's thoughts about her life and the battle that had taken place on the flight deck were interrupted by the presence of Connor O'Dell and the two aliens.

They were near the statue, staring up at the only image of an Arodoni that had been found on the alien ship.

"Commander Lee, could you join us for a moment?" Connor said.

Lori had to hold back her emotions. She wanted to shout at him that she wasn't in the mood for a conversation. How could he not see that? It also seemed like he had overstepped his bounds by bringing the Dudonus to that section of the ship. But she was so disconnected at that moment that she didn't know if maybe Captain Darius had approved it. So, she kept her mouth shut and just nodded.

"I was just explaining to our guests that this statue was made by the original builders of the ship," he said.

"What have you told them about us?" She asked.

"Nothing," he said. "But they know we are not the Arodoni."

Nurek and Ludus were on the far side of the fountain. Lori Lee wasn't sure what they could hear, but she did notice that Connor had the translation device and that it was turned off.

"I guess that was pretty obvious," she said.

"Even before the episode in the engineering section," he confessed.

"So, what do you want from me?"

"Permission to tell them the truth," he said.

"I can't do that, Mr. O'Dell. Only Captain Darius can."

"I didn't want to disturb him," Connor said.

"That's probably wise."

"Will you let him know that we would like to discuss the issue with him when the time is right."

"Yes," she said. "I can do that. I just don't know when it will be."

"I understand. We shall make our way back to the park area once the Dudonus are finished examining the statue."

"Keep your comlink on," she told him. "We'll reach out as soon as we can."

He nodded and Lori Lee moved on. When she reached the

gravity ring, she contacted Ensign Stanislaus to make sure it was safe. After floating along to the command section, she went to the Bridge. Her post was in the Systems Control room, but she needed to see what the status of the ship was, first.

"Commander Lee," Darius said when she stepped through the open Bridge doors. "Everything okay?"

"Aye, Captain. I'm just returning from the engineering section."

"The droids have completed their repairs," Darius said. "All systems are back online and in the green."

"That's great news," she said, even though it felt wrong for some reason. How could everything be okay with Donny and the others dead?

"Did you speak to our guests before returning?" Darius asked.

"Actually, sir, Mr. O'Dell has taken them to the statue in the commerce section of the ship. He wants your permission to talk to them about who we really are."

The Captain took a deep breath. "What do you think about that, Commander?"

"Sir, to be honest, I'm not..." Tears unexpectedly filled her eyes and she looked away, blinking to try to hold her emotions in check.

Darius was suddenly on his feet, one arm around her shoulders, as he walked her back off the Bridge.

"We don't have to discuss it right now, Lori. Are you hurt?"

"No sir," she managed to say, although it was difficult to speak and her voice quivered.

"We've neutralized the threat in the system," Darius said. "And I'm hopeful there aren't any more infiltrators on board. We'll do a full sweep once the Marines are back. For now, I'm sending you to quarters. First, I want you to go to my cabin, fix yourself a stiff drink, then get some sleep."

"I can pull myself together, sir."

"I'm sure you can," Darius said, looking into her eyes. "But you don't have to. Today was a hard day for all of us. And you're clearly exhausted. I've ordered rest for all senior officers. We're taking it in shifts. I want you to sleep for at least eight hours, Commander. I'll see to the ship while you're resting."

"Sir... I... well, I feel..."

"The way anyone would," he said. "We've all been stretched thin, Commander—even me. You talked me out of doing something stupid today. I probably owe you my life."

That got the tears flowing. Her emotions were welling up within her and wouldn't be denied.

"It's true, Lori. You were the voice of calm and reason when I needed it. I probably should have been there for you at that moment, but I wasn't. You stepped up. I can't tell you how much I appreciate that. Now, it's my turn to help you."

"They died because of me," she said.

"No," Darius said softly. "That's not true. They died because of the Ashi. They died to protect the ship. That was their duty, and they will be remembered for it. I promise you that. If anyone is to blame for what happened today, it's me. In war, we should expect the unexpected. We were caught off guard and boarded today. That's a lesson in battle preparedness that I will never forget. Now, it's imperative that you give yourself the rest you need. Drink, then sleep, then we'll figure out the rest when you're awake again."

"Are you sure, sir?"

"Absolutely," he said. "Now, go get some rest, Commander. That's an order."

"And the aliens?"

"I'll see about that," Darius said.

She nodded and headed down the ramp to the officer's quarters on the next level down from the Bridge. Her quarters were right across the hallway from Captain Darius' rooms. She went into his cabin and found the alcohol. Lori Lee rarely drank, partly because she preferred to have a clear head at all times but mostly because she didn't like the taste. But she followed his orders, pouring a small amount of the ardent spirit into a crystal tumbler. It was one mouthful. She swallowed it down quickly, coughing as the alcohol burned her throat and left her tongue numb. It seemed like she was drinking medicine and didn't understand why it appealed to some people. Then a warm sensation bloomed in her stomach and spread out through her body. Her emotions didn't feel so raw anymore. She returned to her room, pulled off her uniform and climbed into the round bed. The blankets and sheets didn't fit the round bed, but she pulled them around her body until she was tucked in on all sides. The pillow beneath her head felt soft and warm. Everything was warm. She couldn't remember what she had been so upset about. Nothing seemed to matter at that moment but closing her eyes. As soon as she did, Lori Lee drifted off into the sweet darkness of sleep.

Back on the Bridge, Captain Darius activated his comlink.

"Mr. O'Dell, do you read me?"

"Yes, Captain," came Connor's voice.

"We are nearing orbit around the planet, and I have to see about the Marines," he said. "But once things have settled down, I will meet with you and our guests. Until then, please refrain from telling them anything about us."

"Oh, alright. I can do that."

"Very good, Mr. O'Dell. Darius out."

He cut the transmission and sat back in his chair, rubbing his eyes. Lori Lee wasn't the only one who needed rest. Nor was she the only one with survivor's guilt and raw emotions, but Darius still had work to do. He had sent the senior officers away to rest. The Bridge was manned with junior officers and enlisted crew. The enemy ships were still running for the edges of the solar system.

"Approaching orbit, Captain," one of the crew members said.

"Very good. I want a high orbit. Don't get too close to the drones."

"Aye, Captain, setting a high orbit now."

He felt a little better being back near the planet. The ship was out of danger; he felt relatively certain of that. No other infiltrators had been seen. The engines, laser cannons, and the power supply via the *Jericho* were all being guarded. He would know if any more Ashi infiltrators came near to the vital sections of the ship. That allowed some of the tension to drain away, but not all of it. He still felt a heavy responsibility for what had nearly been a complete disaster. He reached up and rubbed his tired eyes.

"Someone make contact with our Marines," he said. "I want to know exactly what's happening down there."

"Aye, Captain," a junior officer manning the communications console said.

He reached over and picked up his coffee. It was hot and bitter, nearly scalding his tongue and filling his senses with a heavy, burnt aroma. But that was what he deserved, he thought. There was no one above him to relieve his guilt or take the blame for his failures in the battle. The weight of it fell squarely on his shoulders ... and it took all of his internal fortitude not to cave in under the pressure.

CHAPTER 38

"TAKE US AROUND THE CITY," Remmy ordered.

He and Laila were in the cockpit. It was dark out, but light from the buildings shown around on the hills, trees and gardens that surrounded Kipbur. Remmy noted the guns. They were belt-fed auto cannons that were mounted on four of the buildings, one in each corner of the city, which was laid out in neat rows.

"No sign of the enemy," Laila said.

"They're staying in the dark, trying to see what they can learn before making their attack."

"Do you think they're able to communicate?"

"We should count on that," Remmy said. "Did you make contact with Sergeant Oliver?"

"He's in the command tent now, preparing for the assault."

"The locals are pulling everyone into the center of the city. This could get ugly quick."

"What do you want to do?"

Remmy had been thinking of that. He had no clear numbers on the enemy or the exact locations. GIGI shared images in his mind but it was clear data. The drones had no night vision capabilities, only thermal imaging. The Ashi warriors were moving in groups, which appeared in thermal as just a blob of color.

If they had the manpower and the time, the best option would have been to dig defenses and fight from inside the city as the enemy approached. But that didn't seem like a reasonable option with their limited resources and time.

"They could attack at any moment," Remmy said.

"True," Laila agreed.

"So, my preference would be to flank the enemy on either side of the city," he said.

It was not the kind of tactic that many would opt for but all the Marines on Casasil were special forces commandos. They were all trained to hit unsuspecting enemy forces hard and fast.

"I'll take Izzy and Tex," Laila suggested. "You take Hugo and Leigh Ann."

"Done," Remmy said. "I'll go east; you go west."

We meet in the middle," Laila said.

"Sounds like a plan," Remmy replied. "I'll have Dirk take control of the automated defenses and GIGI has drones in the area. No bombs, but they can still make strafing runs if the enemy closes in on the city."

The dropship landed four kilometers away from the city on the East side. Remmy led Hugo and Poh out, then watched the ship climb back into the dark night sky. There were no lights on the aircraft. It wasn't silent, but it wasn't visible without assistance, either. The problem was that no one knew how good the aliens could see at night. They might have excellent night vision or some type of vision assistance. They obviously weren't afraid to make a tactical move in the dark since they had left their pods and advanced on the city after sundown.

"What's the plan, boss man?" Hugo asked.

"We spread out," Remmy ordered. "You go north, Hugo. Leigh Ann, you go south. Get as far out as you can and still see me in your night vision."

"Copy that," Hugo said.

"Remember, there are automated guns on the edge of the town. We want to hit the enemy hard but don't chase them into the town. In the dark, Sergeant Oliver might not recognize friend from foe."

"Got it," Leigh Ann said. "Rules of engagement?"

"I have no idea how many Ashi there are," Remmy explained. "GIGI picked them up on thermal. They're all about two kilometers out from the city and that means two klicks from our current position."

"What are they armed with?" Hugo said.

"That's uncertain as well. Most of the Ashi that were seen leaving the pods had laser rifles, although some had only hand-to-hand weapons."

"None of the big cannons?" Hugo asked.

"Negative. Unfortunately, these aliens left their pods at night. So, our intel is limited. As soon as you get sight of them, spread the word. We hit them hard and fast, spec op tactics and no quarter given."

"Copy that," Leigh Ann said.

Let's watch our shooting, too," Remmy said. "We don't want to accidentally spray the town with reckless shooting."

"Are the locals undercover?"

"In the process, I'm told," Remmy said. "Better safe than sorry. Let's go."

Remmy waited while Hugo and Leigh Ann made their way from his position into the darkness. When they were at the edge of his helmet's night vision capabilities, Remmy ordered the team forward.

They didn't have to go far before the first group of aliens came into view. They were spread out, facing away from the city.

"I got pickets," Hugo said.

"Me too," Leigh Ann said. "They're expecting us."

Remmy had instantly gone down on one knee the moment Hugo called in over the comlink. He couldn't see any of the Ashi from his position and had no idea if the aliens could see them.

"Any indication they can see you?" Remmy asked.

"Negative, Sergeant. They're at ease."

"Must be the light from the city behind them," Leigh Ann said. "All I can make out is a shadow but it's staring right at me. Hasn't lifted a weapon, though."

"What are they armed with?" Remmy asked.

"Rifle," Hugo replied.

"Mine too," Leigh Ann said.

"What's their posture?"

"Casual, relaxed even," Leigh Ann replied. "The picket on my end has his gun pointed at the dirt."

"Same here," Hugo said.

"Alright then," Remmy said. "On my signal, we go right at them. There's no way to take them down silently. So, we go straight at them, fast march, weapons hot. The moment they catch sight of you, put them down. Remember, aim for their stomach. The lower, the better."

"Roger that," Hugo said.

Leigh Ann acknowledged the order with a click on her comlink. Remmy checked his Nelson LTX rifle. He had a full magazine. The fire indicator was on burst mode and his safety was off.

"Here we go," he said. "Marines engage."

He lifted his rifle to his shoulder and started forward at a fast walk. He was bent slightly at the waist, his rifle sweeping back and forth in front of him as he searched for the enemy. A few seconds later, Hugo fired. Three shots in quick succession echoed across the plain. The suppression shroud on his weapon made the shots sound like dull pops.

A second later, Leigh Ann Poh fired. Her weapon was louder. And suddenly, a group of Ashi warriors rose up in front of Remmy. His finger squeezed the trigger of his rifle without any thought and without even really aiming. They were big creatures and they were straight ahead of him, clustered together. His shots rang out. He fired again and was about to shoot a third burst when the darkness lit up with lasers.

The enemy was firing blind. If any of them had seen the muzzle flash from his weapon, they hadn't taken careful aim. And once more, their height betrayed them. The laser sizzled through the air over Remmy's head. He dropped to one knee and fired back.

Hugo and Leigh Ann joined in. The Marines were mowing down the enemy but there were more of the Ashi than expected. Nearly thirty of the aliens were clustered together. And more pickets from the north and south of the enemy's main position joined the fray. There was no real cover to hide behind.

"Get low," Remmy said, although neither Hugo nor Poh responded to the order. In the heat of battle, orders sometimes when unnoticed. It's hard to think straight when people are shooting at you. Sometimes they just went ignored. Remmy couldn't worry about his companions. He went to his stomach and kept firing at the enemy.

"I've got movement north of my position," Hugo said. "It's another group of aliens."

But the new cluster wasn't moving to help their companions. Instead, they dashed toward the city.

"Switching to full auto," Hugo said. "Cover me."

Remmy kept firing. Most of the aliens in front of him were down. He turned and looked as Hugo charged forward, blasting away at the second squad of aliens. At the same time, the remotely controlled machine gun on the roof of one of the Casian buildings lit the night with high-intensity fire. The Ashi were cut to pieces. It was a slaughter. Remmy didn't even see the group make a single counter shot.

"Enemy down," Leigh Ann said. "My sights are clear."

"Confirmed," Remmy said. The Ashi warriors were all dead or dying. He could hear a few animalistic groans but saw no movement. None of the aliens were standing up. "Hugo?"

"Clear," the big Marine replied.

"Alright, Leigh Ann and I will circle south; you go north. We'll meet on the far side."

"Roger that, Sarge."

"Let's move, Poh, double time, head on a swivel."

"Already going, Sergeant," Leigh Ann replied.

They jogged forward. It was tempting to Remmy to speed up and try to catch up with her, but he knew that was a tactical mistake. The Ashi had bunched together, making themselves easy targets. It was better for the Marines to stay apart in case they ran into trouble.

Leigh Ann took down another sentry, but they were close enough to see the Marine tents at the front edge of the alien town before they ran into any real resistance. One minute, the world was dark. The next, it was lit in blinding flashes of yellow laser light. The beams moved too quickly to be seen; only the flashes were visible. Remmy dove to the ground as Leigh Ann screamed.

"I'm hit," she said.

Remmy returned fire from a prone position. "How bad is it, Corporal?"

"Just a glancing shot," she said. "Burns like hell, though."

"Stay low," Remmy said.

The new group of fighters were spread out in a long, staggered line. They fired and moved. It was much better tactics than any of the Ashi had employed since Remmy had been fighting them. He had trouble tracking them in the darkness.

GIGI, we need help. We're pinned down on the northeast corner of the town, approximately three kilometers from the command tent.

Affirmative. Stand by for air support.

"Leigh Ann, get small," Remmy ordered. "Air support inbound."

"Roger," Poh said.

A few seconds later, as the aliens continued to light up the darkness with their laser fire, a trio of drones dove down and fired across their lines. The dart-like ammo didn't kill any of the Ashi warriors, but most of them turned and fired up at the drones. Remmy used the distraction to fire a few bursts, then he dove to the side and crawled through the darkness. He saw the flashes of return fire and heard the laser blasts pelting into the ground where he had been. It was quickly becoming obvious that he and Leigh Ann were in trouble. There were a lot of aliens. Some had been wounded by the drones, but none were out of the fight. Remmy and Leigh Ann had picked off a handful, but it seemed like there were dozens more, all firing and moving. The only thing Remmy could really do was spray and pray. He set his LTX to full auto, rammed in a fresh magazine and fired a long, sweeping spray of bullets. Some hit their targets, most didn't. He rolled to his right the second his weapon locked up as the last round was fired. He rolled and rolled, ignoring the pain in his body from the rocky ground he hurried over. In the process, he pulled his last two grenades, popped the pins, and threw them. They sailed unseen in the night. The explosions from them made the ground tremble and each one started small fires that shed enough light to allow Remmy's night vision to hone in on the aliens. He started shooting again, targeting the Ashi. Unfortunately, there were too many. The return fire forced him to crawl again. One blast hit the ground close to him and kicked up dirt that flew up under his helmet's face shield. The grit hit his eyes.

He rolled onto his back and used his free hand to try and clear his eyes. When he rolled back over, he could see the enemy. There were too many, at least twenty, closing in on him. He frantically tried to change his magazine. But before he could, a sweeping barrage of projectile fire erupted to his right.

"Stay low, Master Sergeant," Laila called on the comlink. "We've got this."

He lay on his stomach, watching the Ashi fall, their big bodies crashing to the ground like trees being harvested in a forest. He waited, content to be rescued and wondering how he had survived so long.

"Clear!" Laila called.

"Poh! She's hit," Remmy said, getting to his knees.

"On it," Izzy said.

He saw her dash forward. Leigh Ann was still down on the ground.

"How bad is it?" Laila asked.

"Cracked her chest plate," Izzy said. "Some burns around the edges. Looks like her armor got fused with her skin, maybe. She'll need help."

"Stay with her," Remmy said. "Hugo went around the city the other way."

"The Ashi must have circled around. There was none on the west side of the city," Laila said.

"We should go find him," Remmy said.

"We'll do that, Master Sergeant. Check in with Sergeant Oliver and the city officials. I don't think there's enough of the enemy left to be a threat."

It was a pleasant idea. No more enemies, no longer a threat, these phrases were music to his ears.

"Stay here," Remmy told Izzy. "I'll send help to get her to the base."

He set off at a jog and radioed Sergeant Dirk Oliver as he went. The Sergeant was gruff, clearly unhappy, but followed Remmy's orders and shut down the weapons on the corners of town. While Remmy went straight to the city, Laila and Tex set off at a fast jog back the way they had come. When Remmy finally reached the command tent, he felt almost hollow. His stamina was reaching its limit. He needed time to rest and regain his strength, but as usual, there was no time.

"Master Sergeant," Dirk said with a scowl.

"Can you head out with a hover gurney and collect Corporal Poh."

"Is she hurt bad?" Dirk asked.

"A laser blast got through her armor, but she'll live," Remmy said. "How are Rip and Ricky?"

"Thompson will be fine. They removed the shrapnel and fixed him up. Rip's another story."

"That bad?"

"He might lose his arm," Dirk said. "About two inches of bone is missing. They've got him sedated and ready for transport back to the *Renegade*. It's possible that Dr. Lanski can replace the missing bone, but there's a lot of nerve damage, too. Even if he keeps the arm, he might not be able to use it again."

"I'm sorry to hear that," Remmy admitted.

Dirk just nodded and pushed past the Master Sergeant. His feelings were normal, but his insubordination would have to be dealt with before long if it didn't change on its own. Remmy left the tent and made his way into the town proper. He hadn't gone far when a trio of the six-legged, pachyderm Casians met him in the street.

"Is the threat over?" Ernhard asked, his trumpeting language translated by an app on Remmy's helmet. It printed the words on his HUD and he scanned them before answering.

"Almost," Remmy said. "The last of the Ashi warriors are being tracked down north of the city."

"How is it possible," another of the Casians said. "The Ashi are unstoppable."

"We were fortunate to get in behind them," Remmy said. "I think they rely mostly on their size and strength to intimidate their victims."

"Your race is the most valiant I have ever heard of," Ernhard said. "We owe you a great debt."

"You don't owe us anything," Remmy said. "Friends help friends; it's as simple as that. And this fight isn't over. There are hundreds of pods with as many as eight or nine Ashi warriors inside. We will have to teach you to hunt them down."

"We are not equipped to fight the Ashi," Ernhard said.

"I'm going to remedy that," the Master Sergeant explained. "We'll rig up some of the aircraft that will allow you to search out the enemy and put them down from a distance. You'll be outside their reach and much faster than the Ashi. For now, keep your people safe in the center of town until my Marines report the all-clear."

"Where are you going?" The third Casian asked.

"I've got to go find my Lieutenant," Remmy said before turning on his heel and heading back out of town.

CHAPTER 39

THE ASHI eventually came out of the forest. Lieutenant Colt watched them from the same hilltop that Remmy had occupied. They moved slowly. He couldn't say whether they saw or heard the dropship leaving and suspected it was safe to emerge or if they believed the cover of darkness was enough to keep them safe. Either way, they appeared and, after searching for signs of their enemy, moved toward the wrecked skiffs not far away on the battlefield.

Micky Colt took his time and counted the Ashi. There were forty-six warriors, each with armor and the heavy-mounted machine gun that made them so formidable. The aliens divided into two separate groups. One spread around the other, looking out into the darkness for any signs of danger. They held their machine guns, ready to fire. The second group was smaller and went to work on one of the skiffs.

The Lieutenant's targeting computer told him the aliens were nearly three kilometers away. From his slightly elevated position, he could see the skiff that was being repaired. The aliens wisely cannibalized the parts needed from the other hovercrafts around them. A component here, a servo there, some wiring and fuel seemed to be enough to get the device up and running again. Micky Colt targeted the hovercraft with an infrared laser, then waited until the hovercraft was filled with enemy warriors before firing his long-range missile.

From the shoulder of his MECH suit, a panel opened and the missile shot upward. Colt didn't even feel the long-range weapon leap from the suit. He kept the invisible targeting beam on the skiff. It started to move, slowly drifting forward. With his Heads-Up Display zoomed in, he could see the hulking aliens. Two-thirds of them were on the skiff, while ten more of the Ashi warriors walked behind it. They saw the missile shooting up into the air. The weapon used simple rocket fuel that burned furiously to propel the warhead toward its target. The missile arched down, flying straight toward the skiff. Some of the warriors jumped off the hovercraft. Others raised their machine guns and fired at the missile, but it was moving too fast and was too small. It rocketed down and smashed into the skiff. The explosion was so spectacular that his HUD dimmed to protect his eyes.

The lieutenant no longer had the big rifle that was built specially for the oversized MECH. Instead, he would have to rely on the built-in munitions, of which there were several available. None were in range of the aliens at the moment, so Micky Colt waited and watched. He had no idea if the aliens could see him, but the Marine lieutenant could certainly see them. The skiff had been blown to pieces; the shrapnel eviscerated several of the Ashi warriors. After waiting for the smoke to clear and the fire to burn down, Micky could only count seven that were still on their feet. And, as expected, they were headed back to the forest. What surprised Micky wasn't their retreat but that they abandoned their heavy machine guns and armor. From what he could see, they had no weapons at all. The big green warriors had only their kilts and boots after leaving their armor and machine guns on the battlefield.

Maybe it was a trick to lure him in close, but Micky was the kind of man who prided himself on recognizing opportunities when they presented themselves. He saw the seven Ashi warriors running away without weapons and it seemed like a no-brainer to him that he should follow.

Running in the MECH suit was a bit like being on an elliptical machine. Each step was like compressing a spring. There was no jarring to his knee, just a soft landing, and the system cycled back up so that he could run in the MECH suit with minimal effort.

The suit had a long, fast stride. He sprinted toward the forest, moving much quicker than the Ashi warriors could without their heavy armor. Still, he was three kilometers away from the woods and it took a few minutes to reach the edge of the forest, where he slowed down.

Everything he had ever learned or studied about combat tactics told him he was being foolish. Going into the dark, unknown forest was essentially walking into a trap. But he wasn't just a man in his MECH suit. He was more like a superhero and Micky wanted to fight. He recalled his combat in the mountains far to the south. He had taken out four of the aliens in short order without taking any damage at all. How difficult could it be to track down and kill seven more? They didn't even have guns, he reminded himself, before pressing forward through the trees.

The MECH was twice Micky's normal height. He had to climb up into the suit, which opened in the front, and sit on the narrow, curved seat before locking in his arms and legs to the system controls. He had two ways to see out of the suit. The first was a Heads-Up Display on a wrap-around screen. The cameras for the screen were in the MECH's head, along with the long-range communication unit and built-in speakers, so that when he spoke, people not connected with a comlink could hear him. The other was a simple grid directly in front of his face. It was made of thick, transparent material that was similar to plexiglass and nearly inde-structible. It was also protected by two sets of plate armor so that he could only see out of a narrow slit.

It was too dark to see anything through the slit in front of him and the forest restricted his night vision on the wrap-around HUD. He could see but only for a few meters in any direction ... and all he saw were trees. Some were thick, others thin, and they all had signs of being shot repeatedly. He moved forward slowly, trying to minimize the sound of the heavy MECH's footsteps. He dialed up the suit's auditory system, wanting to be sure he heard any sounds that his enemy might make.

Not long after entering the forest, Micky's excitement was gone. He felt like he was alone among the trees. There was no sign of the enemy. They might have circled around, watched him go into the forest, then slipped away into the night. He felt both foolish and disappointed, but he had nearly wiped them out with one blow. No one would argue that the MECH suit wasn't a complete success. There were still bugs to iron out and some new skills to master, like flying in the heavy armor, but he would perfect the design and become a master in the suit. He was convinced it would radically change warfare as humanity knew it. If only he could get back to the Sol system alive, he would be lauded as the man who reinvented mechanized warfare.

Even with the suit's detection systems dialed up, Micky never saw the enemy. Two of the Ashi warriors came at him from behind. One smashed him on the back of the MECH head with a thick tree limb that had been cut down into a shape similar to a baseball bat. The blow knocked Micky forward. The suit fell to its knees. He was shocked by the blow, and even worse, the cameras in the MECH head unit were disabled. His HUD went dark. The display still worked and his suit's computer system was still functional, but he was for all intents and purposes blind.

The second warrior had a thick-bladed, curved knife. He drove it down into the shoulder joint of the MECH suit with all his weight. The blade severed wiring and wedged into the servos, that gave the arm freedom of movement. Alarms went off inside the suit, and by that point, Micky was acting on impulse and training alone. He extended the suit's cutting blade and spun around. The second Ashi warrior was still close to him and couldn't leap away before the MECH blade ripped a gash in his stomach. Internal organs came spilling out of the alien as it staggered backward, wailing in pain.

The other warrior charged Lieutenant Colt, smashing into him. Micky used the sudden momentum shift to get the MECH back on its feet. He could not lift his left arm, but he could move it from the elbow down. He activated the flamethrower nozzle, which extended from his left forearm and ignited. As the Ashi warrior stepped back and raised his club, Micky doused him with fire. The flames roared from the MECH suit and sent the Ashi warrior reeling, his hair, kilt, and boots on fire. Flames also kindled on the shrubs around the trees nearby, giving a flickering light that Micky could see by through the narrow slit in the MECH suit.

Instinct told him to turn and he got the heavy suit moving just in time to catch a third warrior rushing at him with his big knife held high. Micky extended his good arm with the long blade and impaled the alien on it. The Ashi warrior died instantly, but the sudden weight pulled Micky off balance and when he tried to rip his sword free, the blade broke instead.

There were still four Ashi warriors alive and they came at him simultaneously. Micky barely managed to fire a small weapon at one. A finger-sized, short-range plasma cartridge smashed into the alien's chest, spewing the chemical gel across his body. It reacted instantly to the oxygen in the air and ignited. The plasma burned into the alien's body cavity in a horrific display as blood and gore gushed down this stomach.

He fired the flame thrower again and burned one of the three remaining aliens, but not bad enough to kill. Meanwhile, a third Ashi warrior dove into the MECH's legs and knocked them out from under Micky, who hit the ground hard. The suit was made to absorb impacts and protect the pilot, but the sudden change of gravity caused Micky's skull to slam into the bulkhead. It had a thin pad over the hard steel casing but it wasn't made to protect the pilot from such a blow.

The fourth alien drove his knife into the space between the

MECH's head and back. With a powerful wrenching motion, he levered the head off the suit, ripping it away. Wires were torn apart and the power system shorted out. Micky was dazed and left hanging by the safety harness inside the dead MECH suit. The aliens, thinking the suit was a robot, spit on the MECH suit and left it there, surrounded by the Ashi warriors who had been maimed and killed by it.

The battle over, Micky was trapped inside the armor and he soon passed out cold. When he woke up several hours later, his head was pounding and he hurt all over. Worse still, he couldn't move. He had no way to get out of the MECH suit, which did have a manual release, but because he was lying face down, the front couldn't open. To add insult to injury, because the suit had no power, Micky had no way to turn it over and escape. He would have to wait and pray that someone came for him before he died inside the armor he was convinced would be the future of human warfare.

CHAPTER 40

IF SOMEONE HAD BEEN THERE to record exactly what happened, they might have noticed the smoke from the fires around the prone Marine in the large MECH suit disturbed the tiny creature resting on a broad red leaf some fifty or sixty feet above the ground. It didn't belong there. A strong north wind had blown into the forest. The creature was only six millimeters long and looked like a white, hairless caterpillar. Inside its tiny body was a fantastic organ that could spin out a hundred meters of silk each day.

The creature, known on Casasil as a Burturm, was surprisingly intelligent. As the smoke billowed up and filled the canopy of the forest, the creature attached its silk to the wide leaf and slowly crawled off. It didn't fall. The Burturm drifted down, spooling out a line of silk as it sought relief from the smoke. Eventually, it came to rest on the left shoulder of the MECH.

Lifting its tiny head, the Burturm sensed prey all around. The tiny worm-like creature was a carnivore, and while there was plenty of flesh to choose from, only one living creature was within reach. The Burturm began to crawl and made its way from the shoulder of the MECH to a tiny opening where the heat of the armored suit had been. It took the tiny creature a full hour to get inside. It scooted and squirmed toward its prey. If a person had been there to study the creature, it would have revealed a tiny, translucent trail of toxic secretion that was especially susceptible to human brain activity. No one in the entire galaxy knew that fact. Humans had never come into contact with the Burturm, and the tiny worm-like creature didn't have the same effect on the Casians.

The smell of flesh drove the tiny creature almost into a frenzy. The iron-rich blood was intoxicating to the Burturm. It crawled across the padded bulkhead where Lieutenant Micky Colt had been knocked unconscious. From the bulkhead, the creature made its way to one side of the safety harness. It inched along, its long, narrow body scooting across the edge of the strap.

At last, it reached the human. It slithered onto the unconscious officer's shoulder and examined its new surroundings. The Burturm had no concept of clothing but it knew the compression shirt Micky Colt was wearing was not organic. It assumed the shirt was some type of protective shell. So, it continued on, slithering toward the Lieutenant's neck.

When it reached flesh, the Burturm felt a heady rush of euphoria. Nothing the creature had ever sensed was as rich and delicious as the human. And so, with its tiny mouth full of microscopic teeth, it began to eat its way into the man's neck. Blood immediately welled up. The tiny Burturm sucked the blood down in a ravenous, gulping motion that filled the creature with both energy and drove it into a further frenzy. It drove its body forward, biting, swallowing and pressing forward.

Within minutes the tiny creature had burrowed its way into the man. All that remained was a tiny dot of blood that quickly coagulated and dried. No one would likely ever know what had happened. The Burturm had found a home and it worked its way, deeper and deeper, into the human's body. Eventually, it reached the spine. The tiny creature could feel the electrical impulses flowing past.

At the same time, the Burturm felt a new sensation inside its own tiny body. The soft tissue and iron rich blood was not only invigorating, but it was causing the Burturm to grow. Releasing its silky web, it began to circle around the spine, Slowly moving upward, wrapping the bundle of nerves first in its web and then within its own body as it grew larger and larger. Eventually, it would reach the human's brain stem and begin to burrow once more. What effect it would have on the man no one could say. The Burturm had never found sustenance so rich, so wonderfully delicious and invigorating. It was determined to stay and wrapped itself tighter and tighter around the man's backbone and spine. Only time would tell what effects the tiny creature might have on Lieutenant Micky Colt. He was completely unaware of the Burturm's existence, much less the fact that he had become its living host.

CHAPTER 41

"DON'T LEAVE YET," Dirk Oliver said as Remmy passed the command tent. "Captain Darius is on the horn."

Remmy nodded and stepped inside the command tent. The space was filled with ammo crates and communications gear. There were a few camp chairs near the comms unit and Remmy sat in one with a sigh. His fatigue was high, but there was too much work to be done to get any rest. He might be able to sneak in a half-hour nap on the flight back to where he had left Lieutenant Colt, if nothing else had gone wrong.

"Sir, this is Ronan Two," Remmy said into the comm unit's microphone.

"Good to hear your voice, Master Sergeant. Sounds like things got hairy down there."

"Nothing we couldn't handle, sir," Remmy replied, which got a snort from Sergeant Oliver before he walked out of the command tent.

"How many casualties?" The Captain asked.

"Two KIA, sir. Sergeant Jay Thorne and Corporal Jack Fortnoy didn't make it. Four more wounded, including Gunnery Sergeant Chad Rand, sir. He'll be out of commission for a while. And

Corporal Al Van Winkle will need surgery. The med techs said he could lose an arm."

"I'm sorry to hear that, Remmy. Things didn't go as planned up here, either."

"Is the ship okay?"

"She is, but we got hit with an EMP that knocked out our power and at least five enemy soldiers gained access to the ship."

"You were boarded?" Remmy asked, the shock snapping him out of his fatigue stupor.

"Yes. And we lost six crew members. I never even considered getting boarded to be a possibility, so we got caught with our pants down. Frankly, I'd say we're lucky things didn't turn out worse than they did. But we're back in orbit now. There are only three Ashi ships in the system and they're running for the edge of the heliosphere in different directions. I'm not sure what they hope to do, but that's our situation. What's yours, Master Sergeant?"

"There are still Ashi warriors on the ground. We managed to stop most of those from the carrier that made it to the surface, but several hundred escape pods from the second ship came down, too. They're scattered all over the planet. The drones will get some of them, but we need time to recharge and reload them, sir. I've got a plan to equip the locals to hunt down the rest but I need a couple more days here. Lieutenant Colt is about an hour away from Kipbur. I was just about to go and pick him up."

"May I suggest you delegate that task," Master Sergeant. "I want the Lieutenant and everyone you can spare back up here. We're going to have to sweep the ship to ensure there are no more infiltrators waiting to sabotage the *Renegade*."

"Copy that, sir. Staff Sergeant McPherson and I can handle everything down here. I'll send everyone else back up to you."

"Excellent, Remmy. We're damn proud of what you and the Marines did down there."

"Thank you, sir."

"Let's finish this up and figure out our next move. Stay close to the radio if you can."

"Roger that, sir. We'll have ears on down here."

"Very good. Shogun out."

Remmy leaned back in his seat and sighed. No chance for a nap after all.

It took half an hour to get the wounded loaded into the drop-ship. By then, Laila was back with Tex and Hugo. Remmy gave Sergeant Dirk his orders.

"We find the LT then make for orbit?" Dirk asked to clarify.

"That's correct. GIGI will do the flying. Once you reach the *Renegade*, everyone who is able will form a search party and check every compartment on the ship."

"That could take days," Hugo said.

"I'm sure Lieutenant Colt will have a plan. We can't risk the possibility that there might be more Ashi on the ship."

"At least we'll be fighting for our own," Dirk said.

"Go ahead and take off," Remmy said. "We'll wrap up opera-tions down here and see you all in a few days."

"Watch your back, Master Sergeant," Tex said.

"You too, Staff Sergeant," Izzy said. "Don't do anything crazy."

Remmy wasn't sure if Corporal Izzy Berry was talking about combat or if she knew about Laila's relationship with Remmy. Perhaps he should have kept Hugo or Tex with him on the planet, but the plain truth of the matter was that he wanted to be with Laila. He didn't expect there to be trouble and since the decision was up to him, he had chosen who he wanted to remain with.

"Good luck. Once you find the Lieutenant, have GIGI inform me," Remmy said.

They all shook hands and exchanged hugs. The platoon was close. Combat had a way of bonding people almost as tightly as family. Only Sergeant Dirk Oliver seemed to be out of sorts. Remmy was giving him a pass since Sergeant Jay Thorne had been Dirk's best friend.

"Any objection to us picking up Sergeant Thorne's body," Dirk asked Remmy quietly as the other Marines boarded the ship.

"No. You think he'd be happier in space than buried here? I can see to that, if you like."

"Let me," Dirk said. "It should be me."

"Do what you think is best, Sergeant," Remmy told him.

Dirk nodded in appreciation, then boarded the dropship. Remmy watched it go and turned to Laila.

"Alone at last," he said.

"Sort of," Laila replied, pointing past Remmy.

He turned to see a group of locals lumbering toward them.

"Duty calls, I suppose," Remmy grumbled. "Why don't you catch four hours rest? I'll wake you if there's a need. We'll just be reloading the drones."

"I can help," she said.

"So can they and it's time they started learning how."

As Laila turned in for some rest, Remmy met with Casian officials. He assured them the city was safe and took volunteers to help him load the drones with fresh munitions. He taught them how to handle the bombs and what it took to arm them prior to flight. They were suited for moving materials. Their trunks were extremely agile and strong. And even though the Casians didn't utilize a lot of technology, they understood it well enough. Their thermal power plant was put to work recharging all the drones which had come in during the night.

As dawn broke, the first of the recharged and rearmed drones was going back up. Their task was to hunt down the Ashi stragglers and take them out. Remmy, exhausted, returned to the command tent. Despite his best efforts he was nodding off in the camp chair in front of the communications unit when GIGI spoke to him. It took the Master Sergeant a moment to wake up.

"Oh," Remmy groaned as he leaned forward and rubbed his hands over his face. "What did I miss."

Lieutenant Micky Colt has been located, GIGI informed him. *It appears the Lieutenant was wounded in battle.*

How bad? Remmy thought.

The Marines were forced to pry open his armor. He was uncon-

scious. Initial scans show he may have suffered a concussion. Other-wise, he is intact.

I hope he gave as good as he got.

It appears that he did. I registered thirty newly slain Ashi troops on the battlefield and four more were found around the Lieutenant in the forest. We have retrieved Sergeant Jay Thorne's body and are making our way into orbit now. ETA is fifty-three minutes.

Outstanding, Remmy thought. Everything was coming together. He would get the machine guns off the buildings on Kipbur and mounted onto a couple of the dropships. After that, it wouldn't take much training to get the Casians ready to hunt down any of the remaining Ashi. They already had pilots and did occasionally use aerial vehicles to travel the vast distances between their cities. A couple more days and he would be back on the *Renegade*. That was a pleasant thought. Normally, Fleet ships were crowded and dank, but the Arodoni ship was huge, comfortable and surprising. Though it seemed alien to Remmy, he considered it to be safe. At least, he wouldn't be fighting once he and Laila were back on board the ship.

"You look tired," she said as she stepped into the tent.

"Wow, has it been four hours already?" He asked.

"It has. Although I could go back to sleep if you like."

"I wouldn't stop you."

"Is that proper, Master Sergeant? Or do I detect special treatment?"

"Would that be so bad?" Remmy asked.

"No, it wouldn't be so bad. I kind of like it."

"Good," he said, getting to his feet. "'Cause we've got a few days here and I'd like to give you all the special treatment you can handle."

"That kind of talk will get you everywhere," she said.

Remmy smiled. "That's what I was hoping for."

CHAPTER 42

DARIUS SAT down in the pavilion. Connor O'Dell had shown Nurek to the Captain's favorite meeting place on the ship already. The tall alien stood looking out at the park. There was a herd of small four-legged animals only a stone's throw away. Darius could hear them cooing softly. The sound reminded Darius of doves.

"This is a most amazing ship," Nurek said. "There is nothing like it in the known galaxy."

"We're proud of it," Darius said.

"But you didn't build it. You are not Arodoni."

"That's correct."

"You let us think that you were," Nurek said. "I'm not sure how I feel about that, Captain."

"I understand. We weren't trying to deceive you, but we aren't going to talk about our race, not even to our allies."

"You come from an unknown system," Nurek said.

"And we want it to stay that way."

The alien nodded. It might have been approval. Darius hadn't spent enough time with the Dudonus to be able to read their body language. The tall alien sat down across from him.

"You are an interesting species," Nurek said. "You are violent, yet with some compassion. You are guarded, yet you behave with honor."

"It was never our intention to start a war," Darius said. "The Correllian artifact that we call GIGI waited in the far reaches of our solar system for a long time. Eventually, it sent us the plans for a long range ship that enabled us to reach it. I was given that task with orders to return it to my people. Yet, when we took possession of the artifact, GIGI convinced me of the danger posed by the Imperium and provided a way to protect my people."

"This ship," Nurek said. "The Correll were clever. I don't think anyone knew they had located one of the missing Arodoni ships."

"Once we procured the power core on Lawash, GIGI instructed us where to go. Only after we found the ship did we realize that the long-range vessel GIGI had instructed us to build was actually part of the *Renegade's* power system. We also discovered that an Imperial ship was guarding the hyperspace portal we needed to use to get back home. It left us no choice but to fight and then, suspecting that the Imperium had some way of tracking us through space, we came here to the Casa system to test our theory."

"The ship you fought outside the Vangori nebula placed a tracking device on this ship," Nurek said. "That much I can tell you. I was not privy to all the Emperor's intelligence, but he spoke freely around me. Dudonus slaves are non-people to the Ashi and most other advanced races."

"But not because you are less intelligent," Darius pointed out.

"No, but we are not strong, as you can see. We cannot fight. We are easily injured, and so resistance is unheard of. We are used as domestic slaves as we require little rest and live longer than most other races. The investment in a Dudonus slave will pay dividends through several generations on most worlds."

"Slavery is wrong. It was practiced by my people for thousands of years before we ended the foul practice. It's one of the reasons I knew my people would never agree to join the Imperium."

"And those that resist are either enslaved or exterminated," Nurek said.

"That's what GIGI led us to believe."

"It is the truth. Many worlds have resisted Imperial rule, only to be devastated by the Ashi military complex. You saw Lawash. It was poisoned by heavy metals after orbital bombardment wiped out its largest cities. The Ashi are careless in that regard. They view themselves as superior to all other races, even the five core worlds that make up the Prime Council. But as long as the Ashi control the military, no one can resist them."

"Not even if you rise up across the galaxy?"

"No planet or people are allowed to have weapons of war or even defensive systems. The Ashi ensure that Imperial worlds are protected. That is the emperor's sole purpose."

"So, even if there is galaxy-wide resistance, they have the power to crush any uprisings. What about the slave ships? We encountered one that was not an authorized vessel. It had EMP weapons."

"That is true; there are bands of people who live outside the law. Some even have weapons which they have cobbled together or designed. But none can stand toe to toe with an Ashi ship-of-war. They operate from dark corners of the galaxy and have no interest in challenging the authorities."

"So, what now?" Darius said. "We've started something here."

"And word has gone out across the galaxy," Nurek said. "Mr. O'Dell informs me that the hyperspace portal was mined. I believe that was to keep news of the Imperial defeat from leaking to the greater galaxy. But I sent word via a secret network my people have been fostering for decades. That message went out with Sheika Kahn when he fled the system."

"And what did you tell your people?"

"That our hour has come. We must rise up. There are pockets of resistance on every world, Captain. Soon, they will begin to disrupt the Imperial regime in a thousand ways."

"But the Ashi military will just crush those rebels."

"Not if they're distracted by a menace far greater than any they have known for thousands of years," Nurek said. "The Arodoni were the only race the Ashi feared. But the Arodoni were not militant. Their technology was simply too far advanced to be easily defeated. You have proven that with your victories here. An entire armada was destroyed by a single ship! That news must be spread. Fear will grow in the Ashi like a cancer."

"But we're just one ship," Darius said. "Powerful, yes, but just one. We can't hope to defeat the entire Ashi fleet."

"My people are not fighters, Captain. But we have been planning for this rebellion for a long time. And if there is one thing the Dudonus are good at, it is organization. If I may be so bold, I would direct your passage through the galaxy to worlds that can easily be liberated by your vessel's power. The Ashi have many grand ships, but if they are forced to protect every far-flung world, they will not be able to bring their strength against you."

"There's another problem," Darius said. "I don't have the crew to fight a war. We barely
have the manpower to keep things operational during a fight. On top of that, many members of my crew want to return home."

"If you take this ship back to your hidden system, it will be traced. The Imperium will send hundreds of warships to defeat you and destroy your planet."

"Maybe we can find and remove the tracker," Darius said. "I'll be ordering my people to begin that search as soon as I leave here."

"As you should, but be aware, Captain, that the wheels of war are in motion. If you flee, you will only give the Ashi time to build their forces. Your victory here in the Casasil system has already given them a reason. If we do not continue what was started here, things will only get worse. And once the Imperium knows that you exist, they will scour the galaxy until they find you."

"It seems our choices are limited."

"But you are not alone. May I make another suggestion?" Nurek asked. "Let us crew your ship."

"The Dudonus?"

"Some, the Casians and more. People from every world we liberate could be given the chance to join you here. This ship is vast. It has the resources for a crew of well over a thousand beings.

You can train us and we can assist you. It is your ship. No one would deny that and you have the expertise to operate it. Our role would be to assist you with knowledge of the galaxy and by fulfilling the roles you do not have enough people for."

"Would anyone be willing to do that?" Darius asked.

It was actually an idea he had been toying with. The *Renegade* practically begged to be filled with people. Who said they all had to be humans? If he could get volunteers from various worlds, they could properly man the ship and also expand their knowledge from the alien races. It seemed like a win-win to Darius. He didn't know how the rest of his crew would react, but he was willing to give it a try.

"I believe many would leap at the chance. Especially if some are allowed to study the Arodoni technology."

And there was the rub. Not that it had to be a major problem, but Darius could guess what many of his people would say. The Arodoni technology was invaluable. Why not keep it all for themselves? But the more he thought like that, the more he realized that sole possession of the Arodoni tech would only lead to humanity becoming as corrupt as the Ashi. Humanity certainly had that pedigree. Empires had risen and fallen throughout Earth's history. As one nation grew strong, it inevitably conquered the weak. The Arodoni tech would make humanity the strongest race in the galaxy, at least militarily.

"We have no way to pay them," Darius said.

"Freedom is the payment for our service. Pride is the reward we will carry back to our people, Captain. To say that we served on the *Renegade* and helped to defeat the Ashi Empire is an honor many people would gladly rush to accept."

"I have to consider all this," Darius said. "But I think your planning is sound. Would you be willing to put together a roster of worlds that we could show my officers? A game plan, so to speak, of where we could go and how we could help."

"It would be an honor, Captain. Thank you for hearing me out."

"Your input has been invaluable," Darius said. "My people shake hands as a sign of respect."

He extended his hand. Nurek looked at it without moving for a moment.

"Slaves are not allowed to touch their masters without permission," Nurek said.

"I'm not your master and you are no longer a slave, Nurek," Darius said. "If you would serve with us on the *Renegade,* you must be an equal."

The words rocked the alien almost like a physical blow.

"An equal?"

"Yes," Darius said. "No race is superior to another. We have different roles. My crew is built on a chain of command but no one is better than another. We work together, each one doing the unique jobs we were trained for. Isn't that what you want?"

"It is..." his voice faltered. "It is what my people have long sought, Captain. To be equal."

He reached out and took hold of Darius' hand. His long, delicate fingers wrapped all the way around the captain's hand.

"One last thing," Darius said. "I can't give you an answer at this moment. I must consult my officers and make sure that what I'm doing is what is best for the crew and for our people back home. But I can make you this offer: whatever we do and wherever we go, you are welcome to stay with us. You can make your home here. My people would be thrilled to learn from you."

"I... accept, Captain," Nurek said, bowing. "It will be the honor of my life."

EPILOGUE

SHEIKA KAHN WAITED on the platform as the Prime Council gathered in the great rotunda above. Excitement rippled through the Kahn's fat body like jolts of electricity. Everything he had dreamed of and worked for was about to come true. The child Vang Na'Raj was dead. The Imperium lay before him. In a moment, he would be lifted up, adorned with the Imperial crimson cape ... and given the entire galaxy.

The call to order was given. The amplified voices of the Prime Council echoed down to where Sheika Kahn waited. Soon he would be Emperor Ulrach Sheika, the first in a new dynasty of rulers.

Suddenly, the platform began to rise. Above him, the floor of the great rotunda opened, and light poured down on Sheika Kahn. He stood proudly. In the audience were ten thousand beings from thousands of worlds across the galaxy. The rich and powerful stood waiting to see their new Emperor. All would soon bow before him.

When the platform reached the rotunda, Sheika Kahn found himself standing before the five thrones of the Prime Council. Members, one from each of the five core worlds, ruled over every aspect of the Imperium. Theirs was the tedious work of administration. His job would be to give direction; theirs would be to carry out his every whim. And Sheika Kahn knew each of the five Prime Council members well. His job as Kahn to the Emperor had been to help steer both the council and the supreme ruler toward a harmonious governance of the galaxy. The council members were greedy, ambitious and sometimes dangerous beings, but Kahn knew their secrets and how to manage them. It was just one of the reasons he would be the greatest Emperor in a thousand years.

Eng of Wesset was the first to speak. He was a biped with shaggy hair over his entire body and a long, oval face. "We are here to address the Arodoni threat," he said in a creaking voice.

Nic'Tal of Hurz spoke next. She was a rotund, insectile being with a red and black carapace and wings that could no longer fly. "Where is Emperor Vang?"

"The Emperor is dead," Sheika Kahn declared in a solemn tone. "It is my great displeasure to inform the Prime Council that Vang Na'Raj, Emperor of the Ashi and commander of the armies of the Imperium, was killed in the fighting on Casasil."

That statement caused an uproar in the crowd behind Sheika Kahn. He stood, letting the sound wash over him. The council waited too, but eventually, a bell was rung for silence.

When the crowd quieted down, Sheika spoke again.

"The Arodoni have returned. It is my duty to take up the mantle of leadership. I shall raise an Ashi army to crush the alien threat. As the new Emperor, I shall ensure the safety of the Imperium!"

There was a spattering of approval from the crowd, but it was far from overwhelming. Of course, every ambitious being in the Imperium would give up everything for the chance to be named Emperor, but only the Ashi could claim the title ... and among the Ashi, only Sheika Kahn was in a position to seize power. The council would approve, he was certain of that. He had too much leverage over them for the members to resist.

Yet what Miz, the lone Ashi member of the Prime Council said, caught Sheika Kahn completely off guard.

"We have word from the leader of the armada sent to deal with the Arodoni that Emperor Vang lives."

That sent a shock through the crowd. And a vein of outrage erupted in Sheika Kahn but he could not let it show.

Miz continued. "The Arodoni have captured him, but a raid was underway to rescue Emperor Vang. I believe the Kahn's request to be named Emperor in Vang Na'Raj's stead is premature."

Koll of Foxill, a skinny four-legged alien with drooping folds of skin and a pointed head, spoke next. "I agree. Every step must be taken to ensure that we rescue our Emperor. No resource should be spared."

"He may already be free," Eng of Wesset declared.

Groll of Tzingah, a gelatinous alien and the fifth member of the council, hummed and tooted. His words were translated into Ashi via a device that projected them out across the rotunda. "Our duty is clear."

"Sheika Kahn, you must lead the resistance to the Arodoni, but not as Emperor," Eng said.

"Until we have proof that Emperor Vang is alive or dead, you shall remain Kahn," Miz declared.

Before Sheika could argue the point, Koll declared the council adjourned and the platform began to descend once more. Sheika Kahn didn't move or make a sound. He let the darkness close in around him. If the council wanted to see Vang's broken body, he would deliver it to them and stake it out on the rotunda floor. They had made an enemy who would not forget their betrayal ... but the Kahn was not impulsive. He knew that it was better to wait and formulate a plan that could not be thwarted. Perhaps the Arodoni were not as savage as he suspected them to be. They must have realized who they were fighting and recognized the value of holding the emperor hostage. But it would not get them what they desired. Already, the Ashi military forces were gathering. Over a hundred ships of war from across the galaxy were moving to join the Kahn's armada. He would take control, just as the Prime Council had instructed him. Yet, yet ... he would not give it back.

And he would make them pay, every single member of the Prime Council.

If the Arodoni wanted war, he would give them all they could handle. Their ship might be powerful but so was Sheika Kahn. War was one way to acquire power and it had just begun. Soon, he would use that power to strangle any resistance to his rule and establish himself as the greatest force in the galaxy.

AUTHOR'S NOTE

Thank you for reading *Juggernaut*. I loved writing this book. My passion for strategy and tactics probably took over and made this book a little different, but there will be more wonder and discovery in the books that follow. There's still a galaxy to be explored and liberated. Perhaps the crew of the *SDF Jericho* can help achieve that.

My plan had been to release Juggernaut in November, but illness made that impossible. I'm fully recovered and hope to write more of this series in short order. Stay tuned, and follow me on social media for more updates. You can also join my mailing list at TobyNeighbors.com

ALSO BY TOBY NEIGHBORS

Modulus Echo

Zero Friction

Planet Fall

Charter

Jack & Roxie

My Lady Sorceress

The Man With No Hands

ARC Angel

Battle ARC

Broken Crucible

Hidden Kingdom

War INC

Carthage Prime

Cronus Team

Skandia Seven

Mercurial

Magnificus Prime

Incursio

Merlin Appears

Runners

Survivors

Infiltrators

Resistance

Conquest

Occupation

Extraction

The Signal

Battle Orders

Base Of Fire

Hard Site

Recall

Evade

Assault

Space Fever

Staying Alive

Fractal Cut

Blast Zone

Action Zone

Covert Infil

Armor Brigade

Havoc Squad

Thunderbird

Ghost Tactics

Quantum Combat

Infinite Threat

Shadow Threat

Evolving Threat

Lingering Threat

Latent Prowess

Gravity Masters

Gravity Storm

Daughter of the Night

Supernova

Artifact

Blood Moon

Renegade

With Pete Garcia

Apocalypse One Percenters